THE CAESAR CLUE

Previous books by this author
Writing as M. K. Shuman

The Maya Stone Murders

Writing as M. S. Karl

Death Notice
Killer's Ink
Mayab
The Mobius Man

THE

CAESAR

CLUE

A MICAH DUNN MYSTERY

M. K. Shuman

St. Martin's Press
New York

Design by Judy Dannecker

Library of Congress Cataloging-in-Publication Data

Shuman, M. K.
    The caesar clue.
        p.   cm.
    ISBN 0-312-04275-2
    I. Title.
    PS3569.H779C35   1990   813'.54—dc20   89-78088

First Edition

10 9 8 7 6 5 4 3 2 1

This book is for my son Karl

For Ted & Herschel
with the best wishes
memories of a
collaboration few

THE CAESAR CLUE

1

The jetliner leaned into its final approach to New Orleans International, twenty miles out and dropping toward the cypress swamp at twenty feet per second. The night was clear, and in another minute the headlight would go on, probing the darkness below like a cyclops eye. I was on the freeway, coming up on Williams Boulevard, running a little late and hoping the flight wouldn't be early. I exited onto the access road and turned south, to skim the east edge of the airfield, instinctively ducking as a big Delta jet thundered in from the direction of the lake. I had managed to get used to airports in the last ten years or so, but there'd been a time when I couldn't see one of the big jets without thinking of body bags and walking wounded. I curved north, into the airport entryway, and headed for the short-term parking area.

If the plane was on schedule, it would be touching down in a few seconds. I went inside, past the baggage area, up the escalator, and down the long hallway past the various counters. At the one marked Transcaribbean a pert young woman in blue was finishing with a man headed for Houston, who wanted to make an Oilers game the next day.

The sign behind her said the flight from Jamaica was on time, but it wouldn't hurt to check. She gave me a quick once-over and smiled.

"Yes, sir?"

I was getting ready to speak when her phone rang. She shrugged apologetically and lifted the receiver.

The smile vanished and she stumbled against the counter. "Are you sure?" she said in a near whisper. Then she nodded, as if the person on the other end could see her, and licked her lips. Her eyes flicked over to me and then away, as if she were custodian of a guilty secret. "Yes. I'll hold tight."

I made my living working with people in trouble and I didn't like what I was feeling.

"What is it?" I asked.

"No . . . nothing, sir. A slight delay." She tried to smile, but it was a grimace.

I looked around me at the other counters and saw other stricken faces. The people milling around in the hallway, waiting for the flight, were feeling it now, like animals before a thunderstorm, smelling ozone and not knowing what to do. I wanted to leave, because the last time I'd felt this way I'd been on a deep penetration mission that had gone haywire and they'd had to lift us out, or, rather, lift what was left.

A man came up to me and grabbed my left arm.

"What's going on?" he demanded, trying to cover his fear with bravado. When he saw my arm didn't work, he dropped his hand and mumbled an apology. "I thought, *My God, my wife is on that plane.*"

"It'll be okay," I said, not believing it.

Two seconds later I heard the word *crash.*

It came from somewhere on the periphery of the crowd and crackled through like a flash fire. A woman sat down on the floor, her legs splayed at funny angles, and her husband stared blankly ahead as if he hadn't noticed. The phones behind the counter were ringing steadily now and there were booking agents talking on them, or to each other, but none seemed to want to talk to any of the crowd in the hall.

I stood around for another half hour and at some point somebody came out of a doorway behind the schedule sign and made an announcement. I didn't have to listen because I

2

knew what he was going to say as soon as he asked for our attention.

Five minutes later the press showed up, and that was when I left.

I drove back through the night, trying to put together what little I knew. The plane must have exploded a few thousand feet from the runway, because there was no debris on the field. Fire trucks were heading west out of Kenner, and toward the swamp, but they would play hell finding anything until daylight. If it had come in from the east, it would have gone down over Kenner itself, like the ill-fated Delta in 1982. In the swamps, there was nothing to hurt except the trees, some alligators and the fish. Of course, if you were still aboard, it didn't matter.

But the Delta had been caught in a wind shear, on takeoff. This was a clear September night, with visibility of twenty miles.

I got off the highway at Claiborne, sliding down the ramp into darkness. The hospitals were on my right and beyond them the Superdome. The hospitals would be busy tonight, I thought, then corrected myself: Only the morgues would be busy.

Tulane, Canal, and Orleans streets slipped past me and I turned right onto Esplanade without thinking.

Coincidence. That's what my mind kept saying. But it wasn't saying it very loud, because I knew better: Airliners don't crash every day.

I came to Decatur and turned back south, into the Vieux Carre. Another street, and I came to the big wooden double doors that led into the parking area. Tonight, though, I felt too tired to get out and open them and slide them shut behind me, so I parked on the street. Then I unlocked the little pedestrian door to the patio and headed for the outside iron stairs that led to my second floor apartment.

The courtyard fountain was working and spray kissed my face as I went up. For an instant I stopped, trying to use the sensation to blot out the horror of what had happened. It didn't work; the spray reminded me of the wreckage crashing into the swamp, geysering dark water into the night sky. I wondered what the passengers strapped in their seats had felt.

I unlocked my door, went inside, through the kitchen and into the room I used as an office. Everything was as I had left it: file cabinet locked, odds and ends of a few cases scattered around my desk, green light on my answering machine showing there had been no calls.

I flopped into my chair and then, impulsively, reached over to the answering device and set it to Play, because the old message would still be there.

There was static, a click, and then it came on, a woman's voice speaking quickly, as if she were about to run out of time.

"Mr. Dunn, my name is Julia Morvant. I'm calling from Jamaica. I'll be on Transcaribbean 420, arriving at Moissant at eight-fifteen. Please. It's important for you to meet me. I need your help."

The voice sent shivers through me, because three hours ago it had belonged to a living person and now it belonged to a ghost. I took the message tape out of the machine and placed it in my desk drawer.

I stared trembling again and it was hours before I could stop.

2

I sat drinking coffee on my balcony the next morning and reading the *Sunday Picayune* when Detective Sal Mancuso limped up the patio stairs.

"Take what you want," I said, lowering my paper. "My money's in the desk drawer."

"It's early to be cracking jokes," Mancuso said, pulling up a deck chair and leaning back against the wall. "And I'm too tired to laugh."

I moved my head to look at him. He was right: He looked like hell, with his sleeves coming unrolled and his tie hanging limp like three-day-old greens in the French Market. We'd met at a veterans meeting a few years back and been on speaking terms ever since, but it was the first time I could remember his coming to my apartment, not to mention early on a Sunday. Old Mr. Mamet, the caretaker, must have let him in through the patio door.

"Have a croissant," I said, gesturing to the bag on the floor. "There's coffee on the stove."

He sighed and reached into the bag, but he made no effort to get coffee, probably because he'd had a couple of gallons already.

"Bad night," he said. For the first time I noticed the mud caking his slacks and understood.

I thumped the front page of the paper. "Sixty-seven peo-

5

ple," I said. "Sixty-seven people and in two minutes they'd have been on the ground." I shook my head.

"They never had a chance," Mancuso said in a monotone. "You know what it's like in the swamp."

He was looking at me now and it was my turn to nod. "Yeah. Tough break."

"Worse than that," he said and shifted position. For a second I thought he was going to be sick but then he got his words right, so that they came but everything else stayed down.

"It wasn't a fucking accident," he said. "We figure it was a bomb."

"A bomb?" It was my turn to look at him. He was a small man, swarthy, with a kind of intensity that usually gets burned out of cops. But not Mancuso.

"Micah, all the eyewitnesses agree. The fucking thing flew to pieces. One of the scraps we fished up smelled like a dynamite factory."

"Shit," I whispered.

"My thoughts, too." He stretched slightly, but it could have been a shiver. "Look, I came to ask you something. When I got there, I saw you walking away. I haven't mentioned it to any of the federal boys, the FBI or the FAA, but if you had business with somebody on that plane, now's the time to say."

He was right. I put my paper down, got up, and went back inside, with him behind me. I fished the message tape out of the drawer and placed it in the machine. Then I played it for him. When I finished he whistled.

"Jesus, Micah. Who was this Julia Morvant?"

I shrugged. "I don't know. I found the message on the machine when I came back in at seven. From the last name, I'd say she was from around here. It's French. And only locals call the airport by its old name, Moissant."

The policeman shook his head. "Well, it may not be connected. But it's the best shot we have for now."

"I'll see what I can turn up," I said. "Maybe somebody in

6

the Quarter will know this Julia. Maybe some past client. It's a long shot. . . ."

Mancuso made a wry face. "But better you than the feds. If it's the real thing, we don't need a task force chasing everybody into hiding. I'll see what information the airline has. Maybe she bought her ticket by credit card." He stopped at the door. "I'm not on the case," he said. "I was just in the area yesterday when the call came. After I catch some sleep I'll go back to the Mystery of the Missing Hookers. My chief suspect is the Chamber of Commerce. But if you turn up anything, give me a call."

"I will, Sal."

I stared at the door a few seconds after he'd left, listening to his feet go down the iron steps.

Julia Morvant. A French name, not common and, therefore, one that should be easy to run down. If it was real. If she weren't an actress, or a runaway, or a whore . . .

I went back out onto the balcony and picked up my paper. I didn't really care that a UN commission was blaming both sides in the Middle East or that the local congressman was calling for the death penalty against dope dealers. Instead, my eyes kept going back to the front-page photo of wreckage against the cypress stumps. If there was a chance that the woman on the phone was involved I owed it to a lot of people to check it out.

Sandy. She was the place to start.

When she picked up the phone her voice was sleep-fogged, and I detected an undercurrent of peevishness.

"I'm sorry to bother you," I said. "I wouldn't call if it wasn't important."

"Sho'," she said. Sandy was a tall, well-built black woman with a taste for art and finance. She could go from banker to street whore in a few seconds, which probably accounted for her unusual success as an investigator. I gathered she led a full love life, but I made it my business not to inquire, and I hoped *I* hadn't interrupted something.

7

I told her about the plane crash and heard her breath suck in.

"Christ, Micah, why didn't you say so? You mean you've got a gig that connects with *that*?"

So I explained about Julia Morvant.

"She may be anybody, but my guess is she's local. Try the street people, and I'll try the phone directory and the colleges. Maybe between us we'll get lucky. Keep track of your time and . . ."

"Forget it. I may have to ride a plane someday. All I need is some nut to blow it up."

"Well, do what you can," I said, and thanked her.

I showered and got ready to jog. I was missing Katherine fiercely, halfway resentful of the archaeology that was claiming so much of her time. When I'd met her a year ago she'd been the secretary at Tulane's Middle American Research Institute, but she'd picked up more than any of the students for whom she'd kept records and run errands. After a case involving the Institute, she'd realized she was wasting herself and enrolled as a graduate student. I had approved and so had her grown son, Scott, who proudly referred to her as "Mom, the archaeologist." But the Institute had a research focus on Yucatán, and she made frequent trips down to the ruins. She'd been away this time for fifty days, with another three to go, and I realized for the first time how empty my life had been before I'd met her. I wondered what she'd say about Julia Morvant. Then I remembered she'd be coming back from Yucatán on a plane and I shuddered.

The next day I finished up a job tailing a man whose business partner suspected him of stealing from the company. It was the partner's idea that his associate had a woman squirreled away someplace, maybe across the lake, in Mandeville, or in Oak Island East, but he was wrong. I waited outside the office, and when the target came out at lunch, I followed him to the bank and then to a barbershop in Metairie. I waited outside for fifteen minutes, but I could see from my spot across the street that he had gone through a door into the next room, which was something I could have predicted the minute I saw where he was heading. The barbershop belonged to a bookie named Torrelo, and it was a front for some businessmen who broke your legs if you fell behind on payments. A woman in a big house would have been cheaper, and easier to get free of, but that wasn't my problem.

My problem was Julia Morvant. The diction had been Southern, but not the kind of drawl you get in Mississippi or Georgia. Nor had it been Irish Channel or Cajun. Guessing, I'd say she'd had a couple of years of college, at least, and I doubted she was much over thirty. Not a lot to go on.

When I got back I called Mancuso at Homicide.

"I was expecting you," he said. His voice sounded tired, but not so bad as yesterday. "She boarded at Kingston. Paid cash. Gave an address in Gentilly that doesn't exist. All they remember about her in Kingston is thirtiesh, brown haired, Caucasian, good-looking. We checked all the Morvants in the book; nobody knows who she is. She's not registered with Motor Vehicles. And get this: Her passport was phony."

"Did you trace the call?"

"It came from a public booth."

"No hotel? Nobody who remembers her?"

"Too early to say. The feds are taking over and they've made it clear the only place they want to see New Orleans cops is directing traffic on Canal. We aren't smart enough to do anything but wade around in the swamp after bodies."

I murmured a few words of sympathy at his frustration, but I didn't expect to turn up anything new or helpful.

For the rest of the afternoon I sat in a roach-infested loft with a pair of binoculars and a camera, watching a warehouse crew off-load delivery trucks. It wasn't wholesale pilferage, just a case of liquor here and there, and I suspected the owner was hiring me to cover his own embezzlement. But it was his company, so I noted times and took pictures, and tried to think about the yacht races in Pontchartrain the following weekend.

9

It didn't work, though, because my mind kept going back to the voice on the phone. Was it chance she had called me from a foreign country and then boarded a plane that had been blown out of the sky? She'd used a false passport and had called from a public booth. What did that point to? Drugs? Was she a mule who'd decided to bolt the organization? The Colombians hadn't stopped at mass assassination in the past; blowing up an airliner would just be a new wrinkle.

I tried to remember any cases in the last few years that had involved drugs, but there was nothing I could hang onto. I'd been contacted once to try to get back some money from a coke deal gone sour, but turned it down; I didn't give a damn whether drug dealers got burned. A couple of times I'd been hired to track kids or spouses with expensive habits. I'd done a fair amount of security work for industry, identifying people with addictions. Some of the people had been let go, but a fair number landed in treatment programs and some even came back to thank me.

Maybe, I thought, it was a domestic case. She'd run from her husband and then experienced pangs of conscience. But that didn't square with the explosion, nor did the theory that she'd absconded with some money from her firm and had a change of heart. Companies don't generally blow up dishonest employees, not to mention the absurdity of sending someone overseas to plant a bomb.

The work shift ended at five and I left as soon as the warehouse closed. Everybody in the city was on his way home and didn't have but five minutes to get there. I'd learned to dodge and weave in the city traffic, almost as good with one hand as I'd once been with two. My air conditioner had gone out on Friday and I hadn't had a chance to get into the shop, so I rolled down the window. A mixture of exhaust fumes and rotting vegetables rushed in at me along with the heat and the smell of rain.

Julia Morvant. Was this something she had smelled on afternoons like this?

It took me twenty minutes to get to Esplanade, where the

10

old red-brick mint building told me I was almost home. I parked on the street again and went in through the front entrance, drawing the barest arched brow from Lavelle in the downstairs voodoo shop. He was holding an earnest discussion with a black woman. I started for the stairway to my office, then stopped. Something about the arched brow . . .

"What's up, David?" I asked and watched him grimace.

"I told you not to call me that," he protested. The black woman, I judged, was selling him some toads and other necessities and regarded me without interest.

"I'm sorry," I apologized. "You just don't look like an Henri."

"He's right," the woman said. "Don't look like a Lavelle, neither."

The shopkeeper gritted his teeth. "All I need is crap from some one-armed detective."

"Don't make fun of the man, David," the woman ordered. "He can't help hisself, but you can. Some of the grisgris have to be handled by a man that's pure hearted and you ain't, honey."

"Christ," Lavelle swore.

"Was there something you wanted to tell me?" I asked him, smiling blandly.

"No. Isn't my business who goes up to your hole. I hope it's a damn burglar."

My smile started to go away.

"Man or woman?"

"Orang-utan. At least, he had red hair."

"He went up and then came down again?"

"He went up and stayed." He shrugged. "I thought maybe he was a friend of yours that had a key. He was in a business suit."

"How long ago?" I asked.

"Couple of minutes."

I nodded. "Thanks, Henri." I walked through his shop, to the back door leading onto the patio. I shut the door quietly and listened, but all I heard was the gentle gush of the fountain and, behind it, from over the wall, distant car horns.

11

I started up the iron stairs and came out on the second floor walkway. I put my ear against the back door, heard nothing, and carefully inserted my key into the lock.

Cigarette smoke told me that my visitor was in the front room—my office.

I picked up a baseball bat from beside the refrigerator and started for the doorway but my feet crunched down on something.

"Bang, you're dead," a voice rasped from just inside the doorway, and I froze.

"What. . . ?"

A form moved into the area in front of me and I heard a guttural laugh. "Peanut shells. I put 'em on the floor. I figured you hadn't learned anything from Nam."

Years fell away and my mouth opened in amazement as I stared at the man in front of me. The red hair was a little longer, the belly slopped a little over the buckle, and this time he was wearing a rumpled business suit instead of camouflage fatigues, but in every other way he was the same.

"Solly Cranich!" I said, lowering the bat. "For God's sake, I almost brained you. . . ."

"You didn't come close," he laughed. "You're getting soft, Micah. I could've wired this place to blow you into seven million little bitty pieces."

"I guess you could've," I acknowledged, and then grabbed his outstretched paw. "You jimmied my door, too, I suppose."

He shrugged. "Let's just say I let myself in. Last time we were together, in Saigon, we agreed there wouldn't ever be any locks, that any time . . ."

"I know what we said," I chuckled. "We were both drunk."

"Best way to be, back then." Solly's smile faded. "Look, I heard about your getting hurt and all. Tough."

"Lots had it worse."

I opened the refrigerator.

"Oh, I helped myself to a beer," he said. "But I think there's some left."

12

"Thanks."

I got out two more, followed him into the office and took a seat behind my desk. Solly lit up another cigarette and leaned back in his chair.

"So you're a private eye these days," he said. I listened for pity but there wasn't any.

"I enjoy it," I said. "And I'm not bad at it, people say."

"Hell, you'd be good at anything you set your mind to." He watched me pop the aluminum tab of my beer can with one hand but there was no sympathy in his eyes. I was glad.

"Thanks, Solly. So what brings you to New Orleans? Are you out of the Corps?"

"Jesus," he laughed, taking a long pull of beer, "you're never out of the Corps, you know that." He came forward slightly in his chair. "Truth is, I was in range of getting my thirty when I caught a piece of shrapnel in Beirut. Part of a special team they sent in to ferret out our hostages. They put a plate in my head and gave me my papers. I thought I was just another old major, of which the woods are full. But then one day a civilian that liased with us from a spook agency sat down next to me in a bar and asked if I didn't want to make use of my experience. Hell, I jumped at it."

I felt a momentary pang of envy. "CIA?" I asked.

"Not exactly. It's one of these conglomerates, a little bit of everything from DEA to State Department. Tell the God's truth, there ain't a lot of 'em I've got use for. Bunch of little Ivy League shits, most of 'em. But they let me alone mostly. And I got it good. How can I complain? You know me, Micah. I'm an OCS man, never made it to college, don't know anything about management theory and all that crap. I just know how to take an objective if they give it to me. I thought when Evelyn died it was the hardest thing I ever went through."

"I'm sorry."

He waved away my sympathy. "But it wasn't nothing like having to take off my uniform. So when this came along, well . . ."

"I'm glad for you, Sol."

13

"Thanks, Micah." He tapped his ash in the empty beer can.

"So how did you find me?" I asked.

He sighed. "Well, I never was any good at cover stories; that's what got me blown up in the first place. Truth is, they sent me."

"To find me?" A tingle of excitement passed through me. I was happy enough now, I had my own life, but suppose . . . ?

He nodded, expression serious, as if he understood my thoughts and didn't want to raise false hopes.

"It's this damn plane crash. My agency is involved."

The deflation was over in a second. "I see. But why come to me?"

"Don't bullshit me, Micah. We've been through too much. We know about this Morvant woman."

I shrugged. "You probably know more than I do."

"We know she made a call to this number before she got on that plane. It's easy enough to get phone records. We talked to a cop, says she left a message for you."

"I guess that's no secret. But the fact is, Solly, I never heard of the woman before and don't know what she wanted, except for me to meet her at the airport."

He finished his second beer. "Hell, I believe you. But I need to pick up the tape."

I thought for a second, then got up and went to the refrigerator. I brought back two more beers and passed him one.

"Why?" I asked.

"Establish identity, for one thing. They may never find her body. And maybe they can enhance the tape, you know, and play it to some relative, if they ever find one."

"Good try, Solly. But you're right: You can't lie worth a damn. There's more to it."

He grinned ruefully. "Well, I told them a bullshit story wouldn't work, but I tried." He leaned almost out of his seat now, his eyes burning with the old fire I'd last seen on search-and-destroy missions in the Mekong.

"Micah, look, even I don't know everything that's involved here, but what we're dealing with is terrorism. The lady was a part of the group. We think she was carrying the bomb and it went off by mistake. We need to keep a lid on all of this, because we don't know how many of them may already be in the city. Our guess is she called you so they could set up some kind of cover with you as the fall guy."

"She's not foreign," I said. "Her accent was local and she knows the city."

"Lee Harvey Oswald was American." He cleared his throat.

He was right, of course. "And if you catch them, then what?"

"We do what has to be done," he said levelly, then took another swallow of beer. "Anybody don't like it can write their congressman."

"Our congressman would probably agree," I said. "So would almost everybody else."

"Good," Solly said, his face suddenly hard.

I took another swig, all the memories of Nam rushing back, and for a second it was good: the mixed spice and vegetable smells of the markets, the delicate, fragrantly scented women on the boulevards of Saigon, the excitement of another world. Then the other memories returned: smoke and burned flesh, and the sound of rotor blades overhead, body bags on the runway.

I reached into my drawer and brought out the tape. "Here you go, Solly. I hope it helps."

"Thanks, Micah. The group'll appreciate it."

"The group," I said. "Does that make you a groupee?"

He struggled to his feet. "Screw you," he said. "And I'd get a good lock on the door."

"Next time I'll booby trap it," I said. "By the way, if I need you, where will you be?"

"I'm at the Clarion. Call this number," he said and scribbled seven digits on a card.

He stuck out a hand. "Thanks, Micah. Semper Fi."

"Semper Fi, Sol," I answered as he started down the stairs. "Good hunting."

He was older and slower, but even so, I'd hate to take him on, and I felt sorry for the bad guys if he ever caught them. Yet despite his bluff demeanor, I'd always recognized that he was a compassionate man, who hated to kill. Besides the Corps, the love of his life had been Evelyn, who had understood him and supported him. He responded by using the time other men spent in the Saigon whorehouses to write her long letters about the country and its people. Now he was alone, but at least he had something useful to do. I hoisted my bottle and drank once more to his success. People that bombed airplanes didn't deserve much consideration.

The phone broke in on my thoughts and I picked it up, half expecting to hear my father's voice, from Charleston.

"Mr. Dunn?"

It was a woman.

"Speaking. Who's calling, please?"

"I have to talk to you. It's important. I'm a friend of Julia Morvant."

3

My mouth went dry. It was the last thing I expected to hear.

"Who is this?" I asked.

"Never mind my name. Did Julia contact you before . . ." I waited but my caller didn't want to finish the sentence.

"We need to talk," I said. "Can we meet somewhere?"

"I just need to know," the woman said, a thin edge of hysteria in her voice. I judged her to be in her twenties and local.

"We can talk," I said, trying to soothe. "But face-to-face. I'll tell you everything I know."

It was a safe promise and I waited to see if my bluff would work. Finally I heard something like her breath sucking in.

"Okay. Chad R's on Baronne in half an hour. I'll be at a booth in the back."

"Good enough. I'm fortyish and I'll be wearing a *guayabera*. My left arm doesn't work, so I'll be easy to spot."

"I know," she said, and the line went dead.

The clock on my desk read six-thirty. Plenty of time to drive over. Equally interesting, it meant she had called from a radius of a mile. Of course, that included a lot of the city, but my guess was that she'd been at the bar all along, nerving herself, and accepting that it might come to a face-to-face. I thought about calling Sal Mancuso and asking him to try to set up a tail, but then I discarded the idea. Likewise

17

the notion of putting Sandy on her, even if I could have gotten Sandy there in time. The girl knew me, somehow, and for that reason trusted me. The best way to lose your reputation is to breach a trust. No, I'd play it straight.

It was already dusk when I parked across the street. Chad R's was a hole in the wall that had once been a Mexican restaurant and before that part of a mission for winos. The mission was gone but not the winos, and a couple of them looked at me wistfully as I started across the street, eliciting an angry honk from a cab. They were hoping I'd be hit and lie still long enough to let them pick my pockets, but no such luck.

Some New Orleans bars have character and some just have tourists. Chad R's had neither. It was a watering hole for commuters who told themselves they'd wait out the traffic and then said the hell with it, they didn't want to go home anyway. There was a big shrimp net over the bar, implying some nautical connection, and, for no apparent reason, paintings of famous matadors over the half dozen booths against the far wall. No one cared about the incongruity, any more than they cared about a new face in the doorway. The two men in the first booth were already well on their way to incoherence, one declaiming against the Levee Board for some political dereliction while his companion nodded blankly. A woman with bleached hair was draped over a stool, looking bored, and a spark of hope flickered in her face as she saw me and then as quickly went out as I passed.

The woman I'd come to meet was already seated in the last booth, a drink in front of her. She regarded me with sad, puppy-dog eyes that made her seem older than she could possibly have been. Not bad looking, well-dressed, but a little too made up and definitely tired.

"You know my name," I said, sliding in across from her.

She fished a cigarette from the pack on the table and I watched her flick a gold lighter.

"Okay. My name is Belinda, if it's that important."

"It makes conversation easier."

18

The waitress appeared and I asked for a Lite Beer; I'd already had my limit, with Solly.

She stared at me with the doggy eyes as she dragged on the cigarette and then looked away as she exhaled.

"I want to know what she told you," Belinda said.

"You know, relations between a PI and his client are confidential," I said pleasantly. "Maybe you could explain what your interest in this is."

"She's my roommate," Belinda said. "She left a week ago. Told me she was going to Jamaica. She called me the night before last, scared. Told me her flight number and asked if I knew anybody that could meet her at the airport and guard her."

"And you gave her my name."

"It came to mind. You did a job for a friend of mine once."

"Mind telling me who?"

She tapped her cigarette into the ashtray. "It doesn't matter."

"Did she tell you anything else when she called? What she was scared of, for instance?"

Belinda frowned and shook her head slowly from side to side. Her necklace caught the light and shot little arrows of gold at me. "Well, there was one thing she said, but it didn't make any sense."

"Do you remember what it was?" I could tell I was going to have to plumb for every scrap.

"You'd have to know her. She was my good friend, but she's—she was kind of a flake. Always reading heavy things and quoting them. It could piss you off. But she was okay, down deep."

It was clear Belinda wasn't the kind to read heavy things, but that didn't make her unique.

"What did she say?" I asked patiently.

"She said she'd done it, whatever *it* was. And then she said, 'It'll make Marc Antony look like a piker.' Marc Antony. I remember that. He was a guy in some film I saw once. Marlon Brando."

"You're right." The waitress brought my beer and I sipped it, trying to make sense out of the comment.

"Belinda, why did she go to Jamaica? I mean, it obviously wasn't vacation, was it?"

She looked away quickly. "I'm not sure. It's not important."

"It's damned important," I said. "Everything about Julia Morvant is important. Sixty-seven people are dead and the cops can't even find her name in the phone book or the motor vehicle file. Her passport was phony. Now you tell me she was your roommate, but you won't give me your real name—no, I *don't* believe it's Belinda—or any of the details. Why should I help you?"

"Because I have to know if she told you anything, for God's sake." She blushed and then seemed to draw back. "I'm sorry. I just can't tell you any more."

"Then I guess we're wasting each other's time."

A look of alarm flashed across her face. "No! Listen, you don't know her. She's special. She's my friend. She helped me, she was there when I needed her. Can't you understand? I can't just pretend she never existed. I'd have died for her."

"Belinda—or whatever the hell your name is—something tells me you're in over your head, just like she was. Listen, these people, the ones who blow up planes and carry Uzis, are nobody to play with. If you're straight with me, I can help you. I have some contacts, people that can put you under protection, even give you a new identity. Don't try to do this alone. For God's sake, trust me."

"You didn't know Julia," she protested. "I did."

"Okay, you're right. And I want to know why she's dead, too." I searched for a common thread and failed. "Look, is there any chance she could have been carrying a bomb?"

Belinda's face mirrored shock. "A bomb? What are you saying? That she. . . ?" Her head rocked from side to side. "No. That's crazy. Never."

She frowned and then sighed almost inaudibly. "She didn't tell you anything, did she?"

Before I could answer she was rising.

"I have to go to the little girl's room, do you mind?"

I thought quickly, but I couldn't remember any exit, so I shrugged. "I'll wait."

As she got up, a faint aroma of exotic perfume lingered, tickling my nose. It was thirty seconds later when I remembered the door at the end of the hallway that connected with the alley. When I heard the door open and close, I knew I was in trouble.

I laid some money on the table and walked back out onto the street. I was just in time to see the red 280-Z pull away from the curb and squeal off toward the uptown area.

She'd been quick, and I'd been slow, but it hadn't been a complete loss. At least I'd gotten the license plate number. I struggled to pull my note pad from the pocket at my waist, and pressed it against my body with the heel of my hand while I scribbled the license number, using the pen I kept tied to it with a string. The winos watched, half interested. It was probably the best show of the day.

I called for Mancuso but he'd signed out, so I tried him at home.

"I need a license number," I said. "Can you run it for me?"

"Tomorrow," he yawned, and I realized he'd been sleeping. "Can't it wait till then? I've spent the last twelve hours looking for teen-whores that went home to Mommy."

"I'd rather not," I said. "Please, Sal. I'll owe you one."

"Hell, after I fished you out of the river last year, you owe me a couple already. Okay, so what's the number?"

I gave it to him, along with the car description.

"Female cauc driver," I said. "Age twenty-something. And I'd like to know if there are any wants or warrants."

"Is this a criminal case?" he asked suspiciously.

"I can't say at this point."

"If it is, or if it becomes one, I don't want to be the goddamn last to know."

I thought of telling him about Solly, and about my call from Belinda, but stopping the bureaucratic process once it starts is like getting toothpaste back in the tube.

"Understood," I said. "But I really need the person that belongs to that car."

"Okay, I'll call up the night shift and have it run. Will you be at home?"

"I'll call you back," I said.

I drove to a little Greek place, had a gyro and some black coffee, and tried to make sense out of my meeting with the woman who called herself Belinda. Terrorists used naive young women in their schemes, but even if Belinda wasn't a Rhodes scholar, she didn't strike me as very naive, and if Julia Morvant had been her roommate, odds were she hadn't been a fool, either. Belinda refused to say why her roommate had gone to Jamaica, but I had a feeling she knew: Julia had gone there with some purpose in mind, and then things had gone wrong and she'd tried to get back home.

My watch said eight, so I went over to the pay phone in the corner, took out my pad, placed it on the shelf in front of me, and dialed.

"Okay, Micah," said a weary Mancuso. "Get ready to copy and then let me get back to sleep."

I picked up the pencil. "Shoot."

"Car and plates match. Car is registered to a Linda Marconi, Apartment 723, fifteen hundred Causeway Boulevard. No outstanding traffic or parking citations."

"Thanks, Sal."

"Hold up. I'm not finished."

"There's more?"

"A little. There's an outstanding bench warrant from city court. Your Miss Marconi failed to answer a complaint for prostitution."

A couple of call girls, I thought, as I wheeled through the still tight traffic beading the Interstate. I passed over the canal into Jefferson Parish, my hand on the steering knob, and

22

bit my tongue as a Winnebago borrowed my lane with five feet to spare.

It explained a name nobody could trace, and a passport she'd probably gotten from somebody in the shadow world. It also explained how my name had come up; I'd done a job for some businessman, or lawyer, or real estate agent, who'd gone to Linda Marconi for solace. When she needed somebody in my line, she'd called her john and he'd been too glad it was just a name she wanted, and not shut-up money.

The building had a Vacancies sign on the lawn, which said something about the state of the economy, because the structure was a new one, the architectural style Holiday Inn, with windows that looked out over Lake Pontchartrain. Like much of New Orleans, the lake was a phony. When Iberville made the initial exploration in canoes, in 1699, it was an imposing expanse, twenty miles from shore to shore, with a bounty of fish and waterfowl. Nearly three hundred years later it was a muddy agglomeration of sewage and disposable cans. Shell dredging destroyed much of the ecology, and no one in his right mind would eat a fish from the place, if a fish could be found, much less bathe in it. Above the surface, though, the illusion remained, so there were yacht races and motorboat sports, and from a tall building like Linda's, it was a nice backdrop.

I parked on the street and went inside. There was a parking garage, but I didn't want to waste time looking for her car. I wanted to catch her before she'd had a chance to think up a new plan, back her into a corner, and not go away until she told me what was going on.

The security guard gave me a quick once-over and decided a man with a lame arm wasn't going to be a problem. I waited for a woman who looked like a legal secretary, big glasses and a set expression, to leave the elevator, and then pressed the button for seven.

I'd never understood the attraction of these places. Nobody seemed to *live* in them; they just visited until the lease was up and then found someplace else. But there seemed an abundance of floaters, mostly young people, who enjoyed the life-style.

The hallway was deserted, but from behind one of the doors a TV was playing. I found 723 and started to knock. Then I noticed the door wasn't completely closed.

I knocked and rang the buzzer, but a minute later there was still no response. Maybe she's in the bathroom, I thought, or down the hall, with a friend, but the memory of Julia Morvant sent shivers through me.

I pushed the door open and went in.

Faint light from a standing lamp suffused the living room. I closed the door behind me and then spun into a crouch as a figure moved on my left. When I froze, the figure froze, too. I stood up again, slowly, letting my heart go back to normal, and turned up the intensity of the lamp. A mirror, covering the left wall. I'd been scared by an image of myself.

But besides the two of us, the room was empty. I stepped around the coffee table, where pillows provided the seating. A faint smell of sweet incense hung in the air. Two doors on the other side of the room probably led to the bedrooms, while straight ahead, behind a counter, was the dining area. A picture window looked onto a balcony, framing the lake, with the causeway arrowing out in the distance against the water.

Nothing was out of order and the same perfume I'd smelled in the bar lingered on the air. But something about it all bothered me.

I walked to the dining area and stopped. A purse was on the table, and I was sure it was the same purse she'd carried to our meeting. I checked the kitchen, then went back into the living room.

I didn't like going into strangers' bedrooms but didn't see any alternative. I tapped on both doors and waited, then pushed open the first one.

The room was dark so I flipped the wall switch.

Light glowed down from an array of overhead lamps that framed a suspended mirror. In the center of the room was a king-size bed with a quilt. Smaller mirrors lined the other walls, around the closet and bathroom doors. The only other furnishing in the room was a bureau, and on the other side of the bed, a small bookcase.

I checked the bathroom, but it was empty, so I went out, to the other bedroom.

The smell of perfume was stronger in this one, and it was less elaborately furnished, just a bed, some records on a shelf, and some clothes on the floor in one corner. This was Linda Marconi's room, I was sure, and a quick check of the bureau turned up some junk mail and a box of receipts to prove it. The apartment was evidently in her name, along with the utility bills, and some old check registers showed a haphazard attempt to keep track of her expenditures. It didn't seem a problem, because her income looked to be comfortably in excess of what she paid out. I noted the account number and the name of the bank and kept going. The bottom drawer had been converted into a repository for memorabilia. Mixed in with assorted sex aids were pictures of her as a young girl, pictures with boys, and pictures at the beach. I found high-school love letters, and a letter from her mother, with an Alexandria return address. Linda was a pack rat, and I found an Alexandria High class ring from '82 and some old Mardi Gras doubloons. There was also a packet of recent snapshots, mostly pictures from the zoo, as if she were having fun with a new toy, but one showed two young women on a beach. I recognized Linda at once, and when I turned the photo over I saw the names *Linda and Julia* written in the same childish scrawl I'd found in the check register.

I held the photo up to the light and stared down at the other woman. She was in her early thirties, with chestnut hair to the shoulders, and a nice body, suggestively posed for whoever was taking the picture. Her mouth hinted at a smile, but, while Linda wore her sunglasses, Julia's were perched on her head, as if she wanted the camera to see her eyes. I wondered what the eyes were seeing, then shrugged and dropped the packet of photos in my pocket. I shut the drawer and went over to the closet. Some frilly nighties, and some specialty leather gear. There was a stack of clothes on the floor, and when I moved toward the bathroom I kicked some shoes. Besides being a pack rat, Linda was a bit of a slob, which contrasted with the neat habits of her roommate.

The bathroom was empty, but a douche bag coiled like a snake from the shower rod. I went back to Julia's room and started a methodical check of the bureau, writing down the labels from underwear and other possessions, and looking for sales slips. I made a similar check of the closet. Maybe she had a favorite salesperson in whom she confided, someone who could tell me more than I knew so far.

She had the expected inventory of split-crotch lace panties and high stockings. Also, a varied assortment of condoms, which showed she was no fool. I was hoping to turn up her address book, but she hadn't hidden it in the bureau or the closet, so I moved to the bath.

Feminine napkins and tampons were demurely out of sight, in the clothes hamper, but the hamper itself was empty of dirty clothes. I went to the medicine chest. A prescription could turn up a doctor, and I found what I was looking for: a plastic bottle of Elavil capsules, made out to Julia Griffith. I wrote down the prescription number, the name of the pharmacy, the date, the name of the pharmacist, and the doctor's name, L.V. Laurent. The pills had been purchased last month, and the bottle was still full, so she'd obviously stopped having the problem and seen no need to take the medicine with her.

I returned to the bedroom. This time I went to the shelf beside the bed. There was poetry by Dickey and Jarrell, and also Houseman and Yeats. The volume of *Finnegan's Wake* had some pages still uncut, which I hardly held against her, but the single-volume Shakespeare was well thumbed. I went through the flyleaves, looking for inscriptions, maybe from some john who'd seen her as an Eliza Doolittle to his Professor Higgins. Or maybe from a time when she'd used her real name and added an address in case the book were lost.

I almost lucked out with Omar Khayyam. There, on the

inside cover, was a simple legend in blue ink: *To Julie with love, Christmas 1984. From Jenny.*

I put the book back on the shelf, after holding it upside down to see what would fall out. But I wasn't *that* lucky.

The sound of the telephone on the bedside table startled me and I stood listening until the ringing stopped and the answering machine clicked on.

I turned up the volume to catch the message. It was a man's voice, giddy from alcohol.

"Julia, listen, my name is Phil Ander—well, just Phil, okay?" He laughed as if it were all a big joke, but I could sense the nervousness. "I'm in town for two days and I thought maybe we could get together. I'm in Room 450 at the Sonesta. Give me a call. Oh, yeah, Bob from Houston gave me your number."

I reran the tape for the last week and got a mix of similar messages, all from men, all leaving only first names: Gus, Ron, Jack. . . . They seemed to melt together. I wrote down the names and her telephone number, as a matter of course, but I knew I'd find her phone was listed under another name. Then I went to the next room, where Linda had a similar machine. I listened to her messages.

"Baby, this is Ralphie. The old lady's outa town and I want some special, you know, like last time. If you ain't around, how about your roommate?"

There were some other calls with oblique allusions to the chain gang and the beltway, which tallied with the leather goods I'd found in the closet.

But I was missing one item: While Linda Marconi might be content to keep things in a cardboard box in the dresser, her roommate seemed just the opposite. For Julia I had no doubt there would be a safety deposit box, maybe several of them, where she kept anything that could identify, incriminate, or otherwise disturb her orderly existence. The problem was I didn't have time to look for the key.

The smell of smoke seeping up from under the door told me I had even less time than I thought. I cracked the door and coughed as something acrid hit me in the face. A sickening haze was already starting to fill the room.

The damn place was on fire.

27

4

It wasn't as bad as it looked; just a cigarette that had fallen on the rug and smouldered until the synthetic fibers had finally reached flash point and started to release their deadly fumes. I held a handkerchief over my face until I got to the kitchen, then filled a jug up with water and, holding my breath, doused the charred area. I opened the big sliding door onto the balcony and stood over the street, gulping the night air. There hadn't been enough heat to activate the sprinkler system and for some reason the smoke alarm hadn't gone off, so I had some time to try to think it out.

There wasn't much thinking to be done: She'd dropped her cigarette on the rug, and the only reason I could think of was because somebody had surprised her and taken her somewhere by force.

I took a deep breath and went back into the smoky room, noting the shower cap over the smoke alarm, probably something the girls had done because of their frequent use of candles. I went out into the hallway and closed the door behind me.

The security guard in the lobby paid me less attention than when I'd come in, his nose thrust into a paperback thriller. I could have asked if he'd seen her come down with someone, but I didn't want to get hung up there. Instead, I drove a block to a pay phone and called the number Solly had given me.

It was answered in true spook fashion, no hello or drop dead, just the number repeated by a man who obviously wasn't Solly.

I left a message to call me at the pay-phone number and waited. I could have called Mancuso, but Jefferson Parish was outside his jurisdiction. And he'd already told me he was off the bomb case.

Three minutes later the phone rang and I picked it up.

"Micah?" It was Solly's growl and I acknowledged with a brief description of what had happened, not mentioning the packet of photos I'd taken.

"Jesus," he snorted. "Well, you done good, boy. Hang in where you are. Don't move."

I didn't. I went back and sat in my car in the parking lot, watching the traffic slide past.

Two women, both high-class hookers, one dead, the other taken. Worse, each had just contacted me. Somebody had been following Linda Marconi and had seen our meeting at the bar. But how had they gotten onto her? A phone tap? A coldness started to creep through me. The only tap that made sense was on my own line. I made a mental note to have my office swept tomorrow. And if a tap were found . . .

A black Fairlane nosed into the lot, shoving hot air out of the way ahead of it, and Solly Cranich got out. He'd changed from his suit to a loose *guayabera* like my own, but the shirt couldn't conceal the bulge on his right hip.

"Micah," he said, crushing my hand with his paw. "Look, we'll take it from here on. The honcho says thanks, he owes you."

"Sure. Just one thing, Solly: She didn't have a bomb, did she?"

He gave me a funny, sideways look. "You mean the Morvant woman?"

"That's right."

29

He shrugged. "Well, it was just an idea." He managed a gruff chuckle. "Another government theory bites the dust."

I nodded. "Well, do me a favor, will you? Since I've gotten dragged into this, I can't exactly just drop out. Mind keeping me up to date?"

Solly frowned, and then his face loosened up and he gave a wink. "No problem," he said under his breath. "You deserve it." I started away, but his voice caught me. "Micah, look, keep the lid on, okay?"

I drove back to my place. This time there was a message from Katherine.

"Micah?" Her voice came through static and I strained to hear. "Listen . . . going okay . . . calling from Valladolid. Everybody's off drinking, but I was thinking about you. I can't stand it. Isn't that crazy? I feel like a high-school girl. I'll try again tomorrow. Love you."

The recorder beeped and I sighed. She was at Ek Balam, the famous site that had been responsible for our meeting. I tried to visualize her in the field, her jeans dirty and dust smearing her face under the straw hat, but I had trouble replacing the image of her when we'd met, in demure short-sleeved blouse and pleated skirt.

I tried to force her out of my mind, thinking instead of the Marconi girl. I opened my desk drawer and stared down at the .38 Detective Special. No. Guns were a last resort. I never carried except when I was out late, in certain parts of the city no sane person should have gone, and even then I was outgunned. I slammed the drawer shut and walked down to Jackson Square. They had barricades around the Cabildo, from the fire that had nearly destroyed it last year, and I remembered how close the fire had come to the cathedral. I went into a cafe and found a pay phone, where I dialed a wire man named Sessoms.

He listened to my suspicions and promised to come the next day, early. "Meantime, I wouldn't use the phone," he said. "'Less, of course, you got something you want 'em to hear."

I walked back slowly, enjoying the descending cool of

night. It was a Monday and the Quarter was moribund. A few tourists passed, swinging cameras, along with a couple of sailors. The streetwalkers had taken the night off, but then, everybody deserved to rest sometime.

Back at my apartment, I bolted the door and settled down to read a history of yachting. Two hours later I was ready to go to sleep. But first I went back into the front room, took the revolver out of the drawer, and put it beside my bed.

I'd almost finished my morning exercises when Gerald Sessoms knocked on the door. I was glad for the interruption, because after a hundred sit-ups and some other routines that didn't require two arms, I was down to the point of trying some isometrics with my left. The doctors said there was nerve damage and it was true I couldn't feel anything, but I kept forcing myself to place it next to the other one on the chin-up bar, or against solid obstacles, because I was deluded enough to think that one of these days the muscles would get the message, and then the nerves. But doing the exercises meant I had to think about it, which was why I was glad when Sessoms knocked.

We shook hands without greeting and he started to unpack his suitcase. A lanky red-neck of fifty, he'd drifted down to New Orleans from north Louisiana, and now he ran an electronics-supply house. But he made money after hours by doing electronic counterintelligence. He dipped snuff, had a dim view of all kinds of government, and got pleasure at the thought of throwing a monkey wrench into any of Big Brother's machinations. I watched him unscrew the ear- and mouthpieces of my phone and attach his voltmeter. Like most PIs, I left the specialty work to others, but I knew the most common types of phone bugs would cause a minute drop in voltage, a change that could be detected by the kind of instrument Sessoms was using. He played with his dials for a while, shook his head, and then put my phone back together. Then he got out a magnetometer and started to sweep the walls.

When he finished, he put his machine away and went to

31

my window, where he glanced out, spat some snuff into the jar he carried and then motioned me out to the balcony.

"If the phone was tapped, the tap's off now. Nothing in the office, but you got a big window there, onto the street."

"Infrared," I said, then laughed. "But you don't think they're in the old Mint?" It was one of the Quarter's famous landmarks, directly across the street from me.

"Not likely," he agreed and spat again. "Though I've seen stranger things. More likely your other window, the one on the end. It would be an easy shot from the building across the street. That way they could hear everything going on in the room. Clean and simple; no need to get inside, no evidence to keep track of."

"We're talking government, then," I said.

He shook his head. "Not necessarily. *I* can get the equipment if I want to. Hell, today everything's for sale. And, you may not be bugged at all."

I thanked him and tried to give him some money, but he just smiled.

"Professional courtesy," he said. "Just keep them cards and letters coming."

After breakfast I called Sandy's number and left a message for her to meet me for lunch. I had an appointment with a woman in Chalmette who was sure her ex had snatched their ten-year-old. The cops had refused to act and I listened as she went through a pack of Winstons and two martinis, describing in detail what a dirty, depraved bastard her ex had been and probably still was. She wasn't the ideal client, but few of them are and she had a court order, so I laid out my terms and when she didn't blink I agreed to look into it.

Half an hour later I met Sandy at a burger joint on Chef Menteur Highway. She was stylish in a flowing dress and a half dozen gold necklaces and she drew admiring stares from a couple of brothers who whispered together and smiled. She stabbed them with a look and their whispering stopped.

"Sorry to be late," she said, sweeping into the booth. "I had a late night."

I explained about the woman and the abducted boy, and gave her the address on the last child-support check. "It's Mississippi, so the locals aren't all that interested. Figure it's a federal case."

"And the feds don't see any headlines from a custody dispute," she agreed. "Gotcha, babe."

"Anything turn up on the Morvant woman?"

She shook her head, exuding a perfume that smelled like orchids. "Street people don't want to say nothing, but nothing. Your buddies, Mancuso and company, have stirred 'em all up, looking for these girls that got lost. Same in Jefferson. You know how it is: Strung out kid, peddles herself for a couple of months, and moves on, but somebody at city hall has a hard-on, so now the cops are running all over the place, and nobody'll talk because they think I may be the law."

"Well, I'll tell Sal to lay low," I promised.

Sandy smiled and got up. "Right on. And I'll get on this straightaway, Micah. But I'll bet the kid's better off."

"Probably," I agreed and drove back to the central business district. I picked up a check for services at John O'Rourke's law office on Gravier, along with a congratulatory note telling me my evidence had resulted in a settlement. The lawyer was in court on another case and his secretary, Abbie, let me borrow his phone.

The book listed Dr. L.V. Laurent under "Psychiatry—Adult." He had an office on Clearview Parkway, in Metairie, so I called to see if he was in, thinking I'd drive out if he was and try to figure some entrée.

"Are you a patient?" the receptionist asked pleasantly.

"No, I'm an attorney he talked to about . . . well, a matter we discussed. I've looked into it and I need to get in touch with him."

"I see. Well, the doctor's at Riverview this afternoon. You can probably contact him there."

"Thank you."

A few blocks from the Riverside Country Club in Harahan, Riverview Clinic was a complex of brick one stories built in the last ten years, before the oil glut made new ventures unpopular. A border of well-clipped bushes masked a chain-link fence and the wood-shingled security hut at the entrance drive could have been taken from any of a couple of dozen residential developments. I told the guard I'd come to take Dr. Laurent's car to the shop and he obligingly described it. I thanked him, signed in with my real name, and parked three cars away from the psychiatrist's blue BMW. Then I went inside and asked the lady at the front desk if I could have an audience.

The woman appraised me for a second, then pressed a button on the telephone. "What was your name?" she asked.

"Dunn," I said. "Micah Dunn."

She repeated my name into the receiver, nodded with a frown, and hung up slowly, as if the phone were alive.

Half a minute later I was being hustled out by two men who didn't want to hear my reasons. I'd half expected it, but it had been worth a try. I reverted to Plan B, which meant an afternoon of waiting, but waiting was part of my job.

I was lucky, though. He must have finished early, because it was only three-thirty when the BMW passed through the gates and headed north, toward Jefferson Highway.

When he was a block ahead, I followed, keeping far enough behind that my '83 Cutlass wouldn't arouse any suspicions.

If he was headed for his club, I'd have trouble following him in, but as it turned out he was just going back to the office and I caught up on Clearview and slid in beside him, so that I was getting out before he'd finished locking his car.

"Doctor Laurent," I called, hurrying over to his side of the car.

He looked up, quizzical under thick black brows. He was short, with a black beard that hid his features, and made him look younger than he probably was.

"Yes? What do you want?"

"My name is Dunn," I said. "I need to ask you something."

His lips curled down in distaste. "Mr. Dunn, or whatever your name is, I have no intention of answering any questions. You misrepresented yourself to my office and then you concocted some lie to get onto the clinic grounds. I don't have time for this kind of nonsense and if you don't leave immediately, I'll have you arrested. I saw you following me and I called the police on my car phone."

I got the feeling he expected applause but I just shrugged.

"Have it your way, Doctor. All I want to know is why you prescribed Elavil to Julia Griffith."

"Do you think I'll stand here and discuss the details of my practice with a stranger?"

"I don't know, Doctor. I'd just like to know what you were treating her for."

Ego got the better of irritation and he bestowed a patronizing smile. "If you knew anything about psychiatrists, you'd know we're medical doctors, and that patient-physician privilege is absolute."

"Then Julia Griffith is a patient of yours?"

"I said I don't discuss my patients." Once more, though, ego rose to the fore. "But, as a matter of fact, I don't have any patient by that name. Now if I were you I'd leave before the police get here."

"They're pretty slow," I said. "But we could all go down and talk about what happened to the plane Julia was on. It came down, you know. A mile short of the runway. So, you see, she isn't going to sue you for divulging her secrets. She's dead."

He gave me a sidelong look and then darted inside, leaving me in the late afternoon sun.

Something about his sudden escape made me think it had all been bluff; that he hadn't called the law and wasn't going to.

Why?

I went back to my office, stopping at the pharmacy that had filled the prescription. But it was a chain operation, with a few hundred prescriptions a day, many from strangers, and the druggist was only slightly more communicative than the doctor. He didn't know Julia, couldn't remember her, and had work to do, if I'd excuse him.

So I thanked him and left. The westbound lane was already bumper-to-bumper and it wasn't quite four-thirty. In the distance was the shiny helmet of the Superdome, floating above it all. It was a pleasing sight, but I kept thinking about Solly. Somebody had told him to give me a nudge, but he knew me too well to expect me to just drop it all. Still, trying the psychiatrist had been a shot in the dark and I'd expected it to be a dead end, just like the investigation.

When I opened my door the phone was ringing and I caught it before the answering machine cut in.

"Dunn Investigations," I said.

"Right," a tired voice said from the other end and I recognized it as Sal Mancuso. "Look, hotshot, I think you better get up to Wisner, where Mirabeau crosses the bayou. We just made the acquaintance of your friend, Linda Marconi. Somebody beat her to death and dumped her in the water across from the golf course."

5

The first settlement of New Orleans was near the place where Wisner Boulevard now grew out of Carrollton and started up the west bank of Bayou St. John. The first recorded settlers were a small group of Indians. They didn't last long after the arrival of the French, and soon the woods were felled for the Europeans. By the nineteenth century the oaks to the west of the bayou had become a favorite place for duels between young Creoles. Today, the old settlement was under the Fairgrounds, and the dueling oaks were inside City Park. Bayou St. John, once a thoroughfare to the lake, on the north, was a scenic canal, with masonry bridges reminiscent of Amsterdam, and high tone houses on the east bank.

Whoever had done it had been considerate, I thought, as I bulled north on Wisner, through the traffic, and past the golf course on my left, where earnest putters were measuring their shots. No one's game had been interrupted. The action was all on the right, at the water's edge, where the disturbance would be minimal.

I saw them soon after I crossed Harrison, a clutch of police cars on the grassy verge, right in front of the Mirabeau Avenue bridge. There was also an ambulance and a coroner's wagon. I pulled up onto the grass and got out. As I opened my door I saw Mancuso walking toward me, the bottoms of his trousers wet.

"Glad you could make it," he said sourly.

"Try calling when the whole city isn't on the way home," I said. "At least I didn't have to use the Interstate."

"Save it," he ordered and led me toward the water's edge. He was in shirtsleeves, collar loose, with wet places where his 9mm hugged against his torso in the shoulder holster. My nose wrinkled as I approached the canal. The air was heavy with steam, carrying the mud smell of the bayou, along with the less pleasant smells of human excrement and rotting garbage.

A little circle of people were standing in the ankle-high grass along the water's edge, looking down at something. The circle parted reluctantly as Sal approached.

"Can we move her now?" one of the coroner's men asked. "It's been almost three hours. . . ."

"You'll get her soon enough," Sal snapped. "I just want this man to look at her first." He shot me a gimlet stare. "Take a good look, Micah."

I did, but it wasn't something I enjoyed. She was on her stomach, arms stretched out on either side as if she were swimming, her body half in, half out of the water. She was wearing the same outfit as when I'd seen her the night before, but it was streaked with mud and dried brown stains I recognized as blood. The left side of her face was exposed and her eye was open. So was her mouth. There were purple bruises on her face and arms and I winced.

"Know her?" Sal asked through tight lips.

"I met her once," I said. "When was she found?"

"Three hours ago. A jogger. Coroner figures she's been there all night."

"Was she killed here?"

"Who knows? My guess is they dumped her off the bridge and she washed up here." He took a deep breath. "Look, hike your ass over here where we can talk."

I followed him to a spot out of earshot and he put his hands on his hips.

"Now, goddamn it, what's going on? I did you a favor last night, damn it, and you promised to keep me abreast. So

38

what happens? First thing I know I get a call that a body's been found in the bayou. They call me because I'm supposed to be in charge of all the dead and missing whores and maybe this is one. No good telling 'em that if this is a whore, she's a high-class one, not a streetwalker; that this is a murder and all the others are disappearances; and that this one looks like a beating, which probably means a pissed-off pimp or boyfriend. I'm the whore finder, so I have to come. Then imagine my surprise when I find out her prints make her the same lady one of my supposed friends asked me about just a few hours before somebody tried to remove her head. I might almost think I'd been had. So talk, Micah. I want to know what's happening."

He was right. I had no reason to hold out on him. Whatever primacy Solly and his people enjoyed had disappeared with the death of Linda Marconi. It was as much a city homicide as a federal case now.

When I finished explaining he shook his head and swore under his breath.

"Bastards. Come in here like gang busters and think they've got all the answers. Okay, I'm sorry I acted pissed, but you've got to understand."

"I do. And I don't blame you."

His features had softened. He took out a cigarette and lit it. "So now I've got *two* cases. Disappearing hookers, and *this*. There's no way I'll be able to explain to the lieutenant that they're different. He knows it, but it's all politics now. Dead white girls are high visibility."

I thought for a minute. "Have they turned up Julia Morvant's body?"

"I told you, I'm off the thing." He lowered his voice to a whisper. "But, just between us, I *was* a little curious. But the coroner's man says the bodies are so jumbled up they don't know what they've got. Or who."

I told him about Dr. Laurent. "Her name may not be Griffith," I said. "It would be nice to have some prints."

He nodded. "I'll call the Jefferson folks and make arrangements to go out and check her apartment for prints. If the feds haven't turned everything upside-down."

I slept fitfully that night. Ninja warriors kept trying to get into my apartment and I kept blasting away at them with my .38. There were too many and I fell back into the office. Suddenly Solly was next to me, telling me not to worry, he'd take care of the bastards. He had some kind of laser gun and he was melting them down, laughing while he did it, and when he'd finished he broke down his ray gun and went over to the window.

Something warned me and I yelled at him but it was too late. A death ray from across the street burned through in a shaft of red light and he vaporized before my eyes.

I was still groggy when the phone rang and I heard my father's voice.

"You still asleep? Is that what they taught you at the naval academy?"

The same old Captain.

"I'm fine," I said. "Just didn't sleep well."

"Why? Sleeping alone again? I thought that archaeology woman was going to tie an anchor to you."

"She'll be back in a few days."

"Not good for a man, being alone. I don't sleep by myself any more than I have to."

Bravado, the mark of the old sea dog.

"They say there's a depression in the Caribbean," he went on. "If it slips in between Cuba and Yucatan you'll have a hurricane on your hands."

"We've had them before," I said. "So what's new in Charleston?"

"Nothing. Everybody here makes money off what's old. You could, too, if you'd come back."

"We've been through that before." I tried to put the events of yesterday out of my mind. "You could come down here for a visit," I said.

"Not me. Seen enough of that town. Tourist trap. I was

40

there for Mardi Gras in '61, on the *Stoner.*" He chuckled. "Strange people in that town."

"True enough."

His voice turned serious. "What's wrong, son? It's not just loneliness, is it? Something bothering you?"

"Just tired," I said. "Look, I'll talk to you later."

A brief silence, then a cough. "Sure. Didn't mean to bother you. Fathers shouldn't butt into their sons' business. I got my own life, anyway. I'll, ah, write when I get a chance."

I sensed his hurt, but there wasn't anything to be done while I was still unsure of the phone. I made myself breakfast, fumbling the kitchen implements even worse than usual. I'd resisted special equipment, because I'd seen people manage with worse handicaps than my own, but I'd finally succumbed to a specialized can opener and a few other so-called improvements. This morning, though, I kept forgetting and expecting my left arm to work, like this was before Nam, before the academy, even, and I was living in Charleston, helping a wealthy friend race his yacht. Things had been simple then. Good was good and bad was bad, and I was going to help save the world.

But the world was beyond saving and all anybody could do was make it from day to day, except that when airplanes exploded and young women turned up dead in the bayou it was harder, because you never knew what would happen tomorrow or if you wanted to be there to see it.

I went down, nodding to Lavelle, who was reading the *Picayune,* waiting for victims.

"Hell of a thing," he said indignantly, thumping the paper. "Did you see this?"

"What?"

He flourished his paper at me and I caught something about assassination on the front page.

"That silly asshole Stokley got blown up yesterday."

"Stokley? Emerson Stokley?" I asked, surprised.

41

"The honorable himself, the man the good citizens around here sent to Congress to throw money at the military."

"What happened?"

"He was in the Virgin Islands on a tour. Somebody lobbed a grenade into his cabana." He shook his head. "I don't agree with all his politics. But he's no worse than most of 'em they've got up there."

"You sound unusually tolerant today," I commented.

He shrugged. "What can I say? The man did me a favor once when he was on the council. A bunch of fundamentalists were trying to zone me out of business."

"Perfidy everywhere," I said.

For some reason I was glad to get out on the street, where the morning sun was already raising little heat waves from the tar street. The people I saw were not interested in Caribbean terrorism. I passed tourists with cameras, businessmen in seersucker suits that were already wrinkled, and a few winos leaning back against the walls of buildings, not knowing if it was day or night. All in all, it looked like a simpler world than the one that seemed to be reaching out to drag me in.

I wasn't sure where I was going; I just needed a chance to think, and I did it best on the street, with a flow of bodies around me. I hadn't been that way before Nam, but something about the green loneliness of the jungle made the loneliness of cities more tolerable now.

Twenty minutes later I was standing on Canal, outside the Clarion Hotel, watching a bellhop unload a limo while a woman in a big hat fretted about some gewgaw she couldn't locate.

I realized now I'd been thinking about Solly. This was where he was staying, he'd said, but I hadn't come to spy on him. I wasn't sure why I'd come, in fact. So I just stood there, sweating, as people passed, and then, when it was too late, I turned around and saw the man behind me and knew there was no longer any choice but to go in.

6

Another one met me in the lobby and they formed an escort into the elevator. Before anybody else could get in they pressed the button, the door closed, and we began to rise. Five flights later the elevator halted and one of the men motioned for me to get out. I'd seen them before, not the same faces, but the same men, nevertheless; gray suits, dark glasses, conservative ties, and an earpiece and lapel pin each. Under the sports coats each would have a .357 or maybe, things being what they were, a Berreta 9mm. They were part of an army, but it was not one I'd ever wanted to belong to.

We walked down the narrow hallway, past rooms with breakfast trays out front. It was an old hotel, with an air of faded middle-class memories. Many of the rooms were small, and the restaurant wasn't four stars, but it saw its share of conventions.

The man behind me had been mumbling into his lapel mike, and one of the doors ahead of us opened suddenly and a third man in the same uniform stood aside for us to enter.

If I expected a spook setup, I was in for disappointment. Some breakfast trays were on the bureau and luggage stand and a newspaper was spread over one unmade bed. There was no communications center, which meant they either had a suite or, more likely, a house nearby. The only concession to the electronic age was a VCR, hooked to the television, but then, maybe they liked girlie tapes.

Solly was sitting in the chair farthest from the door and he managed a smile when he saw me.

"Micah. I'm glad to see you." He got up and gave me a handshake I thought was a little too hearty.

Everybody seemed to be waiting for something, and that was when I realized water was running in the bathroom. The door opened then and a fifth man came out, wiping his hands on a towel.

Older than the others, he sported a bushy black mustache and a silk shirt that must have cost fifty dollars. A PPK, the CIA's favorite handweapon, hung from a Berns-Martin fast-draw rig, and a pack of cigarillos stuck out of his top pocket.

"Excuse me," he said, giving me a steel grip. "But New Orleans's famous food is about to do me in."

His English was accentless, which is what happens when you spend a little bit of your life everywhere. Since he wore a West Point ring, though, I figured he'd spent at least four years in one place.

There was silence while he reached for his cigarettes, found the pack was empty, and threw the container into the trash. One of the men handed him a fresh pack and he broke the cellophane.

He waved me to a chair and lit the thin, brown cigarette while the others watched. "Captain Dunn, you must be psychic," he said finally. "We were going to invite you over but you came on your own. Remarkable. Maybe there're something to this ESP crap after all."

"Linda Marconi is dead," I said evenly. "Somebody killed her. Then they dumped her in Bayou St. John."

He shook his head. "Hell of a thing. But, take my word for it, there are worse things happening. I'd like to tell you about some of them. My name is Cox. I'm in charge of this operation."

The lights went off suddenly and one of the agents pushed the buttons on the television. The screen sprang to life.

44

"Nothing we're about to discuss goes beyond this room, I hope that's understood."

"I don't make blind promises," I said. "I don't know what you're getting ready to show me."

I caught some alarmed glances but my host seemed unruffled.

"Fair enough. You've paid your dues. I don't think anybody could doubt your patriotism."

I was looking at a car, or rather, what had once been a car, before something had reduced it to twisted scrap. A gendarme was standing to one side and a news crew was at the fringe of the picture.

"Marseilles, February third of this year," Cox said. "Tally: two dead. One was the American resident DEA agent. News reports called him a tourist."

The video ran for an instant longer than I needed; I'd seen bombed cars before, in the streets of Saigon, and it brought back smells and sounds I'd have rather forgotten.

Next was a sailboat, moored to a wharf.

"The *Recife Queen,* out of St. Croix. Owned by a Dutchman named van Guilder. The boat was found drifting in the Caribbean on May twenty-first. There was blood on the planking." In confirmation, the camera zoomed in on the deck and I saw brown stains. "No sign of van Guilder, but a satellite picked up a yacht in the area, headed for Colombia. Too late to intercept." He paused. "Van Guilder was a contract agent for the CIA. He was checking into drug traffic in the islands."

A third picture. This time a brick building with the front blown out and a fire truck playing a steady stream of water on the ruins while people ran back and forth.

"This was taken in Cuernavaca, Mexico. One of the chief DEA informants for that area ran a laundry here and lived in the back. He was killed, along with his wife and three children. That was on July fifteenth."

I should have expected the next part, but it caught me by surprise. I was staring at a cypress swamp, but something was wrong with it. The usual tranquility seemed somehow disturbed, and then, as the camera zoomed in on the hunks of metal sticking into the mud, I understood.

"Transcaribbean Flight 420," Cox intoned. "I don't have to tell you about that one. Sixty-seven people killed. Innocent people. Just to get Julia Morvant. At first, as Major Cranich told you, we thought she was the one with the bomb. But now we know better."

The camera lingered for an extra, unnecessary ten seconds and then one of the agents pushed a button to stop it.

"Sixty-seven people were killed to get one," Cox said. "That tells you something about the people we're up against." He nodded and the tape started again. This time it was part of one of the morning's network newscasts.

"Yesterday evening," said the voice of the newscaster, "an attempt was made on the life of Louisiana Congressman Emerson Stokley. Stokley, a senior member of the influential House Armed Services Committee, has recently called for stricter enforcement of drug laws and increased use of the military in curtailing drug traffic. The congressman was on a fact-finding mission in the Virgin Islands when a bomb was thrown into the house where he was staying."

The scene shifted from the television studio to a rustic street, where blocks of a wall had been blown into the road and a tile-roofed house smouldered from the great hole in its side.

"Congressman Stokley was taken to a nearby hospital with superficial wounds to the head and face. His wife, who was in the room with him at the time, suffered a possible concussion and flash burns."

The screen flicked to a file picture of the Stokleys and I thought, looking at her, that she reminded me vaguely of Katherine.

"Both the congressman and his wife were evacuated by military aircraft and are expected to recover. Meanwhile, local police were carrying out a search for the would-be assassin and FBI agents are expected to arrive within hours to make a full investigation."

The screen faded and abruptly a man's face appeared. It was a police photo, and he was looking through the camera as if by so doing he could pretend he was somewhere else. He had thin black brows, a pugnacious jaw, and Latin features. The signboard around his neck was marked Guatemala. The sign said his name was Angel Cordoba.

"Don't let the sign fool you," Cox said. "His real name is Rivas. Adolfo Rivas. He used Cordoba when he was picked up last year in Guatemala. They held him on a firearms charge, and then he bought his way loose before we could send agents to take him back to the U.S." The tape shifted to a black-and-white street scene, a man getting into a Renault, then looking back over his shoulder, as if he sensed he was being watched.

"Rivas was born in south Texas. So he's a U.S. citizen. His parents were Mexicans. He was a militant in the early seventies, but the movement wasn't militant enough for him, so he went to Cuba. From Cuba we think he may have gone to the USSR for formal terrorist training. He showed up again in the early eighties, as a hit man with connections to the Nicaraguan government and also with Panama's Noriega. Looks like somewhere along the line his ideology got lost in the shuffle, because we know he carried out a couple of hits for the Colombian cartel. This year he's been in his full glory. The pictures we showed you first are his work. He seems to feel like he's striking a blow for the revolution if he can bring the U.S. down through drugs. Or maybe he's just greedy. We know he can command a million a hit."

Now I saw Rivas with a mustache, lounging on a patio with a swimming pool in the background and jungle foliage visible over a garden wall. His body was squat and muscled, his chest matted with thick hair. I wondered where the photographer had been, and admired his guts.

"Rivas blew up the airplane. We think it was because they were afraid of the Morvant girl, that she was turning on them, ready to inform. We think he then took a hop to the Virgins, where he threw a bomb into Stokley's house. Only this time he wasn't so lucky. The congressman and his wife were in the next room."

"You have some proof?" I asked, my stomach suddenly weak. I'd felt like this during the briefings for intelligence missions in Nam.

"He was IDed at the airport. Also driving away from Stokley's on a motor scooter," the man by the TV said.

I looked over at him, vaguely surprised, as if a mannequin had spoken. Cox nodded agreement and exhaled a cloud of smoke.

"The girl in the bayou, too?" I asked.

Cox nodded. "Her, too. We found a late night who saw a man pushing something out of a car, into the water. His description wasn't perfect, but close enough."

"Jesus," I breathed.

"So now you have it." He tapped a folder that had appeared mysteriously at his slide. "This dossier includes his vitals, habits, known associates, but I'm afraid it won't help much, because he's a smart bastard, always changing his appearance and his habits. He always works alone, and uses people like they were toys."

Now the weakness was spreading. I looked over at Solly, but he looked away.

"Why are you telling me all this?" I asked, already knowing the answer.

"Because, Captain Dunn, we need your help. He's in New Orleans and we think he'll strike again."

"What can I do about it?" I asked, once more knowing the answer before I spoke.

Cox looked at me without smiling. "Captain Dunn, we want you to find him for us. And if he resists, we want you to kill him."

7

There was a long silence and then someone cleared his throat.

"I'm not an assassin," I said finally. "I don't hire out to kill people."

"We know that," Cox snapped. He tapped another folder. "In fact, we know all about you, Captain. We know what you do now, and what you used to do, and how well you did it. We know you hold the Silver Star, Purple Heart, and a few dozen other decorations. We know how you were treated when you came home." His jaw set now and I sensed he was no longer talking about me. "We know how *everybody* was treated. But you especially."

"Lots of guys had it worse," I said, but his words burned. It wasn't something I liked to think about, a part of my body that wouldn't work, a marriage gone sour, the loneliness of trying to find a new occupation.

"*Lots of guys* aren't Captain Micah Dunn," he said. "We have Solly Cranich's word for that."

Solly gave me a self-conscious smile and I knew he was uncomfortable. His forte was action, not words.

"Solly's your man," I said. "Solly's the best there ever was."

"Major Cranich is as good as you say," Cox agreed. "Maybe even better. But he doesn't know New Orleans like you do, Captain."

"Listen," I said, "knock off the *captain* shit. I'm out. I have been for twenty years. I don't need flattery."

And the constant use of my former rank was getting to me, as he probably knew it would.

"No flattery," Cox said. He shot a hard look at Solly. "You didn't tell him?"

Solly shook his head morosely.

Cox turned back to me. "Cranich over there retired as a major, as you know. When he came to us his commission was reactivated. He really is a major, on detached active duty."

"Congratulations," I told Solly, my heart starting to thunder. Cox held up a sheet of paper.

"Do you know what this is?"

"Tell me," I said, already sure of the answer, and yet afraid to ask.

"This is a request," Cox said. "Made out to the Secretary of the Navy by the head of my agency. All I have to do is sign it and forward it through channels. But that's a formality, because I already have a verbal agreement with all parties." He leaned toward me and I got a whiff of his cologne. "If you come aboard, your commission will be reactivated, just like Solly's, and you'll be returned to detached active duty as a captain in the Marine Corps."

I was starting to shake now and hoping he wouldn't see it. Twenty years. The dreams, the hopes, the envy as I watched others rise through the officer ranks . . .

"And, of course," Cox went on, "once we get Rivas, there'll be others. Our work isn't likely to dry up in my lifetime, or yours, or theirs." He motioned around the room, then turned back to me and extended a hand.

"Congratulations, Captain Dunn."

I knew I was shaking now, as I accepted his handshake.

"Look," I began weakly. "I said I don't kill people. And all this was twenty years ago, anyway. You don't need a one-armed agent."

"You remember what Lincoln said about Grant when they called him a drunkard? Send a barrel to my other generals? Maybe we need more one-armed agents. That's what Solly says. I agree." He chuckled for the first time. "And we aren't asking you to kill anybody. We aren't in that business. When we lay hands on this bastard, we aim to turn him over to the U.S. attorney, who holds a warrant for drug trafficking, and when they finish with him, we'll give him to the state for prosecution for murder. If they don't fry him, he'll spend the rest of his days in Marion."

"Unless he puts up a struggle," I said.

Cox shrugged. "That goes without saying. And, to be realistic, he probably will. If he's killed, nobody's the loser. If not, we get him."

"And if I'm killed?"

"Do you want to be a private detective forever? Spend the rest of your life looking through bedroom windows? Last year you almost got killed in a shootout on the wharves here. Come on, Dunn, you're too good for that. Christ, man, we're giving you an out."

"I'd like to think it over," I said.

Cox rose from his chair. "Sure," he said, faintly annoyed. "Take a day. We don't have any more. Rivas doesn't give a damn about our personnel situation."

"I understand," I said and got up myself.

Solly started forward, then stopped, his face confused. He was wondering why I hadn't jumped at the opportunity, of course. And so was I. After all, it was an attractive proposition and he almost had me, but something about the last part, attacking my profession, hit me the wrong way.

Back in the sunlight, I wandered south along Canal and then, when I got to Baronne, turned south. My shirt was sticking to me, but it wasn't entirely the sun that was making me sweat. I had to go inside, sit down, put my thoughts together.

I came to O'Rourke's law office and went in. The receptionist's desk was empty and I heard a rustle of papers from the inner sanctum. A second later O'Rourke himself came out, a legal pad in his hand, his shirt open at the collar.

"Hell, I thought it was a client," he said. "I hope you're not looking for work."

Lanky, my own age, with longish brown hair and a wry sense of humor, John O'Rourke had helped me years before, when I'd been desperate for work. These days I did his investigations and we met every couple of weeks for lunch, always trying to find the perfect spot. He, too, was divorced, but unlike me, he had yet to find a companion to suit his requirements.

I went back into his office with him and flopped in the chair before his desk.

"I don't need work," I said. "I've just been offered a permanent job."

His eyes narrowed slightly behind his horn-rims and he leaned back. "Really. And what kind of job is that?"

"To tell you the truth, John, I don't really know. At least, the ramifications are a little obscure."

"And you don't know if you should take it, or you wouldn't be here."

"You got it. Look, what I'm about to tell you is client to lawyer, right?"

He nodded and I told him about the Morvant phone call and everything that had happened as a result. "So now I'm being offered a return to active duty, and I've got to admit it's tempting."

He balanced a pencil between his palms. "But you're still not sure."

I exhaled and the shaking started all over again. "Christ, John, if you knew how many times I've dreamed about something like this or gone over the day when I hit that mine, thinking about how different it all would've been. . . . I'm not complaining about the arm, you understand. I can do fine with one. There are guys with no legs or with no movement below the neck. I just mean the having to leave the Corps. I loved it. I loved it better than anything else in my life."

O'Rourke, who had been a draft protester in those years, sucked in his breath. He had his own injury, a slight limp from a Chicago policeman's club.

"It's hard to give up what you love," he said softly.

"But," I began again, arguing the other side, "that was

twenty years ago. Everything's different. My life is different. We're at peace, at least theoretically. I might be a misfit. Hell, we were fighting what we thought was a good war, but it turned out to be a rotten war. I can't ever be the person I was."

"No."

I got up. "Mind if I use your phone to call the captain? All of a sudden I think I need some fatherly advice."

He pushed his phone toward me and started to get up but I waved him back down and dialed, hoping my father would be home.

After six rings I was about to hang up when I heard his voice.

"'Lo?"

"It's me," I said. "Look, I couldn't talk much earlier because I was afraid the line was bugged."

"Bugged?" he exploded. "Jesus, lad, what kind of mess have you got yourself into this time?" Beneath the bluster, though, his tone was warm and I knew he was glad I'd called him back.

"Well, I thought maybe you could help me with it, actually. Of course, I don't want to make problems for you. I know you're busy and, like you said earlier, you have your life and . . ."

"I can make time. Now what the hell is this all about?"

When I'd finished telling him there was a long silence.

"Dad?"

"I'm thinking."

More silence, then,

"You know, I never thought much of your idea of joining the jar heads, always figured it was some kind of juvenile rebellion, passing up a naval commission for one of theirs after the academy. But a man's got to do what makes him feel alive. For me it was always the waves and a steel deck under my feet, and thirty knots into the battle. But that's because I'm a destroyer man. You aren't. For you it's man against man. I can understand that. The question is, does this thing that's being offered to you make you feel good again, like you did before?"

53

"I . . . I'm not sure," I stumbled. "I guess most of all I'd like things to be the way they were and yet . . ."

"Yet they never will be. Everybody you knew is gone. There's a new crew. Most of 'em haven't ever fought an honest war, ship against ship or army against army. Still, I guess somebody has to do it. Do you want to be one of those people?"

I couldn't think of any answer, because I was trying to see myself without the apartment, in a foreign city. Would Katherine even want to come?

"Another thing," the Captain said. "Whatever these people are telling you, you have to realize a man with one lame arm isn't going to do much undercover work. Will you be happy working out of an embassy or consulate? Watching the others do the black stuff?"

"That's occurred to me," I said. "But at least I'd have my commission back."

"True enough. So in the end it's a decision only you can make, which you damn well knew when you called."

"I know. But I needed to bounce it off somebody."

"Hell, that's what I'm for. But there's one other thing I can do, maybe. I still have a few contacts on active duty. And one or two in the intelligence community. Let me ask some questions about this so-called group. I'd kind of like to know who they answer to. Maybe you would, too."

"That's for sure," I said fervently. "Thanks, Dad."

"Aw, hell."

I replaced the receiver and turned to O'Rourke.

"Well?" he asked.

I shrugged. "I haven't made up my mind." I sat back down. "Look, what do you know about Emerson Stokley?"

"Stokley?" O'Rourke's brows rose. "Actually, I probably know pretty much." He chuckled. "He's one of the few politicians I've ever sent money to."

"You?"

"Well, it was him or that asshole Bordelon, who wanted to get us out of the U.N., impeach the liberal members of the Supreme Court, and send the troops to Nicaragua. Stokley's

54

a moderate, but he has to pay lip service to certain elements or he wouldn't get elected around here. And I think he's more than just a pretty face for the cameras."

"God, and you're the man who marched in sixty-eight."

"Hell, nowadays Jerry Rubin's a Yuppie." He put his hands behind his head and leaned back again. "Actually, I've known Em Stokely since we were in Tulane Law School. I was a year ahead of him. He wasn't a bad guy. He comes from a rich family, but there was nothing stuck up about him. I think he actually had a few original thoughts. He felt the war was right and he served two years right after he graduated. I disagreed about the war, but he had the courage of his convictions. In fact, he might've been in Nam while you were there."

"We never met," I said.

"No. Anyhow, when he came home and opened up a law office we met every once in a while. I always had the feeling he was restless, looking for something; his niche, I guess." O'Rourke looked through me, into the past. "He went through a raft of girl friends and then he married a truly beautiful lady and he seemed to settle down. First thing you know he was being elected to the city council and then to Congress. For the last twelve years he's been quietly building his seniority and working behind the scenes to form coalitions on important issues. Just between us, I have a feeling he's a closet liberal."

"That really is damning news," I said.

The lawyer laughed. "And, he gives excellent constituent service," he went on. "I had a client with a tax problem and Em's office worked overtime to get things straightened out. He's built a good organization. And he tries to make it home every weekend, to tend to constituent problems."

"He sounds like everybody's buddy," I said. "Except that somebody obviously doesn't like him."

"Well, from what I hear it wouldn't have mattered what his name was. He was just getting a little too zealous for the drug lords."

"Apparently," I agreed, turning over everything in my

55

mind for the fortieth time. "Tell me something, John: Since they've brought him back home, where do you think he'll be? One of the private hospitals?"

"There or at home. The family has a plantation called Godsend down near Twelve Mile Point. If you want, I can find out. I'll call his local office."

I stared out of the window as O'Rourke dialed and identified himself to the person on the other end. Through the blinds I could see the shadows of people passing on the sidewalk. Adolfo Rivas. Was he out there somewhere? Might he even be trailing me at this moment? Christ, I was being paranoid. What would Rivas want with me? I was incidental, at most. There was no way he could know about the offer Cox had made me.

O'Rourke's voice brought me out of my thoughts.

"He's at the estate," he said, hand cupped over the mouthpiece, "him and his wife, under heavy guard, of course. They'll probably be there for the next week or so. This is supposed to be top secret, but this guy owes me. Anything else?"

A sudden impulse hit me. "John, ask if I can get in to talk to him."

"What?"

"Look, just vouch for me. Tell your friend I'd like a few minutes of the congressman's time. If I'm going to get as involved in this as I seem to be getting, I think I ought to talk to the only victim of this Rivas who's still alive. Maybe he saw something, I don't know. And if Rivas tries again, I'd like to have some idea of the layout."

O'Rourke's brows went up again and he swiveled his chair away from me, as if the negotiations would be too delicate for other ears. I got up and went into the front office.

There was still time to back off. I'd gotten in out of professional curiosity, and because a woman who'd wanted to be my client was now dead, and I took that personally. But now it was more than personal: It was a deep-seated itch that needed to be scratched, vanity and a longing for a past life. It was an abandonment of all objectivity and I told myself I should know better. This wasn't sixty-eight and Rivas wasn't some elusive VC organizer. All we had done twenty years ago had been for nothing, even, I thought, flinching, my arm, and yet here I was proposing to get into the game again. Why should it be any different this time? Because the cause sounded purer? Or did the cause matter at all? Was it just the need I'd suppressed, which Cox had so cleverly brought back up to the surface?

O'Rourke's chair squeaked and I heard the phone being replaced. He came back into the reception room.

"He'll call back after he checks it out. I had to do some heavy begging. I may even have to go to a Saints game."

John O'Rourke was a devout hater of all organized sports.

On another impulse, I lifted the phone on the secretary's desk and dialed Sal Mancuso's number. Luckily, he was in.

"Anything on the girl's apartment?" I asked.

"Nothing. Goddamn feds could fuck up a train wreck. They turned the place upside-down. And somebody managed to wipe away all the prints. We not only can't prove which body, or part of a body, belongs to the Morvant woman, but we can't get a set of her prints. Now, that's a hell of a thing. I'm so pissed I could wire the attorney general. We ran the name Julia Griffith and all variants and came up with a sixty-five-year-old retired schoolteacher from Marrero who has an unpaid parking ticket."

I thought of mentioning my talk with Cox but decided against it. All I needed was to get between two feuding agencies.

"Sorry, Sal."

"Sure," he said, disgruntled. "Let me know, will ya, when the next body turns up."

I stood quietly for a moment, my hand in my pocket. The apartment, wiped clean, almost as if somebody wanted the Morvant girl's identity kept a secret. . . .

And then I remembered something. The pictures I took from the apartment. One of them was of Julia Morvant. Maybe I had her prints after all!

8

I went back to my apartment. The photos were where I'd left them, locked in my desk drawer. I found a Ziplock bag and started to place them in it, stopping to look at the photo of Julia. Was there humor I detected in the curve of her lips or was it superiority? Whatever it was, I felt a strange attraction to her that I couldn't explain, as if she was someone I might have been close to years ago and suddenly met again.

The ringing phone jarred me from my reverie. It was O'Rourke.

"The word is *okay*," he said, sticking to our prearranged code. "You know how to get there?"

"It would be hard to miss. What time?"

"One. Good luck."

"Thanks, John."

I drove over to Central Homicide and stood around while they called Mancuso from his desk. I took him into the hallway, where no one would see us, and dropped the bag with the pictures into his hand.

"From Marconi and Morvant's apartment," I said. "Some of the photos show the Morvant girl, according to the writing on the back."

"And you've been holding out on me?" he asked, squinting.

"I forgot about them until just now. But look, my advice

58

is to check them all for prints. There's a good chance, if she showed any of them to Julia, then there'll be some prints still on them."

"If there are, we'll find 'em," he vowed. Now we were even.

I took the bridge east, to the West Bank, a geographic anomaly explained by the fact that the West Bank extends all the way north to a cusp in the crescent that holds the city. There's a lot of history in Algiers, but it's long ago been replaced by shipyards and government facilities. There's a naval station, a naval hospital, and a border patrol unit. There's the Fisher Housing Project, where you wouldn't want to go without a couple of ranger platoons, and an Abrams tank for support. But there are also middle-class neighborhoods, with comfortable houses and shade trees, a golf course, and even a psychiatric facility.

The main highway is a four lane called General de Gaulle Drive, after a visit years ago from the French leader. It passes banks, shopping centers, and fast-food joints. I stopped at one to eat an early lunch.

Sitting alone at the plastic table, I thought about Julia Morvant and wondered what it might have been like to meet her. Now, of course, I would never know.

I left at twelve-thirty, heading southeast, across the Intracoastal Canal Bridge, and down the other side. At the bottom I went right onto a blacktop, past a Vietnamese culture center that seemed strangely out of place, and a mile and a half later I reached the levee, where I turned right again.

Now I was in a rural area called the Lower Coast, passing straggly bits of forest and roads that went nowhere. Here and there, on the right, were handsome estates, set back discreetly from the road, and beside them, curtained off by more forest, shacks with stacks of old tires in front and chickens pecking at the roadside.

Godsend was one of the larger holdings, set back well from the road. A single wooden pole barred the shell drive, as if any barrier were necessary to tell people that you didn't come here uninvited. The drive itself wound through an alley of pecans, across a manicured lawn, to a white mansion in the antebellum style. O'Rourke told me that it had been built in the 1930s, on the site of the original Godsend, which had been constructed before the Civil War, between a bayou, to the rear, and the Mississippi.

As I pulled into the driveway a man appeared from a guardhouse concealed in the nearby foliage and asked my name. I gave him my driver's license and he checked a clipboard, then called to confirm on a hand radio. A few seconds later he nodded and the wooden pole lifted.

My tires crackled on the shells and I drove slowly, as if entering a sacred place. To the left of the house was a gazebo, which conjured up an image of lemonade, poetry readings and sedate conversation. On the other side of the drive, an ancient black man rode a mower over the last few rows of offending grass.

I slowed even further as I neared the house. There were two cars already parked in front, a Mercedes and a Lincoln Town Car. Both had congressional plates.

There were homes like this in Charleston and I'd visited my share, but no matter what my commission said about being a gentleman, I was not of the gentry and money always made me faintly uneasy, as, I suppose, it does many people.

The front door was opened by another elderly black man in coat and tie.

"Yes, sir," he said. "This way."

I entered a large, tastefully furnished room, but I'd hardly had a chance to take in my surroundings when another, younger man appeared. With skin as fair as the old retainer's was dark, and carefully styled brown hair, he seemed to fit in with what I'd seen so far. He squinted behind thick glasses and a couple of pens stuck out of his top pocket. There were some ink smudges on his fingers.

"Mr. Dunn," he said, offering me a quick handshake that showed he didn't have a lot of time. "My name is Nelson

60

Benedict. I'm the congressman's aide. I hope you won't object to a search."

As if on key, another man appeared from nowhere with a magnetometer and I held out my right arm as he passed it over my body. He started for my left side, where my other arm hung limply, but Benedict waved him away.

"It's all right. I'm sorry, Mr. Dunn, but after what happened we have to take precautions."

"Are the congressman and his wife able to see me?" I asked.

"The congressman is," said the aide. "He'll decide whether you can speak to Mrs. Stokley. They're both resting upstairs."

"Were you there when it happened?" I asked.

He shook his head. "I was in the village, picking up some supplies. There was going to be a sort of an intimate little dinner with some of the local officials." He ushered me toward a staircase. "I understand you've been recommended to help work on this," he said, lowering his voice.

"It's been suggested," I said.

"I hope you find them," he whispered.

"I haven't agreed to anything yet," I said.

"I see." He stopped in front of the door, then turned to face me before knocking. "You'd best know: The bomb left the congressman temporarily deaf. You'll have to write out your questions, though he can answer well enough. But not too much, please: He was almost blinded, as well."

"Thank you for telling me," I said.

He rapped twice on the door, and, without waiting for an answer, opened it.

The room was dark, so dark I at first had trouble seeing the figure propped up in the chair beside the bed. The air smelled faintly of mint and I realized it must have been a medicine used in preparing dressings.

Benedict started to close the door behind him.

"Thank you, Nelson," said a voice. "You can leave us alone now."

The aide started to protest, then realized he wouldn't be heard and looked from one of us to the other.

"It's all right," the congressman said. "I don't think we have anything to fear from Mr. Dunn."

I thought I detected a hurt cluck, but the door closed, and the congressman and I were alone.

"Excuse the darkness, Mr. Dunn. The explosion almost blinded me as well as left me without my hearing. The doctor told me to take it easy on my eyes for a few days. And I may talk a little loud."

My own eyes had started to adjust, and as I came forward to shake his hand I saw that he was swathed in bandages that covered the sides of his face and the top of his head, like an old-time nun's habit. But there was no mistaking the features; I'd seen them enough on the news.

I started to mumble sympathy and he nodded at the movement of my lips.

"Thank you. But I don't intend to let it get me down, any more than you let your own problem get the best of you. There's too damned much to do. Right now, though, I'm a hell of a lot more worried about *her*." He nodded toward the bed, and for the first time I realized there was someone in it.

I turned to look down at her. She was sleeping, the sheet drawn up almost to her neck, her face peaceful. Gauze patches were taped across her eyes, which had suffered from the blast.

"H-O-S-P-I-T-A-L?" I mouthed.

"She's only resting. It was a shock. But she'll be all right. I only wanted to keep her company."

I looked down at her again, this time critically. She was a beautiful woman, with pale gold hair and refined features. I tried to remember if they had any children but I couldn't recall hearing of any.

"Cox sent you," the politician said. "So we don't have to beat around the bush."

I nodded. "Yes."

"He said you'd be working for him. He recommended you highly. John O'Rourke's call was just icing on the cake."

Cox seemed ahead of me all the way and I resented it. I pulled a chair near to where he sat, sat down myself, and then pulled my notepad from my shirt pocket. With it resting on my knee, I used the attached pen to scribble out an answer: I HAVEN'T MADE UP MY MIND.

He squinted over at it as I held it up and then nodded. "I understand. Don't let him push you into anything. Don't let *anybody* push you into anything. This thing happened, but I'm convinced it's over with, at least so far as our being targets. This man, whatever his name is, is long gone."

I shrugged, hoping he'd get my meaning.

"Yes, I agree. He did hurt a lot of people." The congressman's voice caught. "That's the terrible part. But, you know, maybe he's one of these people that really can't help themselves. A man with a compulsion."

PSYCHO? I wrote.

He nodded. "Basically. What can you do in a case like that? It's a fact of life."

My expression must have been telling, because he nodded again.

"I know." He tried to shake his head but it was an effort. "I'm publicly for the death penalty, but if I were in that little room at the penitentiary, with my hand on the switch to end a man's life . . . I just don't know."

CAN YOU TELL ME EXACTLY WHAT HAPPENED? I wrote.

He stared past me in the gloom. "We'd just gotten in from the beach. We were going to have a little informal dinner for a few of the local members of the party. We were changing clothes in the bedroom when we heard a crash, like glass breaking. Aline opened the door into the parlor and I heard her gasp. I went toward her. I saw it on the floor and shoved her behind me. That was when it went off. I don't remember anything except waking up outside. They said I dragged her out."

It was useless to ask for details; I was beginning to think I'd already overstayed my time, but there were one or two more things I needed to ask him before I left:

HAVE YOU RECEIVED THREATS?

It was his turn to shrug. "All the time. You can ask Benedict about that. I never pay them any attention. At least, until now."

WAS IT A GRENADE?

He nodded the affirmative.

HAVE YOU EVER HEARD OF JULIA MORVANT?

He squinted at the page for a second, then shook his head. He moved his hand up to rub his eyes.

I understood and mouthed thanks.

"Thank *you*, Mr. Dunn. I hope—"

His sentence was interrupted by a moan from the woman on the bed. Stokley saw my head move and followed my eyes. He was on his feet in an instant, bending down over her.

"Aline. Aline, are you all right?"

The door opened then and Benedict rushed in, all efficiency. "It's okay, Congressman, she's all right." He looped an arm over his boss's shoulder and eased him back into his chair. The woman in the bed moaned again and turned on her side. Nelson Benedict readjusted her sheet, nodded reassurance to Stokley, and walked with me to the door.

"It's time for her medicine," Benedict explained. "We wanted her in the hospital but the congressman wouldn't hear of it. We have a nurse, of course, but he wanted to spend some time with her, alone."

I followed him down, pausing at the bottom to look at a small framed photograph on a credenza. It showed a man and woman on their wedding day, and though the faces were younger, I recognized the man and woman upstairs.

Trauma had strange effects, I reminded myself, as I shook hands with the aide and went back out to my car. I had seen men recover from terrible physical injuries and others, who had suffered no obvious wounds, retreat into a shell-shocked daze. There was no predicting the strengths and weaknesses of human beings.

When I got back home my message light was on and my heart missed a few beats when I played the message. Then I went cold all over.

It was Katherine, calling from Yucatán, giving her flight number, and asking me to pick her up at the airport.

9

I was an hour-and-a-half early, pacing the long hall-way in front of the ticket counters, and asking every five minutes or so if the plane was on time. She was flying out of Mérida, which meant a transfer in Houston, and it would be late afternoon before her flight got in. The counter personnel were very patient; after the disaster of a few days ago they were getting a lot of anxious questions, especially with a depression in the Caribbean and the possibility that a hurricane would develop within hours.

For my part, I could tell myself that what had happened to Transcaribbean 420 had no relation to the Delta that was still on the ground in Houston. But I could not blot out Julia Morvant's voice, asking me to meet her.

Solly had the tape, and all I had now was my memory. And the hell of it was that in my memory it kept sounding like Katherine's voice, which sent shivers through me.

I headed for the bar, for a drink, then stopped myself, an inner sense telling me to stay alert.

We had missed Rivas. That was the logical conclusion. He'd killed Julia presumably because she had defected with information about the drug cartel. He'd killed Linda because she knew something, or plausibly, because he was afraid she might know something, being Julia's best friend. He'd attempted to kill the congressman, and therein had been his only failure. But he'd been successful in stopping Stokley's tour and giving a graphic lesson in what happened when the cartel was crossed, so had his mission really been a failure?

Still, he seemed to have no problems with travel: He'd put a bomb aboard a plane in Kingston, Jamaica, then flown in to New Orleans and killed Linda. Only hours afterward he'd flown back to the Caribbean, this time to St. Croix, where he'd bombed Stokley's cabana. There must have been airport surveillance, but the cartel could bribe officials. Hell, they could even provide a plane for a man who loved his work that much. And that was exactly what bothered me: A rational man would have gone on to other things, but Rivas seemed obsessed with his work.

And an obsessed man would refuse to accept unfinished business. If he had missed Stokley once, that could only mean he would try again. I knew that was Cox's analysis and I couldn't fault it.

The plane was five minutes early and I watched through the big glass window in the lobby as it rolled toward the gate. I moved to the gate area and waited as the passengers debouched with their parcels and luggage.

Surely she'd made it. She would have called if there'd been a problem. . . .

Then I saw her, the thirty-first person out, a slim tanned figure in her slacks and *huipil* blouse. A floppy straw hat shaded her face, but when she saw me there was no mistaking the smile.

We ran the last ten feet and I breathed a prayer of relief.

"God, I missed you," she said aloud and I smiled at the thought of the prim, efficient secretary I'd first met a year ago in the staid halls of Tulane University.

"I missed you, too," I said, looking around. "Let's get out of here."

"I have to collect my luggage," she laughed. "Then we can go anyplace you want. Anyplace, that is, where I can call Scott and let him know I'm back."

Scott was her son, now a Tulane junior.

"I'm scared to see the house after two months."

66

"Scott and I had lunch just last week," I said. "He's a fine boy. Everything's okay, you'll see."

I hustled her down the escalator to the baggage claim, my eyes searching every face. But there was no one who resembled Rivas.

She was telling me about the new temple group they'd discovered, and how it combined elements of Puuc style with the earlier classic architecture. I nodded, alert now as more bodies crowded into the confined baggage-claim space.

She looked up at me sharply. "You haven't heard a thing I was saying. What's wrong? You aren't mixed up in some other big case again?"

"Nothing much," I put her off. "I'm just tired."

She gave me an appraising look, but said nothing.

We were already on the expressway, when she mentioned the crash.

"We heard about it in Yucatán," she said. "It makes you wonder about flying."

I didn't say anything, just whipped us through the clots of traffic.

". . . seemed to be a multicomponent structure," she was saying, and I nodded. She stopped suddenly and looked out the window. I wanted to listen, to make myself understand what she was telling me, but I still couldn't wrench myself away from the last few days.

Twenty minutes later we were unloading in front of her house on Prytania. It was a two-story Victorian structure, with a tiny front yard and a patio out back with banana trees for shade. She stopped on the walkway and looked up at the old house.

"It's so weird, coming back from another world," she said.

She picked up a valise in either hand and I followed with the last bag, suddenly conscious of my infirmity. She opened the door and waited for me to come in.

I remembered the first time I had been in this house, a

year ago, and with a pang I thought of the first time we had made love, in the bedroom at the top of the stairs.

Her laughter took me away from my thoughts.

"My wonderful son," she said, holding up a sheet of paper.

I read the words and smiled: DEAR MOM: I CLEANED A LITTLE BIT. FOOD IN THE FRIDGE. CHAMPAGNE COLD. KIND OF BUSY. SEE YOU TOMORROW.

"You called him from Mexico?" I asked.

"Of course. You don't think I wanted a delicate situation, did you?" She smiled and put her arms around me. "And as charming as it is, I feel a little cramped in your place. If a beautiful woman came in with a medieval falcon, I might have to brain her with it."

She turned her face up to me and I leaned down, tasting her lips. All at once her mouth was against mine and she was pulling my head down, pressing against me, making urgent little sounds. I held her with my right arm, drawing comfort from knowing she was back, while at the same time worrying about the complication it introduced.

First things first, though, I told myself, as we started up the stairs, hand in hand: I would have time afterward to worry about the complications.

The first shadows were beginning to fall when she uncurled herself from the crook of my arm and raised on one elbow.

"All right, so what is it?" she asked, once more the determined lady I'd first known. "I've waited for this for eight weeks with all my fantasies working overtime and when it happens, I find my man is in another galaxy."

"I'm sorry," I said. "It's nothing you did."

"I'm sure of that," she said. "I mean, it's not like I didn't skimp on the food down there, so I wouldn't gain a pound, and you know how much I love *cochinita pibil*. Why is it I have the feeling you're up to your eyeballs in something you don't want to talk about?"

I sighed and rolled out of bed. Standing by the window, I

68

was aware of the light falling on my left side, highlighting the crisscross of scars on my arm, and I shifted to get that part of my body back into darkness.

Remembering her love of puzzles, which was part of what had brought us together, I realized it would be futile to try to hold back. Besides, it concerned her. If I took Cox up on his offer, it would mean some decisions for us both.

"It has to do with a woman named Julia Morvant," I told her at last, and let the story pour out. She listened intently, deliciously oblivious to her nakedness, and try as I might I could not keep my eyes from her breasts, twin globes in the room's twilight.

"And you're scared for me," she said finally. "Scared I'll be caught in the crossfire."

I nodded. "If this Rivas finds out I'm after him, he may go after whatever—*who*ever—is closest to me, to draw me out. I can't have that happen."

"Rivas doesn't bother me," she said quietly. "He's only a man."

I knew what she was saying. It was the possibility of my leaving New Orleans and what we had.

"I want you to be happy," she said. "You know that."

"I want us both to be happy," I told her.

"Come sit next to me," she said, and I went back to the bed. She reached up and traced a line along my shoulder with a finger. "You loved the marines, I can understand your wanting to go back. When somebody finds something they love that much, they have to go after it."

Slowly, I turned toward her, aware as never before of her attraction. I loved her; I'd told her that many times. I had a life here with her. Why was there always the word *but*?

I wanted her then as never before and put my hand on her breast, feeling her erect nipple. She closed her eyes and moaned.

"Oh, God, Micah, let's not talk anymore."

We got up again at nine and had an intimate dinner of filet mignon and wine. We said no more of what was on both our minds, pretending, instead, that nothing at all had changed. I listened to her description of their field season and the unexpected cache of ceramics they had found below a living floor. We could almost, for a little while, believe that there was no one else in the world but us. We went to sleep in each other's arms, secure, and slept until almost eight.

Then, like a fool, I called for my phone messages and heard Mancuso's voice.

"Micah, the pathologist just gave us a readout on the Marconi woman: She was probably thrown from a car, but her death was from drowning."

Before I could react he went on to the punch line.

"But what I was really calling about was the pics you gave me. They really did the trick. Call me if you want to know the identity of Julia Morvant."

10

This time Mancuso came out to meet me and escorted me into Homicide like I was royalty.

"I really owe you, Micah," he said under his breath, as we walked to his desk. "Two of the pictures turned up fingerprints that matched some in our files. For once I'm glad you screwed around with evidence."

I knew a few of the other men in the room, but none as well as I did Mancuso, and for the most part they ignored me. Mancuso bent over his desk and thumped a folder.

"This is it," he said, handing it to me.

I laid it back down on the desk and flipped it open.

Julia Morvant stared out at me.

The picture was a mug shot, and her hair was lighter, but there was no mistaking the dark brows, the almost whimsical expression of the mouth, as if she knew this was a game and when it was over she would take her things and go home. Which was almost certainly what had happened.

"Her name is Mary Juliette Folsom," Mancuso explained, pointing to the charge card. "She's from Bogalusa. The chief of police there knows her father, gave me his address. I'm supposed to meet him at ten-thirty. You wanna ride up with me?"

I looked back down at the face of the dead woman, the woman who had cited Shakespeare just before her death, the woman who now was only one of a host of mangled body parts in the morgue.

"Thanks, Sal," I told him. "I think I'd like that."

We took the long bridge across Lake Pontchartrain, heading out of the city smog for the pine woods of the north shore. Once there, we arrowed northeast onto the two lane and then due north, running a few miles west of the Mississippi border. We reached Bogalusa just after ten and turned west, off the highway, onto a shady street that led toward the center of town.

A thriving sawmill town in the first years of the century, its glory days were long over. There were some historic buildings and a park with a couple of museums that were seldom open. The National Guard armory sat on a hill where there was once an Indian mound. There was a bar on the main street, with a machine that makes frozen cocktails and a pool table, if you were a beer drinker.

We found the police chief at the local hot-dog stand. A friendly, heavy-set man of fifty, he wore a blue uniform with his rank on his lapel and a small American flag on his right shoulder. We introduced ourselves and he shook our hands and then threw his cup in the trash barrel at the edge of the parking lot.

"Poor Will," he said, shaking his head. "He never had any luck with women."

We followed him south, and then west out of town. It was pretty country, gentle hills broken by streams and the clean smell of pines in the air. Neither of us spoke, each dreading the ordeal of having to break the news to her father.

Five miles out of town we came to a gate and the police car turned in. We followed, stopping before a frame house with a pickup truck under the carport. In a field to the left, cattle grazed, and there was a barn in the rear, with a tractor visible in an attached shed.

The chief got out and we followed. He started for the house, then stopped and squinted. There was movement in the back pasture and he nodded, pointing.

"He's back there, splitting wood." He waved his arm and a second later grunted in satisfaction. "He sees us. He'll be here in a while, if he's a mind to."

"He lives here alone?" Sal asked.

The chief nodded again. "Yep. For the last twenty-something years. Raises stock, splits wood, bales hay. I don't think I ever seen the man rest." He shrugged. "Hell, he'll probably outlive us all."

I could see him now, a lean, grim-looking figure with a slight limp, coming toward us in his own time, as if to let us know that on his land he would not be hurried by outsiders.

When he was fifty feet away the chief raised a hand in greeting.

"Hello, Will. Sorry to bother you, but there's some men here from New Orleans wanted to talk to you."

Will Folsom appraised us both with narrow eyes and nodded.

"I was about finished anyway." His eyes went from Sal to me and back again. "Police, ain't they?"

We nodded.

Folsom spat on the ground. "So what is it now? What do you want from me?"

Sal cleared his throat. "It's about your daughter, Mary Juliette, Mr. Folsom. I'm sorry, but we've got some bad news."

"Mary Juliette," Folsom repeated. "That's all she ever was: bad news. I've had all the bad news I want. I got no daughter now, so there's nothing you can tell me would matter."

"Yes, sir." Mancuso shifted his weight to the other side. If he had thought the chief was coming to his aid, he was disappointed. The local lawman evidently had dealt with the older man before.

"The fact is," Sal started again, "Mary Juliette is dead."

But Will Folsom was already wiping his face with a blue bandana. When he finished he folded it carefully and put it into the pocket of his overalls.

"Is that all?" he asked.

"Well," Sal began, "I . . ."

Folsom shook his head impatiently.

"Look, Mister, fact is she made it clear she didn't want no part of me or this place. She was in junior high school when she started giving me pain. First the boys, always coming around, so I never could get no work out of her, and then she started running away. Well, I wasn't surprised. It was same as her mother done before her. Like daughter, like mother. Scarlet as the whore of Babylon. Nothing on this place that satisfied. There always had to be more. The big city, excitement, that was what she wanted. Wasn't nothing I could give her was good enough."

For a moment I wondered if he was speaking of mother or daughter and then I realized it didn't matter; he was talking about both.

"Many's the time I had calls in the middle of the night from some stranger, asking for her. Or from the law, saying she was in some scrape. After a while I got tired of it. I got a place to run. I got my pride. I'm a God-fearing man, and Chief Ainsley there'll tell you I never cheated a man in my life or broke the law."

The chief nodded agreement.

"I got tired of being a doormat, a place to come back to when there wasn't no place else to go. I got tired, you understand?"

It was Sal's turn to nod. The old farmer half turned, then gave us a sideways look.

"So how did she die?" he asked softly.

Sal looked him in the eyes. "In a plane crash. The one across the lake, the other day."

For the first time Will Folsom seemed genuinely surprised.

"You mean it was an *accident?*"

"Well, we aren't sure," Sal equivocated.

"But a plane crash," Folsom insisted. "I mean, it had to be accidental, right? The things fall down sometimes."

"Yes, sir. But in this case, there may have been a bomb."

"A bomb?" His jaws worked silently for a moment. "Well, she couldn't of had nothing to do with that."

74

"No, sir, we don't think she placed the bomb. After all, she was killed."

"Right." The whole idea seemed novel to him. "Where was she going to?"

"She was coming back from Jamaica," Sal explained.

"Jamaica. God. I guess she was on vacation, with one of those men she was always with, the ones she got to buy her presents. Was he killed, too?"

"We think she was traveling alone."

His look told us he didn't believe it.

He rubbed a veined hand over his forehead. "Well, am I supposed to go pick up her body? Is that what the law says?"

Mancuso coughed self-consciously.

"She hasn't been identified," I said.

The old man nodded. "Well, when she is, call me up. I'll do what has to be done."

"Don't you worry about that, Will," the chief soothed.

Mancuso had the photo of her in his hand now and he was holding it up. "Just for the record, sir, this *is* your daughter."

"That's her. Who's the other girl?"

"A friend," Mancuso said.

"Yeah. I guess I know what kind of friend. Probably let Julie lead her around by the nose like she did all of 'em."

"Is that how she was?" I asked.

"Since the day she was born. Just like her mother. Thought she knew better than anybody. Regular little know-it-all. Always better than any of the other kids. If one of 'em read a Bible verse, she had to try and quote some writer. Some of the books she brought into this house I was ashamed to have people know were here. I took a whole bunch and threw 'em out." He shrugged. "But there's a few of 'em still here," he acknowledged, his voice weary now. "I guess I just got tired of trying to keep ahead of her."

The self-possessed woman on the beach shifted in my mind and I was seeing a teenage girl, restless, defiant, questioning.

"Do you mind if we look at them?" I asked suddenly.

"What? The books?"

"Whatever you have of hers."

Folsom spat again and his jaw twitched and at first I thought I had said the wrong thing, but then he turned around and started for the house.

"No harm in that, I guess."

We followed him in through the screen door. The living room smelled of pine oil, like the boards had just been scrubbed. There was a small table with a big black Bible, and on the wall the head of a handsome buck. A large television sat in one corner, across from a vinyl sofa, but other than that the room was Spartan in its furnishings. Folsom vanished into the hallway and reappeared a few minutes later with a large cardboard box.

"Keep it in the closet," he explained, setting it on the sofa. "Got no cause to look at it. Probably ought to throw it away." He stood back, allowing us to examine the contents.

If I expected a surprise, I was disappointed. There was a paperback dictionary, a copy of *Mexico on $5 a Day*, an outdated catalog from the University of New Orleans, a couple of cheap mysteries, and, oddly, a paperback of T. E. Lawrence's *Seven Pillars of Wisdom*.

"Trash," Folsom commented, but I wasn't sure whether he was singling out Lawrence or the entire collection. I fished around in the contents and this time I came up with an inspirational volume by Og Mandino. The pages were thumbed and notes had been scrawled in the margins. I laid the book beside the others, on the couch, and looked down at what was left. All I saw was a comb, a makeup kit, and a small spiral notebook. I opened the latter and skimmed through it. It was a journal, and from the dates it seemed to have been written in a couple of months during 1974. It quit abruptly after twenty pages of entries and the rest were blank. On closer inspection I saw that some of the pages between entries had been ripped out, leaving whole days missing.

"That's all there is," Folsom pronounced. "I cleaned out

the room. When she disobeyed me, I cast her out, just like the Book tells you."

We started for the door, the old man following.

"She didn't start out that way, you know. She was a good student in school. Learned the whole Gettysburg Address. She was the princess in the fourth-grade play. But somewhere she just went wrong." He let the door slam behind him. "Somewhere they both went wrong, just like their mother."

Mancuso and I stopped together. "Both?" I asked.

"Her and her sister, Jennifer Ann. The one that's in the asylum right now."

11

To Julie with love, Christmas 1984. From Jenny. Of
course. Omar Khayyam.

Mancuso started to say something but I put my hand on
his arm.

"Would you mind telling us what happened?" I asked
quietly.

Folsom snorted. "Ain't nothing to tell. Jennifer Ann was
just like her sister. Only Mary Juliette was five years older.
Taught all her willfulness and disobedience to Jennifer. In
the end, Jennifer Ann was just like her. Ran away, left me
alone here, after all I done." He kicked at the ground. "Had
some hopes for Jennifer Ann. She didn't have all the high
and mighty notions like Mary Juliette. I thought there was
more of me in her. But like it says in the Book, the evil
drives out the good. She had a temper, just like Mary
Juliette; you couldn't tell her what to do. So one day she up
and went to the city, God knows what she got involved with,
whether it was drugs or liquor or what kind of men. I don't
even want to know. All I know is one day I get a call from
Mary Juliette, telling me Jennifer Ann's in a mental hospital,
wants me to help get her out."

The chief sighed and folded his arms. "Will, you never
told me that. My God, man, if you'd of let me know . . ."

"Don't need no help," Folsom declared. "Besides, like I
told Mary Juliette, hospital was the best place for her.

Maybe get some of the wildness out of her." He shrugged. "Anyway, that was the last I heard."

"When was this?" Mancuso asked.

"I dunno. Month ago, I guess. Tell the truth, I tried to wipe it out of my mind."

"Do you remember the name of the hospital?" I asked, already knowing the answer.

"I think it was something-by-the-river, or something like that."

"Riverside," I suggested.

"Yeah. Probably. You know it?"

Mancuso said, "It's a very nice place. She'll get good treatment."

"I guess. Least she won't be on the streets."

An awkward silence descended and the chief checked us from the corner of his eye. When he was satisfied, he turned back to the farmer.

"Well, then I reckon we'll be on our way, Will. I'm sorry to have to bring you this kinda news. But at least Jennifer's still alive."

We were getting into the car when the old man's voice caught us. He hobbled forward, his face red.

"Are you gonna see her?"

"We'll try," I said.

Folsom considered and then, with a show of effort, got out the words, "When you do, will somebody let me know? She's all I got."

We were back on the highway, headed south for the city, when Mancuso spoke. "All right, so what's with the sister? You know something I don't."

I explained then about the medicine bottle. "Obviously, Mary Juliette, or Julia, as she called herself, went to Laurent on some pretext, to try to find out about her sister, and he gave her this prescription."

"Why not the other way around?" Mancuso asked. "Couldn't she have been going to Laurent and then have referred her sister to him?"

79

"Possible, but then why would she call her father to try to get Jennifer loose?"

"Good point. Well, I may be able to use a contact in Jefferson Parish to find out what's going on. Or we could try for a court order, if we can show it's connected to a crime. It *is* connected, isn't it?"

"I don't know, but I plan to find out." I was thinking about the woman who wanted me to get her little boy back from her ex-husband and wondering how Sandy was coming. It hadn't sounded like a difficult case. "Don't start anything yet," I said. "Let me try something. If it works, we may find out a lot more about Julia Morvant, or Mary Juliette Folsom."

Katherine was at home, having just come in from the University, and we had a light lunch. I was glad to be able to sit down away from the office, because I knew Cox would be sending Solly after me to find out my decision and I needed more time to make it.

"So you think the father ran his daughters off," Katherine said, chewing thoughtfully.

"It wouldn't be the first time it happened," I said, "or the last. I looked in Julia's notebook and what I saw was a lot of unhappiness. I didn't have much time to read it, of course, because Folsom was standing there, but there were some sentences about how much she hurt and one about how she didn't want him to come again. Lots of pages were missing and I think he may have torn them out and just missed that sentence."

"What are you getting at?" Katherine asked in a low voice.

"I think he abused them," I said. "If not sexually, at least physically. He's a proud, intolerant man, unable to bend. His wife couldn't take it and neither could the two girls."

"Why would he keep all that stuff, then?"

I shrugged. "Like most people, he's ambivalent about the people he's emotionally attached to. I think it's his way of holding onto her." I took another sip of beer. "God, it must have been hell growing up there. To be young and energetic and sensitive, and to know there's a whole big world out there. . . ."

She gave me a fishy stare. "Micah, you aren't hung up on this woman, are you?"

My laughter was forced. "Which woman? Julia or Mary Juliette? Anyway, she's dead. How could I be? I guess I'm just obsessed with the fact that she called me. I keep hearing her on the tape, asking me to come get her. Maybe I feel guilty in an odd sort of way."

"Well, so long as she stays dead," Katherine said with a smile.

"I don't think there's any problem about that." A picture of debris floating in the swamp came to mind and I tried to force it away.

"And then there's the comment she made about Marc Antony," I said. "I keep asking myself what it means. She was going to make him look like a piker. A piker, for God's sake. Now what in the hell does that refer to?"

It was Katherine's turn to shrug. "Well, what did he do? 'I come to bury Caesar, not to praise him,'" she quoted.

"And Antony stirred up the crowd against Brutus and the conspirators," I said. "The conspirators trusted Antony and he pulled the rug out from under them."

"Do you think she was going to drop a dime on the cartel?"

"That could get somebody killed, all right," I agreed.

"But why blow up a plane when they could have killed her as easily on the street?" she asked.

I shrugged. "Maybe it was an example to others. And our boy Rivas seems to like things that explode."

"Well, if he killed Linda Marconi, he was willing to change his method," Katherine pointed out. "But I agree. That quotation seems to imply she was going to pull some kind of deception."

She raised her wine glass. "That is, unless that wasn't what she meant."

"What do you mean?"

81

"What's the rest of the quotation? 'The evil that men do lives after them, the good is oft interred with their bones,' right? Maybe she was thinking of that part of the speech."

"Maybe," I said doubtfully. "But how could it apply?"

"Beats me. But I like the 'interred' part. It sounds like somebody was going to get buried."

"True," I said. "But since it turned out to be her, I don't see how it would work. I somehow don't see herself as the kind who blows herself up to make a point."

"So what's the next step?" she asked. "And please don't say you're going to use yourself to bait this Rivas. I don't think I could stand that."

"Well, not yet," I said. "Right now I have another idea. But I need Sandy to carry it out."

It was five-thirty when I got Sandy at home.

"Damn, Micah, I been calling you for two hours," she complained. "Are you off on vacation?"

"I'm at Katherine's," I said and heard her knowing chuckle.

"That's my man," she said. "So she came back after all."

"Yeah, bad luck for you," I joked.

"Life is a vale of tears. Now, you wanna hear how I wrapped up this exceedingly complex case or not?"

"I'm all ears."

"Well, first I drive up to McComb and go down to the co'lud quarters. I find somebody knows somebody works for the gentleman in question, so I visit her, and she says it ain't a bad family, they treat her okay, but there ain't no kid in it. Mister came back from New Orleans by himself, moved in with his momma. In fact, she happens to know the mister is pretty broke up about losing his kid and she's heard him talking to a certain local lawyer about what to do to get him back. And she's heard Momma say she never liked that woman anyway, and there ain't much she woulda put past her."

"So naturally you went to the house and checked it out yourself," I said.

"Naturally. Except in McComb, black gal don't exactly bop up to the front door and ask to see the man of the house. All I could do was a rolling survey—you know, check for toys on the front lawn, make a few passes and see if the kid was outside."

"Which was all negative, or you wouldn't be drawing this out."

"That was day before yesterday, right? It was getting kind of late. I was wondering how I was gonna wrap this up when I remembered something Lakeesha—that's the maid—told me. She said Wednesday was her day to work four hours at the house. So I went back to Lakeesha and asked her how she'd like to make thirty dollars for not working four hours instead of fifteen for working." She tittered. "Wasn't no contest."

"So I guess you were her cousin," I said.

"You got it. Cousin Lula, taking over for her sick relation. Micah-man, you shoulda seen me with that feather duster. I was hell on wheels."

"But no kid."

"How did you guess? I did some snooping in desks and such and as far as I can tell the kid hasn't been there for a month. I found a checkbook with a stub for the last support payment, too."

I remembered my misgivings about the woman who'd hired me.

"So he wasn't in Mississippi," I said.

"No. I came back yesterday afternoon and followed our dear client all morning. I followed her to Maison-Blanche to buy clothes, and then to lunch with some sleeze bag who kept trying to put a hand on her thigh under the table, and finally to a house in Westwego that I find out just happens to be owned by a woman who bears her a striking resemblance. And lo! When she parks in front and the front door of the house opens, who do you think comes running out?"

"The boy," I said.

"Call you Sherlock Holmes. She had him stashed with her

83

sister. She was willing to pay a detective just to stir things up against her husband."

"Christ," I muttered. "How did you leave things?"

"Alone, of course. I figured you could call it from here. Naturally, I got some photos of her with the kid and with her sister."

"We'll let it run a little longer," I said. "The boy's safe, so there's no hurry, and I want to be sure our bill is steep enough. Just make sure the pictures come out. They're our ace."

"Amen. Anything on the other case?"

"Actually, that's what I was calling you about," I said. "You did such a good job as a domestic, I thought you might want another starring part."

"What kind of starring part?" she asked, suddenly wary.

"Well," I said, "I was kind of hoping you could go crazy."

12

It was that night, just after ten-thirty, when the station wagon stopped at the guard shack in front of the Riverside Clinic. There was little I could see from my place across the street, but I knew what was happening: A call had been made from a black member of the city council and a name had been placed on a list. The guard who was looking into the car now had verified that the name on the list belonged to the disturbed young woman lying in the back. Even as I watched he stepped back and the car passed through the gate and down the drive. It stopped in front of the building and I saw shadows pass back and forth in the headlights. Attendants would be coming out now to open the tailgate and assist the patient out. The driver and the elderly woman who claimed to be the patient's mother were going inside now to sign the papers. The papers would guarantee payment and would describe the medical history of the patient. The medical history was false. Payment would come from the black politician, and afterward the favor he owed Sandy would be wiped off the books.

Ten minutes later the man and woman came out and got back into the car. Twenty years ago they would never have gotten past the gate. Today the city was in its second black administration, and the money of middle-class black families was as welcome as anyone else's.

The car came back out and disappeared down the River Road.

I gave the clinic a last look and started my engine.

Sandy was a resourceful, determined woman, tough as diamonds and twice as sharp. Still, I couldn't help but have some misgivings about my idea.

Solly was waiting when I got back to my office. This time, though, the bluff demeanor had vanished, replaced by weariness.

"Jesus, Micah, what's going on with you?" he asked, rising from his chair. He'd picked the lock, of course, and gotten himself a beer, but I didn't mind. "I thought we were going to hear from you," he said.

"I've had a lot on my plate," I evaded.

"*You?*" he snorted. "Look, buddy, I put my ass in a sling for you. I told 'em there was one man that could do this and it was you. Then I told 'em you wouldn't touch it unless they treated you right afterward. Hell, I thought you'd jump at the chance, like I did. I mean, old days all over again, just like Saigon. We'd be working as a team again, you and me, in country."

"It'll never be just like it was, Solly," I told him. "We're both older and we're different people."

His face reddened. "You don't have to tell me that, goddamn it. I'm not five years old. Maybe the war's changed, but the rules are the same and there's still work to do. If you don't want to be part of it, that's okay. I'll just tell 'em I made a mistake—" He lurched to his feet and I realized he'd had more than the beer he was holding in his hand.

"Sit down, Solly," I soothed. "I didn't say I wouldn't work with you. As a matter of fact, I've been working on it ever since I left you people. I just have my own way of doing things, you know that."

His face relaxed and he smiled sheepishly. "I should of known, Micah. You always were an insubordinate bastard." He chuckled. "You remember that time you disappeared for three days? You were already listed as AWOL when you

86

came back with our man, the one you pulled right out of that V.C. village. You'd have gotten another Silver Star if they hadn't been so pissed about how you did it."

"I remember," I said, thinking about it for the first time in a couple of years.

I went over to the window and lifted a blind to look out onto the dark street.

"Well, I'll tell Cox, to cut you some slack," Solly declared, rising to elbow me fondly. "He'll do like I say. But Micah, when this is over"—his face was inches from mine now as we stood looking out into the night—"I hope you'll want to come aboard."

It was a window in the building on the corner, fifty feet away. Maybe it was just my imagination, but I didn't think so.

I let the blind fall and turned back to Solly.

"There's something I have to ask you," I said.

"Shoot."

I headed into the kitchen for the refrigerator, took out a beer, but, instead of going back into the front room, went out through the back door to the balcony. The fountain made a rushing sound, but I knew that could be filtered out. Still, where we were standing was the safest place I could think of without going out onto the street.

"Are your people wiring my office?" I asked.

I wondered if the question would make him angry, but it didn't. There was a long silence and then he leaned forward, his hands on the iron rail.

"I don't think so," he said finally. He turned to me and the bluff heartiness was gone from his face. "But you've got to understand, Micah, they don't tell me everything they do. Cox is a bastard. Sometimes I think he's too smooth. Hell." He shrugged. "Twenty years ago I'd of told him to get his prep-school ass out of my line of fire. But, like you just told me, things change. Now his kind are the ones in control. If I want to work, I got to do what they say. Ain't ideal, but it beats being a civilian."

"Yeah," I said, and patted his shoulder.

He left via the outside stairway. I followed him into the patio and let him out the pedestrian door beside the vehicle gate. Then, when I was sure he was gone, I went back up and stood beside the window. It took five minutes but once more I caught what seemed to be a brief flash in the window on the corner. Maybe my imagination, but maybe not.

I went to my desk, took out the .38, and slipped it into my pocket, along with a small flashlight and two pieces of wire. Then I went down the way Solly had left. A minute later I found myself in Barracks Street. If someone was watching the side entrance, they were well hidden. I walked away, toward Chartres, and then turned right, toward Esplanade. So far today I hadn't picked up any obvious tails and I didn't think they'd sent Solly to nail down my location. So maybe they were just playing a waiting game from across the street with an infrared beam, content to listen in on what happened in my office. If so, they were less competent than I expected, because there was little reason to expect me to transact all my business there. And why did it matter what I did? Were they expecting somebody to call me again?

I didn't like it and the only thing I could think of was to go to the source. Because if it wasn't Solly's people, then that left only Rivas, though why was unclear. Then the thought came to me as I reached Esplanade, the boulevard that forms the northern boundary of the Vieux Carre: Suppose there was something I knew that Rivas didn't? Something that endangered him or the people he worked for?

It was an attractive hypothesis, but I could think of nothing that fulfilled the condition. Unless he was using me to get to somebody else.

Even Esplanade was quiet, the only car a cruising police patrol, a white ghost in the darkness. I crossed Decatur, walking in front of the old Mint, my eyes alert to changes in the texture of shadows. But there was nothing.

I reached North Peters and turned back toward Canal, roughly paralleling Decatur. Their observation post was between me and my window now; I planned to approach it from the south, coming around the French Market and up

Nicholls, then right onto Decatur until I was beside their own building and across Barracks Street from my own. It would be tricky, and if they had a lookout I would probably fail. But in that case, it would probably be Cox's people. Rivas worked alone and I doubted he would take someone else into his confidence.

When I came to the corner of Governor Nicholls and Decatur I stopped in a doorway and waited. So far, so good. I crossed the street quickly and slid through the shadows toward the next corner. The building had been unoccupied for six months and there was a realtor's sign on the brick wall. I put my hand on the door handle and pushed gently but it was locked. I'd expected as much.

Years ago, when I was in the navy hospital, they'd told me a man with one arm could do a lot more things than I thought. I hadn't believed them, but a year later, at a VA Rehab Unit, I'd run into a man with no hands at all. His name was Charlie Mix, and he had an escape act, à la Houdini. He showed me some things I hadn't realized a two armed person could do and he got me to forget my own problem.

One of his tricks involved his bare feet and a couple of pieces of wire. It was easier for me, though; all I needed was to put one of the pieces of wire between my teeth, to hold the pins down while my hand held the other wire that jiggered the tumblers.

It took me forty-five seconds and I was in.

I stood in the darkness for a while, listening. The old structure creaked and invisible rodent bodies scampered through the darkness. But from somewhere upstairs came a telltale sound. It was a floorboard taking weight and then releasing it.

For a moment I considered my options. If I could hear him, then if I started up the stairs he would be able to hear me, and if he was good there was no telling what booby traps he might have rigged.

It would be better to get him down, into the street.

I closed the door behind me and left as quietly as I'd

come. I used the pay phone in a bar on Esplanada. Then I hurried back to my apartment and waited.

Five minutes later I heard the sirens, and then flashing blue and red lights strobed the street outside. Through my night glasses the scene was bathed in an eerie green. Ghostly figures fled in and out of my vision as firemen hammered at the downstairs door of the abandoned building and then broke it down. I counted three of them heading inside, followed by a cop. Maybe I was wrong, I thought. Maybe I hadn't seen anything at all. Maybe the flashes in the window were from passing traffic. Maybe the soft red glow was nothing at all. And maybe the sounds I'd heard had been the expansion and contraction of old timbers.

Except that as I watched, another man came out quickly, shouting something at the waiting firemen. They seemed momentarily confused, which was understandable, since he wasn't one of the men who had gone in.

He was counting on the confusion to get away, of course. I raced down the stairs and out onto Decatur. He was fifty yards ahead of me, going toward Jackson Square. I wanted to run, but held myself to a fast walk. Someone called out something behind me but I ignored it.

His form was only a flicker of shadow now and I hurried to keep up. *One man. Rivas. It had to be Rivas.*

He reached St. Philip, a streetlamp catching his body for the merest instant. I couldn't let him get to Jackson Square. Even at one in the morning there would be people around, bodies to confuse, alleys to lose himself in.

My mind sped ahead, trying to plot out the possibilities. So far he didn't seem to know I was behind him. There was just a chance he wouldn't change direction when he got to the square.

It was the thinking ahead, losing track of the here and now, that was my mistake. Normally, I would have been aware of footsteps behind me, but my mind was with the quarry, and I never stopped to realize that I might have been the quarry myself.

When I turned it was too late. He was only ten feet away,

on the opposite curb, half in and half out of shadow. Instinctively, I reached under my shirt for the gun in my waistband, but I knew it was too late. He stepped off the curb, a machine pistol in his hand and a smile on his face.

Even though I had seen him only on videotape, there was no mistaking the face: The man who would be my murderer was Adolfo Rivas.

13

A string of shots buzzed past my ear and I threw myself onto the sidewalk, landing clumsily on my right side and trying to slap the pavement judo fashion, to break my fall, without dropping the pistol. The pain of the fall throbbed through my arm, ruining my aim. He wouldn't miss again and yet, incredibly, he didn't even try. Instead, he was crouching, looking at something off to his left, by the levee, and I realized, dimly, that someone else was firing. I got off a pair of quick shots, but the ache in my forearm made me miss, and the bullets ricocheted off a brick building behind him.

Still, the crossfire did the job and, after a quick spray from the machine pistol, Rivas ducked into the shadows and I heard his footsteps slapping the pavement as he ran. I raised myself, prepared to follow, and then the sound of a moan from the direction of the levee caught my ear. The man I was after was disappearing, damn it, but the man who'd saved my life needed help.

There was nothing to do but let Rivas go.

I made my way to the other side of the street and stopped, amazed.

Solly Cranich was smiling at me from where he sat on the sidewalk, a silly expression on his face.

"Lucky shot," he lamented, holding his shoulder and letting me help him to his feet. "As for *this* thing"—he gave a contemptuous glance at the Beretta in his right hand—"if I'd of had my 1911A1"—he thrust the offending weapon into his waistband. "Well, we can talk about that later. Christ, Micah, get me outa here. Lights are starting to go on. I don't want to spend the rest of the night answering questions in the cop house."

An hour later I watched one of Cox's anonymous agents finish bandaging Solly's arm. We were in a safe house off West End Boulevard and Cox sat on the arm of a ratty sofa, his cigarillo smoked down to the filter.

"I wish you'd clued us in," he said. "Calling a false alarm wasn't the coolest thing I've heard of."

"No?" I shot back. "Then why were your people spying on me? Why the hell didn't you play straight with me, instead of putting a goon in a window with a laser beam?"

The "goon," who straddled a chair on the other side of the room, half rose, but Cox motioned him back down.

"No need to be all pissed off," he said. "It was for your own good. We were trying to protect you. We knew once Rivas figured you were after him he'd try to neutralize the danger." He shrugged. "We were right, too, weren't we? He must have picked you up outside the congressman's place when you left, and followed you. A little research would show you were a PI and after that he could add things up. I figure we saved your life."

"Like hell," I said. "It isn't that simple. I don't think I was followed and even if I was, why assume I was after *him?* I think there was a leak. I think you need to check your own people and see which one of them's selling you out."

This time all three of the agents rose, their eyes killing me. Only Solly and Cox remained in their places, and for a while, as Cox smoked thoughtfully, I thought he was going to let them have me. But he finally extinguished his cigarette in a Coke bottle and sighed.

"My people are all vouched for, Dunn. There's not one who hasn't been cleared to the top-secret cosmic level. And rechecked. They've all passed lie-detector tests and a psychological battery. It's a tough program. The CIA designed it and I improved on it. Most people can't get past the first cutoff. How do you think you'd do?"

"That's your problem, not mine," I said.

"It's both our problem, if you come to work for me," he said. "We like independent people, people who can think on their feet, make quick decisions. So long as their decisions are the right ones." His brows rose slightly. "But mavericks who fight the system can be a pain in the ass."

"Your ass is my last worry," I said. "Right now I'm more worried about Solly almost getting killed because you didn't tell him what was going on. Not to mention myself."

"Oh, hell," Solly said, putting on a fresh shirt. "I'm okay. I'm just glad I decided to come back to get my lighter and saw you coming down the steps."

"Look," Cox said, getting up. "It's after two in the damn morning. We aren't going to get anywhere arguing. We're all tired and you need some sleep. We all do." He moved to the door. "Hays here will give you a ride back. Get some sleep and cool off. Then get back in touch with me, okay? The offer still stands."

"I'll think about it," I said.

I slept until ten and woke up feeling like I'd left my best years in the street the night before. I had *beignets* and coffee at the Cafe du Monde and tried to pick up any talk of trouble in the Quarter last night, but there wasn't any; people were more interested in the depression that had turned into a tropical storm and was nudging its way into the gulf. Afterward, as I neared my place I found Mancuso's car at the curb. I opened the door on the driver's side and got in.

"I hear there was some excitement down here last night," the policeman said. "Right after a false alarm. Funny thing: The firemen found some pretty sophisticated electronic equipment in one of the vacant buildings."

"The Quarter's going to hell," I said.

"Ain't it?" he pulled away from the curb. He waited until we were out of the Vieux Carre before he spoke again.

"So's how's she doing? Any word?"

94

"Too early," I said, as much for my benefit as his. "She'll need two, maybe three days minimum. And she may strike out completely, but I thought it was worth a try. I can't think of any other way to get close to the girl."

"I'd like to know who's paying the bills," Mancuso said. "Doc Laurent doesn't do anything for free. That's an expensive place. But without a court order, I can't find out who's picking up the tab."

"I've wondered, too," I admitted. "Julia seems to have made good money at what she did, but if she called her father to help get her sister out, it doesn't seem like she was the one footing the expenses."

"Yeah," Mancuso said. "And Jenny's main asset was the first half of the aforementioned word, apparently."

We fell into silence and I stared out of the window as the old neighborhood went past. We were on Esplanade, headed for Carrollton, a route I often jogged, but somehow today it seemed as if we had been on it forever. It was the photograph, of course: It seemed to swim in and out of focus, and the only thing I could see clearly was the curve of her lips in the ironic little smile. Somehow, to me, the case was not about a congressman almost being assassinated, but about a woman who had asked for my help, help I'd never had a chance to give.

"There has to be a way to find out more about Julia," I said. "If I could know what the hell was going on inside her head right before the crash . . ."

"That would be kind of hard," he said. "I don't think science has got us quite that far."

"No," I said, watching more houses go past. We were in a black neighborhood now, with kids playing on porches and in front yards. Then I turned to face him. "But we could do the next best thing. How about some of the johns she dealt with?"

Mancuso gave me a wary, sideways glance. "Don't go overboard on this thing. The girl's dead."

"But now that you have her prints, you could search the files for police reports, see if she was ever arrested and if any customer was named."

95

The detective sighed. "Well, I guess I owe you something. Once we IDed her yesterday, I made the rounds of banks with her name, description, and social security number. We turned up a bank box at Hibernia."

I faced him, my hand gripping the dash. "You've opened her deposit box?"

He shook his head. "Not yet. I talked Judge Broussard into signing a court order, even though we don't have an official death certificate. I called her father. He's coming down to be there when we open it at one o'clock. Maybe you want to be there, too."

"Thanks, Sal."

"No problem. But next time call me before you get the fire department, okay?"

He let me off downtown and I walked over to O'Rourke's office. His leggy secretary, Abbie, greeted me with a smile and sent me into her boss's office without a knock. I told him about my meeting with the congressman.

"I hear they're moving his wife to a hospital," he said, playing with a pencil on his desk. "So is there any word of this Rivas?"

"He's in town," I said. "I was wrong and Cox was right." I described what had happened last night.

"Jesus," O'Rourke swore. "And you haven't told all this to Mancuso?"

"Maybe I ought to," I admitted. "But then he'd have to go to his superiors with it, there'd be meetings between commissioners and U.S. attorneys, and he'd probably end up being kicked off the case again."

"I see what you mean. So where to now?"

"Well, I'd like to call the Captain for starters. I don't trust my phone and I hope they haven't bugged yours."

He pushed the phone over to me. "I hope not, too. Otherwise, they're going to hear some pretty lurid things about a divorce case."

I dialed the captain's number and waited. This time it answered on the first ring and his voice was breathless.

96

"Hello? Son, is that you?"

"It's me. Are you all right?"

"*I'm* fine. But I've been worried to death about you. And, damn it, I don't like to worry. Is your phone safe?"

"None of them are safe these days," I told him, "but this is probably as good as any. Have you got any information?"

His voice dropped to a whisper, as if he thought someone might be in the room with him.

"Well, it wasn't easy. I'd rather take a battlewagon into a mine field than try to get anything out of these security types. And now I've got to go deep-sea fishing with Percy Fennelly, for Christ sake. And I've never liked the man."

"Who's Percy Fennelly?"

"An ONI type, retired now. But not before he got his flag. His own flag, if you can believe it! And I remember when he ran an LST aground in fifty-nine! So he ass-kisses all the brass, and pretends he's still active. Joined some goddamn policy group that calls itself the Committee for Six Hundred. You know, the six-hundred-ship navy—which means carriers and other targets, not tin cans—but they think it gives 'em a right to mouth off about everything else. They give money to the right candidates, and sponsor speeches, the whole business. I had to ask him over for drinks last night. Pompous little bastard, hasn't changed since the academy. We hazed the hell out of him, you know. Anyway, his wife isn't much better. A twit."

"Had he heard of this group?"

"Not per se, but he'd heard of Cox. Thought he was a hell of a guy. West Point, sixty-two; captain in Nam, Silver Star, retired with the rank of major, in seventy-eight."

There was a silence as he waited for my reaction.

"Okay, Dad. You made your point, so I'll ask: Why does a man who's West Point and has *beaucoup* medals leave the service as only a major?"

"Right," he said, pleased I had caught it. "Just what I asked. But Percy only acted aggravated, said he didn't know, that he heard there were lots of offers he had and he could take his pick. But you and I both know a man doesn't

97

just step out for no reason. So I called Frank Gilbert's son. You remember Frank? He had the *Manion* when I was skipper of the *Gordon Faust*. His son, Lee, is working for the NSC these days, detached from the CNO's staff. Hadn't seen the boy since he was a midshipman, but I called him anyway. He was very helpful."

I knew I couldn't speed him; he'd tell me in his own time.

"He did a quick check, made a call, and got back to me just half an hour ago. Turns out this Cox didn't just change jobs; he resigned his commission under some very dubious circumstances."

Somehow it wasn't a surprise.

"What kind of circumstances?" I asked.

"Nobody seems to know. The records were purged. He was just in one day, out the next. But you remember, that was during the Carter administration. There was a general cleanup then, and all the spook services took their licks. Lee felt it probably had something to do with some screw-up in the field."

"So he isn't what he claims," I said. "And poor Solly only thinks he's back to active duty."

"Not necessarily," the captain corrected. "Just remember, in eighty everything changed again. People that were out came back in. Spook types got a new lease. The Reagan administration promised to build a six-hundred-ship navy. A smart man like Cox could find a new niche, end up in the driver's seat of some outfit buried so deep in the Pentagon nobody in Congress ever heard of it."

"Except," I said, "the members of the Armed Services Committee."

"Yeah, maybe them." He coughed. "Well, steer into the wind, son. And watch out for that storm in the gulf."

"Aye, sir."

Next I called Katherine at Tulane's anthropology department and assured myself that she was all right.

"So now what?" O'Rourke asked.

"I guess," I told him, "that I find out what Julia Morvant was saving in her safe-deposit box."

*   *   *

Mancuso was already waiting at the bank. It was the Carrollton Branch, on the shady old boulevard that had once been the main street of the town of that name. Carrollton had been annexed by New Orleans in 1874 and its once-thriving market had become a small plaza on a back street, with a brass plaque. Now, the boulevard was the site of old houses, shopping centers, and the north-south extension of the streetcar line. I got out in the parking lot and recognized Mancuso's unmarked car.

He met me just inside the door. Will Folsom stood beside him, in his blue jeans and a baseball cap. I started to offer my hand and then decided against it. It wasn't a social occasion.

At that moment a woman in sedate silk blouse and tie came out from one of the offices with a paper in her hand. She might have been pretty, I thought, except that her severe clothing suppressed her femininity. But then, I was comparing her with Katherine, whose sensuality no clothes could hide, and that was hardly fair.

"This seems to be in order," she said crisply, handing him back the court order. "We sent for a special master key, since you were unable to furnish us with the client's. I have to tell you, this is the first time that's happened since I've been manager of this branch. Anyway, we'll open the box, and we'll take it into my office. You can remove objects and look at them, and then, when you're finished, we'll ask you to put them all back in the box and we'll replace it. One of my people will stand by as an observer, on behalf of the bank."

"One thing," I asked. "When was the last time she went into the box?"

The manager gave me a surprised look, as if I hadn't really been there until I'd spoken. She issued a crisp order to a clerk, taking out her annoyance on him, and a second later he came back and whispered in her ear.

"It was exactly one week ago," she replied. "Now . . ."

Mancuso nodded and we followed her into the rear.

She spoke to a young man who nodded and led us into the vault. He climbed onto a stool and unlocked the box. Then

99

he removed it and, holding it like a baby in his arms, descended slowly to the floor.

With ourselves as an escort, he went behind the officers' desks to one of the rooms in the rear, where he deposited the box on the desk.

We crowded around as the young man lifted the hasp and opened the top.

The box, at first glance, seemed to be full of envelopes. The young man took out the first, a brown mailing envelope with the bank's return address, and held it for us to see that it was not sealed. He removed the contents and there was a collective gasp as he placed a handful of certificates of deposit on the table. Each was for ten thousand dollars and he thumbed through them quickly.

"One hundred thousand dollars purchase value," he said, and, replacing them in the envelope, went on to the next.

This envelope contained cash, mostly hundred dollar bills.

"Twenty-five thousand," he said, putting them in their envelope. He removed the third envelope and took out two small objects that I recognized as passbooks. He showed each to us in turn. One, I saw, issued by the National Bank of Commerce, showed a balance of five thousand dollars. The other, at a Texas bank, indicated a balance of thirteen thousand and change. The last deposit had been made the month before, for five hundred dollars.

I sneaked a look at her father, but his face seemed carved from stone. I wondered if he realized that he stood to inherit everything now before us.

A fourth envelope cast a new light on things. It held a birth certificate issued to one Julia May Morvant and a social security card in the same name. The latter may have been genuine, but the birth certificate had to be a forgery. Mancuso and I exchanged glances but the others seemed not to have caught it.

I knew what Mancuso was thinking, of course; that the birth certificate and social-security card could have been used to get other documents, like a passport and a driver's license, and they, in turn, could have been used to take out another safe-deposit box. Mancuso wrote down the number on the card and the data on the birth certificate. We looked back at the box. All that was left was a small, spiral notebook with a brown cover and a gold necklace with an imitation sapphire.

The officer removed them both, as if handling the bones of a dead person, and carefully set them beside the other items.

It was the notebook that interested me, of course. And when he'd opened it I saw that it was what I had been looking for: A list of first names, all men's, followed by a final initial, for the surname, and a telephone number. Mancuso reached out, took the book, and flipped through the pages to the middle. Here, each page bore a set of initials at the top, and under each was a series of dates, indicated by numbers and slashes, and a place, sometimes the name of a hotel, and at other times a reference such as "apt." or "his." Beside the latter was always an address. And beneath that, the particular services she had performed, the price, and any comments. For *Ron V. G., 7/12/87,* for example, she had written, *His—1210 Chamberlain, near Topaz. French. $250. Tlk abt wife, Elsa, kids. Stocks.*

We went through the other entries and I got out my note pad and set it on the desk.

The bank officer looked uneasy but he said nothing as I copied some of the entries. When I finished he whisked the notebook away and started to gather the envelopes.

I was wondering what Will Folsom must have been feeling, but then I caught a glance from Sal Mancuso and looked over at the old man. He was holding up the gold necklace, oblivious to the rest of us, and his lips were moving silently.

"Mr. Folsom," Mancuso said softly. "Mr. Folsom, it's time to go."

He shook his head, handing the necklace to the bank officer.

"I gave her that on her thirteenth birthday. Her thirteenth birthday. I thought she lost it a long time ago. I had no idea . . ."

I realized then that he hadn't noticed the book with the names and I was glad.

14

The shop smelled of dust and I stifled the urge to cough. Books overflowed the shelves and in the center of the room a big table was piled high with volumes that were long out of print.

"Hello, anybody here?" I asked, threading my way through the narrow aisle toward a long counter at the rear. The counter was stacked with more books, and its display glass showed a haphazard collection of old coins and archaic military medals.

I heard movement and a minute later a woman came through the open door behind the counter and stopped when she saw me. She was tall and thin, with her gray hair done up in a bun, and a pair of bifocals had slid down her aquiline nose, making her tilt her head backward slightly to see me.

"May I help you?" she asked, coming through the swinging gate to face me. "I have an excellent first edition of Thomas Hardy. I happen to know that it will be gone within two more days."

"Sorry," I said, "I stick to comic books."

She gave me a pitying look.

"Well, you have that military air," she said. "A little on the stiff side. Maybe you'd like a copy of Charlemagne's memoirs."

"How about a Gutenberg Bible," I asked. "I'll wait for you to finish printing it."

She smiled first and then we both broke into laughter and she threw her arms around my neck.

"Micah, you old reprobate. I was wondering what had happened to you. You must have found yourself a new girl."

"You'd like her, Samantha. But she'd be difficult: She's into Mayan codices."

"My God, that *is* a hard one," she said, pursing her lips. "But it can be done. There was a man once, a doctor from New York, who wanted a genuine Mixtec codex, so . . ."

"I don't want to hear it," I said, holding up my hand.

She pouted. "You won't even allow me to brag? And I get so little opportunity these days. I can't do it with my bridge club."

"No," I agreed, "I guess not." Samantha de Villier was a member of old New Orleans society. She had graduated from Newcomb in the late forties, married a rich engineer who had taken her around the world four or five times, and then had died, leaving her with leisure and twice as much money as before. He had been her one true love, it seemed, because after that she'd married two or three more times, but none of them had lasted more than a couple of years, so that now she was by herself and loving it. After hours she hobnobbed with the elite, and during the day she ran a small, eccentric used-book store on Tchoupitoulas, a stone's throw from the river. The books brought her only a small income, but it hardly mattered, because the shop itself allowed her to have a working address, where she could take full advantage of her art degree.

"But I can't believe you came here just to invite me to lunch at Commander's," she complained. "You have that look in your eyes. You're going to exploit me, I can tell."

"Now, Sam . . ."

"And whenever you call me that, it's a certainty."

"What can I say, except that I saw something earlier today that made me think of you and I just had to come over."

"Made you think of me?" She frowned. "What do you mean? Not some of my work?"

"It was so good it had to be."

103

"Don't you know how to get to a woman's heart. Now you've got me all curious. Where was it and for God's sake, *what?*"

I looked back over my shoulder to make sure that the shop was unoccupied except by ourselves. Satisfied, I turned back to her.

"It was a birth certificate," I said. "And a social security card."

"Well," she sniffed, "social security is nothing. Anyone with an offset outfit can do that. Birth certificates aren't very much more difficult. I assume it was a Louisiana birth certificate? I've done some nice British ones lately, for a man with some business in the Caymans."

"American," I said. "For a woman." I described her.

She stared at me for a moment and then nodded. "Of course. Now I remember. It wasn't that long ago." She drifted over to the table with its ancient volumes. "She bought a passport, too. Now what was the name she had me put on it? Something French . . ."

"Morvant," I said. "Julia Morvant."

Her face brightened. "Of course. That was it. You know her then. She's not in trouble, is she?"

"No trouble, at least anymore. She's dead."

"Oh, dear." She wrung her hands. "I hate it when that happens. Not a client of yours?"

"Not quite. She was on the airplane that crashed the other night."

"Oh, that was terrible." She crossed her arms and clutched her shoulders, shivering. "Poor people."

"Yeah."

She looked up at me, frowning. "But how did you find her documents? Weren't they destroyed?"

"The passport was. The other things weren't used. They were in a safe-deposit box."

"I see." She pondered a moment. "Well, I don't imagine they'll be traced here. I don't usually leave a mark."

I knew what she meant: Her forgeries were as close to perfect as any I'd seen, or the police either, for that matter.

And since she was very careful in her clientele, she'd escaped the law.

"What can you tell me about her, Sam?"

"The girl I made the documents for? Well . . ." She steadied her hair with a hand. "She was very attractive, for one thing. Almost *too* attractive. That was one of the things I noticed right off."

"How so?"

"Well, she was trying a little too hard. The elite never try that hard, if you know what I mean." She chuckled. "Everything about her was perfect, as if a hair out of place would be a disaster. Look at me"—she ran her fingers through some stray gray strands—"I've given up. And it doesn't bother me. I had the feeling it would have bothered her. Funny . . ."

"What is it?"

She shook her head. "When I see anyone that perfect I usually tell myself they're a zero. You know, surface only, and straw for brains. But this girl wasn't like that. She spent a good time looking at the books. She seemed to really appreciate them." She came over and picked up a volume with a torn dustcover. "This is a first edition of Sinclair's *The Jungle*. Not in the best condition. I wouldn't try to pass it off as anything especially valuable, but the important thing is that she knew about it, and knew the book had been bowdlerized to remove a lot of the socialist rhetoric. Very few people know that. I was impressed."

"Interesting. So you think she'd studied literature?"

"I doubt it." Samantha ran her hand fondly over the books, as if renewing an acquaintance with old friends. "You see, that's one of those snippets you can pick up on public radio, or by reading reviews, or"—she gave me a meaningful look—"by sleeping with an English professor."

"I see."

"Yes. I talked with her a long while, asked her quite a few questions. It was obvious that her knowledge was extremely eclectic. Some subjects she had delved into in considerable depth. The poems of Yeats, for example, and Swinburne.

She was passionately fond of Swinburne. Of course, everybody knows that kind of gloomy, doom-laden romantic poem is out of vogue now. I suppose Yeats has fared a little better, but then, he was a greater poet. But when I mentioned the Bloomsbury Circle, and other poets from about the same time, late Victorian to early Edwardian, she seemed completely blank."

"Anything else you noticed?"

"Well, when I said she was too perfect in her dress, I didn't mean there was anything garish or clashing. She *knew* how to dress. You know"—she looked up at me with earnest blue eyes—"I think the whole thing was that she was trying so hard to be liked. She *wanted* my approval, almost as if I were her mother."

It was my turn to frown. Of course. It made sense.

"I almost felt sorry for the poor child. She asked a lot of questions about the books, you know, and I sensed she was probing, trying to learn as much as she could in a short period. I had the feeling she was a sponge and that everything I said sank in."

"Did she say anything about herself? Where she came from or why she wanted the documents?"

"Well, you know I don't ask my clients questions, so long as they come here with the right reference. And she had the best. A judge, whose name I'll leave unsaid. I'm sure you'll understand. I called him, though. He's in one of the older krewes. A fine man. I once did a favor for his son. The boy was in love with a foreign woman who lived in a country where they didn't want to issue an exit visa, so I volunteered to help. They were all exceptionally grateful. Of course, I took a chance by offering, but it worked out extremely well. In any case, she came to me with his recommendation and that was good enough. I didn't ask why. But she did volunteer one or two things about herself."

My skin started to prickle. "Oh?"

"It seems her father was a diplomat, killed by a bomb in one of those Third World countries ten or fifteen years ago.

106

Her mother went insane and she was shuttled from one girl's school to another."

I exhaled. "What do you think she wanted the passport and birth certificate for?"

"She said she'd had an unhappy marriage and her ex-husband was badgering her. He had some sort of government connections, she said, and she wanted to put him off the scent and just sort of disappear. Well, my last husband, Luther, was a bit like that, but I didn't run from him. I was more constructive. I hired a charming investigator who put the fear of God into the poor man."

"I remember," I said. "But, to be truthful, it wasn't one of my harder cases."

"Don't sell yourself short, darling. Anyway, it's how *we* met." She sighed. "For whatever that's gotten me."

I gave her a smile, but I kept trying to see Julia, standing where I was now, picking up the old book, trying to impress and yet at the same time being impressed and struggling to absorb every bit she could. How often had she been in that position? Every day?

"Micah, come back."

I looked up, taken aback. "What?"

"Come back to the world. You were in outer space. Is she that important to you?"

"Yes. For some reason she is."

"Because she's dead? That way, you know, you don't have to worry about seeing her as she really was, with all her imperfections."

"I don't know, Sam. I honestly don't. I just know she called and asked for my help and a few hours later she was dead."

"Ah." She put a hand on my shoulder. "Poor Micah. Trying to be the gallant knight. Listen, Sir Knight, I cater to the genteel trade. But that's mainly a fiction I allow myself. We both know that most people who need forged documents aren't really very nice. This girl, she was bright and energetic

107

and had a nice personality, but doesn't it occur to you that she might not be very nice, either?"

I nodded. "Yes."

"So don't let yourself get drawn in. She's dead. Let her rest."

I put my own hand over hers. "Thanks, Sam. You always have the best advice going."

She sighed again. "But advice you won't take."

"Well, you never took mine to get out of this business. You'll get caught sooner or later, you know, and then what?"

She clapped her hands together. "*That's* when the fun begins. Can you see the headlines? 'Grandmother Arrested.' The book will sell a hundred thousand copies, at least."

"Sam, you're priceless."

"That's what all my husbands said."

15

It was evening and I sat in my car, at Lakeshore Park, looking north, over the gray water. The radio said the storm in the gulf was building to hurricane strength and in a couple of days it might make landfall anywhere along the coast, but the present bad weather was unconnected, just a September squall from a low pressure area that had crept in from the north overnight. Even as I watched, a low growl of thunder rumbled in from the distance. Two miles away, on my left, I could see the glint of tiny autos crawling across the causeway. It was Friday afternoon now and all over the city traffic was backing up in the hurry to escape for the weekend. A line of rain marched across the water, toward me, and a few seconds later drops spattered my windshield. There would be wrecks on the interstate and on the bridges and for some the weekend would begin hours later than planned.

For others, like Julia, there would be no weekend at all.

I wondered how many of the names in the book had learned of her death. Just one that I knew of: I'd called him a couple of hours ago and told him to meet me here.

The thought of the names sickened me slightly, which was odd, because in my work I saw the worst side of human existence and I thought I was used to it.

But this was different: It had something to do with Julia, and who she was, which was even more important than the superficial matter of *what* she was. An old man had given her a costume-jewelry necklace and she had kept it for twenty years. Her father had kept her odd assortment of books, which attested to an inquiring mind; with a university education she'd probably have gone somewhere in the literary world. As it was, she dabbled in the classics and hours before she died had recited Shakespeare. That had to mean something. I had to think she was keeping the book for protection, not blackmail.

The rain was beating down hard now, a million tiny fists, pummeling the car in as many places, and I watched a line of water form at the top of the windshield where the seal was giving way.

I had been looking for a special name in her book and I hadn't found it. Not that Stokley would have used his own name, of course, but she was too shrewd to have been fooled. A few of the names bore such notations as minister; there had been at least one priest, and assorted lawyers and bankers. But there was no congressman.

Not that I believed Stokley was involved; it was just one of those possibilities to be looked into and this one hadn't checked out.

I glanced at my watch: five-twenty. The man had said five, but the weather could be a factor. I decided to give him another ten minutes.

A blinking red light was visible now on the rain-shrouded causeway and a minute later it was joined by a red and blue pair. I was glad I wasn't in a slicker right now, trying to stop bleeding, giving mouth-to-mouth. I'd done enough of that twenty years ago to last a lifetime.

My right arm started to ache where I'd slammed it on the pavement. I had a nasty burn from scraping the concrete but I reminded myself that it was a small price to pay, considering my chances five seconds before. I worked my fingers, satisfying myself for the twentieth time that I could handle the gun under the newspaper on the seat beside me.

I didn't expect to have to use it but at this point anything was possible.

A car turned off Lakeshore and slid into the park. The driver hesitated and then pulled up beside me, on the right. I could see that it was an Audi, about twenty thousand new, but through the rain it was impossible to make out the driver's face. It didn't matter, though: I already knew there would be fear on it. Fear and maybe even anger. He opened his door and I slid the gun from the top of the seat to just under it, between my feet.

He came toward me, oblivious of the rain that had already soaked him, and yanked open the door on the passenger side.

"Get in, Mr. Gautreau," I said. "You'll catch your death out there."

He nodded and slid in, shutting the door with a sigh. The rain had plastered his seersucker suit to his body and thin wisps of blonde hair clung lifelessly to his bald scalp.

"How did you get my name?" he asked with a hint of Cajun accent.

"It was in Julia Morvant's notebook," I said. "At least, your first name and your address and some other particulars. The rest I got from the crisscross directory."

"God," he breathed and started to shiver. "I didn't even know she was dead."

"No?"

His head pivoted in my direction, water still dripping down from his face and glasses.

"You don't think I had anything to do with it, for God's sake? I mean, it was a plane crash. Everybody knows it was a plane crash. You said she was on that plane. . . !"

"It was a bomb," I said quietly. "They just haven't let it out to the public yet."

His bifocals were fogged and I couldn't see his eyes. "But don't you see? I called her while she was gone. If you check her tape you'll find my voice. That proves I didn't even know she was out of town."

"You could have called just to divert suspicion from yourself," I said. "You could have taken another plane, to find her or hired somebody."

111

"Oh, Jesus, you think I'd blow up a plane and kill all those people? Why? Tell me that, for Christ's sake? *Why?*"

"I don't know. I can think of several possible reasons, but, for what it's worth, I have to admit it doesn't seem likely."

"Thank God for small favors," he said. "Then why did you call me to come here? I guess you want money." He reached inside his coat then and removed a manila envelope. "All right. Here. It's all I could raise in an hour. It wiped out my account but take it. Then leave me alone, *please . . .*"

His hand was shaking. I stared down at the envelope, with the tips of the bills showing where it was open. From the looks of it there was at least ten thousand.

"Put your money away," I said sharply. "I'm not here to blackmail you."

He held the money out a moment longer and then stuck it back inside his coat.

"What then? What is it you want? Why are you involving me in this?"

"Because I want to know who really did kill her," I said. "And I hope you can tell me."

He took off his glasses then and tried to wipe them, using the bottom of his coat, but he only succeeded in smearing them.

"If I had any information, of course, I'd give it," he said with relief. "But I don't have any." He shrugged. "I mean, I didn't know her, exactly, socially, it was just a, well, an occasional relationship. She never talked about her private life, her friends."

"Still," I said, "you must have formed some impressions of her."

"Impressions?" Another shrug. "I guess so. I mean, sure. Look, who are you? Is this going to come out in court or anything? Maybe I should call my attorney."

"If you want," I said. "We could all sit down, you, me, your lawyer, and the police."

"The police?" He turned a shade paler. He was forty, give or take a year, going to fat, and he used an expensive co-

112

logne. Next week or next month somebody at the brokerage house where he worked would talk him into a membership at the health club and he'd pride himself on getting into shape. But it would only be an excuse for continuing the martinis at lunch and the double shots when he got home. "Look, I don't want the police. I don't *need* them right now. I've got a family, a decent job. I work my ass off, sometimes seven days a week. You don't know how much time I put in just to keep even, to make sure my family has what it needs."

I'd heard the spiel before and I knew it was best to wait until he was finished.

"My son is at Jesuit. His ACT was the highest in his class. He's got a shot at Ivy League colleges. My daughter is vice-president of her class."

For a minute I thought he was going to bring out his wallet and show me their pictures.

"I've worked for what I have," he declared, as if I had called it into doubt. "There's a lot of pressure, a lot of demands made on me, but I perform. Everybody says I perform. Is it so terrible that I need some relief, some relaxation sometimes? I never hurt anybody. I made sure of that. I never hurt my wife. And it's not like I'm the only one. Christ, as long as you take care of your family, as long as you perform . . ."

"I'm not here to judge you," I said. "All I care about is her."

"*Her?*" He hesitated and then he realized what I was talking about and his shoulders slumped. "Well, what is it you want to know?"

"How did you meet?" I asked, looking away from him and at the rain cascading down the windshield.

"No big deal there," he said quickly. "It was about a year ago. There was a guy used to work for the firm, he mentioned her one day when we were having drinks after work. Said he'd tied up with something really special. Said I ought to check her out. I didn't think much about it, but then he got this other job, in San Diego, and I remember, at his

113

going away party, he was with this beautiful girl. He wasn't married. I thought she was his girl friend or something, you know. She seemed to like me. On the way out I asked him who she was, if she was going, something like that, just polite talk. He was a little looped and he told me he was going to give me a present. He took out a piece of paper and wrote a number on it and her name. Then he wished me a happy life."

"You didn't know she was a pro?"

"No. I mean, I never associated with people like that. I've always been, well, on the shy side. I never went after the pretty girls. I was sure none of them would want to go out with me. I settled for a girl I figured was safe. Not so pretty, but solid, you know. And she's been a good wife, Elsa. God, this would kill her."

I wondered why people like Ron Gautreau always assumed their wives were deaf and dumb. I started to tell him that Elsa probably knew, but was too smart to raise it as an issue. Or maybe she just loved him too much.

"You called her," I said, helping him along.

His head bobbed once.

"You won't believe how long it took me to dial that number. Or how many times I got all the way to the last number and then hung up." A car went by on the boulevard behind us, sending up geysers of water. "Maybe I should have the last time, too."

"But you didn't."

He shook his head mournfully. "No. I think if I'd gotten her answering machine, though, I'd have let it go. I mean, I couldn't have left my name and number for a stranger, could I?"

"It's been done."

"Yes." He reached up to loosen his tie. His trembling had stopped and he seemed to be settling in. "Anyway, I got *her*. You don't know how scared I was. I mean, I didn't plan on anything; I just wanted to introduce myself, tell her I'd enjoyed meeting her. I thought, since she'd been friendly at the party, well, maybe a drink or something, you know?"

I waited.

"Oh, hell," he said suddenly. "I guess that's not true. I wanted her, I just didn't want to admit it. I kept telling myself I could stop halfway, there was no harm just talking."

"Go on."

"She was friendly. She remembered me. I asked if she wanted to have a drink or something and she said sure and named a bar."

"Then you found out she wasn't just a nice girl at loose ends."

"Well, not immediately. I mean, we had drinks, talked, and she really acted interested in me and in what I did. She seemed to know something about the market, asked a lot of intelligent questions. She seemed to get a kick out of seeing how surprised I was. Of course, I just figured she'd picked up a lot from Jack, but I have to tell you, in a lot of ways she seemed to know even more than he did."

I had a picture of her in the cozy booth, dazzling the slightly awkward broker with her enthusiasm for his field. Had it all been a put on, I wondered, or had the enthusiasm been real, a craving to learn what she hadn't been able to on the farm?

"After a while," he said, "she got up and asked if I wanted to see her home. Not take her home. *See* her home, like I was an old-fashioned date or something. I realized then that she didn't have a car, at least not with her, so I drove her home. It was an apartment over on Causeway, a big building . . ."

"I know it."

"Oh. Anyway, I went up with her and she invited me in and all the while I was thinking, What the hell am I doing here? But it seemed so natural, so *right*. I felt so comfortable with her. She told me she shared the place with another girl, but the other girl wasn't around. We had another couple of drinks and she asked me about myself, where I came from. I told her from Reserve and she seemed to know all about it; it was amazing, it was like she grew up there or something.

115

She came and sat next to me, and she started to unloosen my tie. Well, after that . . ."

"Right."

"She didn't ask me to pay her. I didn't even know she was, well, professional. She just asked if I had any good tips and whether I'd set up a small account for her."

"Which you did."

"Sure. Why not? Every week or so she'd call and ask how it was doing. I never charged a commission. And sometimes I'd set up a date with her. If she was busy she'd tell me and we'd reschedule. But she always made it seem like she'd rather be with me, like I was somebody special."

"You must've figured out she was a pro."

"Yeah, it didn't take long. I remember, at first I was disillusioned, and she realized it, but she told me I was different, not like the others. Maybe she told them all that, but at least I could pretend."

The flashing lights on the causeway had been joined now by others. Multiple injuries, I thought, maybe even deaths.

"Did she ever tell you anything about her life outside your relationship?" I asked. "Her friends, for instance?"

"She had this roommate, Linda. I met her a few times. She was nice, but not too smart, you know? It was obvious Julia led her around, and Linda kind of depended on her. I invested some money for Linda once, right before the stock split two-for-one, and she made about a fifty percent profit. But she didn't seem to understand. I got the impression she thought she was supposed to make more money than that. I tried to explain about the market but she wasn't interested. Between the two of us, I think without Julia to help her along she'd have been on the street. She didn't have Julia's taste, either. She tended to be tacky in the way she dressed. Julia got on her about it once, told her not to wear a certain blouse. It made Linda mad, but she did what Julia wanted." He gave a lopsided smile. "Come to think of it, I have the feeling a lot of people did what Julia wanted."

"She didn't say anything about any of her other clients?"

"Never. And I didn't ask."

116

"Family?"

He exhaled and a cloud formed on the inside of the windshield opposite him. "Well, she said once that she came from a rich family. Said they had a home in the Garden District, servants, butlers, a limo. Her father was a surgeon and they used to go to Europe every year. But I never knew whether to believe that or not." He looked over at me. "Do you think it's true?"

"I wouldn't count on it," I said, thinking of the grizzled old farmer.

"Once, she told me about her husband and baby. I didn't know whether to believe that, either."

"Her what?"

He gave a nervous little laugh. "I didn't expect it, either. We were . . . that is, we'd just, we were lying there, you know, and she asked me about my children, about how they'd been when they were little, and getting up in the middle of the night, taking them to the doctor, and all. She seemed really interested, asked me all kinds of things, little details, and then she sprung it on me."

"What did she say?" I asked, my throat dry.

"'I had a baby once,' she said. 'But it died. So did my husband.' It caught me by surprise. I mean, there we were one minute, you know, and all of a sudden she's telling me this. I asked her how it happened. She said they were in a car crash. That their car went head-on off the road, into a bridge abutment. She said her husband and her baby burned up."

Even secondhand, the words sent a shudder through me.

"Where did this happen?" I asked.

"She wasn't specific, just in another state. She said after that she couldn't have a normal life."

"Interesting," was all I could think to say.

"No," he contradicted. "The interesting thing was what she said next."

The rain was slackening now, as the squall passed over.

"She said," he went on, "that the accident was the fault of the car manufacturer; that they'd done a lousy job of inspection. But when she went to them, they stonewalled, refused to admit any fault, wouldn't even discuss it."

"Then what?" I asked, knowing there was a punch line and afraid of what it would be.

"Well, she said there was nothing else to do, that the lawyers were all crooked or too expensive, so it was up to her."

He put his glasses back on. Glare from outside reflected in them, hiding his eyes.

"So?"

"So she said she took care of it on her own."

"How?" I asked.

"She said it was an eye for an eye. They ruined her life so she ruined theirs. She said she got a detective to find some dirt on their company. She found out it was stored in the main computer and she got it out by agreeing to sleep with a programmer. She told me she ruined them, had them begging when it was over. She said after that, nothing mattered for a long time and it didn't seem so bad to sleep with other men for money. To tell the truth, I figured it was a crock of bullshit, some kind of melodrama she cooked up to excuse how she got into the business, and yet by the time she got to her baby and her husband she was crying, like it really happened. But it couldn't have, could it?"

I thought of Will Folsom and the cardboard box of books. Was it her father she had destroyed in her fantasy? Was it a scenario she had dreamed up as the fulfillment of a wish?

"Who knows," I said. "Look, does the name Rivas mean anything to you? Short, stocky guy, Latin?"

He shook his head, befuddled. "No. Can't say it does. Was he one of her . . . one of the others?"

"I don't know. It's just a name that surfaced. Did she say anything to you about leaving the country, say on vacation?"

"I didn't know until I couldn't get her to return my call. Then"—he cleared his throat—"you called and said she was dead. It's so hard to believe."

"Right." I pulled out my final question: "Did she ever tell you about a sister?"

"A sister? *Her* sister? I didn't know she had one."

He sounded like he was telling the truth.

"When was the last time you saw her roommate, Linda?"

"Linda? I don't know, a month or so. We were never close."

"You don't read the paper?" I asked.

"Sure, usually. Why?"

"They dragged her out of Bayou St. John the other day. Somebody killed her."

A look of horror contorted his face. "Oh, my God, you don't think I. . . ?"

"It's just across City Park from your house."

It was really a couple of miles, but I thought it was worthwhile to see his reaction. It was a good one. If he was guilty, he was a damned good actor.

"As God is my witness, I had nothing to do with that."

I nodded. "Calm down, Mr. Gautreau. I believe you, at least for now. Go home, enjoy your family. I'll call you if there's anything else."

The relief fought with the awful possibility that he might hear from me again.

"Please. Not at home."

"It probably won't be anywhere," I said.

"Thank you." He reached for my hand with both of his and shook it fervently. "Thank you so much. You have to understand. She was the only woman besides my wife who ever found me attractive. I was always so self-conscious. I felt so different, and she made me feel normal, like it didn't matter."

"What do you mean?" I asked.

He frowned and tapped his right foot and for the first time I saw the built-up shoe.

"My foot," he said. "You can't know how it is to be different, and to meet somebody that makes you feel whole."

He opened the door and I sat stunned as he limped back to his car.

16

The halls smelled of death, death and moisture from the mud that sucked at the old building's foundations and kept trying to drag it down like everything was eventually dragged down here.

"You'll go," Katherine had said last night, as we lay quietly in bed upstairs. "You won't be satisfied if you don't."

She was right. My talk with Gautreau had left me in a melancholy mood, the worst I'd experienced since just after my divorce. The picture of Julia Morvant had altered. Behind the self-sure smile I saw the frightened Mary Juliette, living her fantasies. Then the image shifted once more and I saw a woman with unusual compassion. Another fantasy, I told myself: Mother incarnate, giver of comfort. And finally I saw her on the airplane, frightened, but confident, playing the biggest role of her life, and never knowing that for the ones she had crossed it was no game, and they would have the last word.

There was no way to hide my mood from Katherine. At first she asked if I wanted to talk, but I couldn't shake the images. At first I pretended interest in what she was saying, but I kept losing her words in midsentence. And that night, when she'd bathed and put on an especially sexy negligee, and applied a perfume she'd saved for the occasion, I realized it was no use.

"It's not rational," she said, turning in the bed to face me.

"But it never is. The way I felt about Gregory Thorpe all those years wasn't rational, but that didn't make it less real. What I needed was a strong dose of reality. Maybe that's what you need, too."

I reached over and touched her face. How had I ever been lucky enough to find her?

That was when she said I ought to go.

At first I protested. I'd seen enough bodies in Nam, and I'd been in a few morgues since then. It was never a pleasant experience.

"And there probably won't be any way to tell," I said.

"Probably not," she said. "But just going there may help. The knowing that one of the people there . . ."

"I can do without it," I said, but she knew she had me.

And she was right. That night I dreamed of a plane falling from the sky, a brilliant pinwheel of smoke and light, like the space shuttle exploding. Only somehow I was on the craft, a lone survivor standing hip deep in the swamp, with nothing but desolation around me. I tried to raise my arms to grab a cushion and that was when I realized my left arm had been yanked from its socket. Strange, I thought, that it's only numb. Then I saw the bodies floating around me.

When I awoke she was shaking me and telling me it was all right. A few minutes later I drifted back into a dreamless sleep and when I awoke this time it was daylight. At eight-thirty I called Mancuso and asked him to make arrangements at Charity's morgue.

"I still don't know what you expect to find," he groused as we stood in the hallway, waiting for the pathologist, Dr. Schwartz. "By the way, any word from Sandy?"

"None so far," I said, trying to sound unconcerned. It had only been a day. I'd allowed three.

A nervous little man in a white coat came through a set of swinging doors, shook hands with Mancuso, and then regarded me balefully.

"Is he a relative?" he asked my friend.

"A close friend of one of the victims," I said quickly. "She doesn't have any relatives."

The doctor shook his head skeptically. "Well, there isn't much to see, unless one's morbid." His look implied I might fall into that category. "And in a disaster of this magnitude, we have to use a number of different hospitals. Most of the victims have already been identified. Fortunately, most were still strapped in their seats."

He led us through the doors and I saw a series of tables, each with a sheet-covered form. I produced the photograph Mancuso had handed me on the way over.

"Have you seen this woman?" I asked, my throat catching.

The pathologist gave it a quick glance and shook his head.

"It's impossible to say. I may have. But then again . . ."

I looked around at the white forms. The walls wanted to close in and I felt perspiration on my arms and back.

"Are all the bodies accounted for?" I asked.

"Well"—the little man shrugged—"there are always some it's impossible to identify, and a few we never find. Some probably still in the swamp. And the sheer trauma confuses things." He made a sour face and I noticed he had a twitch. "There are stray arms and legs, torsos. Not pleasant at all. Some of it's guesswork. There's room for mistakes. Suppose you get the wrong arm with a torso?"

We murmured appreciation of his difficulty.

"That's right." He warmed to the subject. "No easy answers. Oh, we do blood tests and the like, take fingerprints, but there's always the chance of a screw-up. You may've read last month about the woman the funeral parlor took out of the rest home. They got her on the slab and found out she wasn't dead. It was her *roommate* they were supposed to take. Incredible, you say, but these things happen more often than you'd think. And in this case it's worse. Any explosion that rips up bodies makes a mess. Not enough body parts, too many body parts. You name it. We have that problem here. We . . ."

"In other words," I interrupted. "There's no way to really know she's dead."

"Technically? Not at this point. Maybe before too long,

but we're still sorting them out. Where there's fire, of course, it sometimes becomes almost impossible for even a dentist. Now if this friend of yours had a dentist you could put us in touch with . . ."

"I've already checked that," Mancuso said quietly. "So far we've struck out."

"Well, then," the doctor said primly, "it'll take longer. But we'll find out eventually. The odds are overwhelming. Look"—he moved toward one of the lockers that lined the wall—"we found a hand, a man's left hand. Waterlogged. That makes it hard to get the fingerprints." He started to pull out the locker, then thought better of it and reached for another, underneath. "Or even worse, how about a foot? Not much to work with. The disaster crew almost didn't even recognize it, floating on the surface. But with photographs, blood types, I'll bet you fifty to one we place it."

"That's okay," Mancuso said, putting a hand on the other's arm before he could open the locker. "We'll take your word for it."

"Whatever. But you see the point I'm making: Something like an ear or an arm, even a head, the real problem is finding it. After that, we can generally place it, if there isn't complete incineration." He smiled lopsidedly. "But if there was incineration, then nobody would've found it, would they?"

We couldn't argue with that.

"So do you want to look at some of the remains?" he asked, completely enthusiastic now. "If you don't find the lady here, she might be at one of the other hospitals. But I'd better warn you: If that hurricane hits, it's going to slow us down considerably. Not"—he shrugged—"that we'd ever have another disaster like Galveston, at the turn of the century. But even thirty or forty extra bodies . . ."

"Right," I said, turning away. "Well, if you turn up anything unusual, I'd appreciate a call." I handed him my card and he thrust it into a pocket of his lab coat without looking at it.

"Sure," he said, walking back out with us, through the

swinging doors. "I know what you're feeling. Everybody wants to think their loved one isn't here. But if she got on that plane, she's here." He twitched again. "We'll find her sooner or later."

I didn't want to think of her anymore; in that sense, Katherine was right. The sheeted forms on the tables, the smell of disinfectant, the drains in the floors, all made me want to turn away. There was no use wasting time on speculation. She'd been on the plane. Mancuso had checked the passenger list. Julia Morvant, in black and white.

I thought of calling Solly, but I decided to go to O'Rourke's instead. He lived in a big house in the university district, a few blocks from St. Charles, which made it easy for him to take the streetcar to work every day, since he hated to drive. I knew that on Saturday he often took bike rides, but today he was home. And I was glad.

He opened the door dressed in T-shirt and sweat pants. A piano concerto sparkled in the background. If my friend was surprised to see me, he didn't show it.

"What's up?" he asked as we went inside. "You don't need a quick bail hearing, do you?"

"No, just an objective ear," I said and told him about Gautreau and then about my visit to the morgue. "I didn't expect to find her. But I know, intellectually, that she's dead. John, I've got to screw my head back on."

He listened thoughtfully. "You will," he promised. "What's the status of this Rivas? Any news?"

I shook my head. "My guess is he's gone to ground, at least for a couple of days. He knows he almost got ambushed the other night and now he'll be wary. Unless he goes for the congressman now."

O'Rourke shook his head. "Unlikely. I talked to Stokley's aide. The congressman and his wife left yesterday for a hospital back east. She has to have plastic surgery."

"Walter Reed?"

"Maybe."

"How many people know they're gone?"

124

"Not many. They're still pretending they're at the plantation."

I thought for a moment. "I'm sure Cox's group set me up to draw Rivas. Somebody managed to get word to him that I was after him and had to be neutralized."

"A leak in Cox's organization?" the lawyer asked.

"Cocaine buys a lot of loyalties," I said. "My guess is somebody's playing both ends. Or maybe Cox has somebody planted in Rivas's camp and used them as a pipeline to get the message to Rivas about me."

"It's happened before," he said philosophically. "You know it was pretty coincidental, your friend being there when he was needed."

"I've thought about that," I said. "But I know Solly. He wouldn't be part of any double-dealing with his friends."

It sounded good; the trouble was that I was having trouble keeping myself convinced. Solly and I had been apart a long time. They'd given him something he wanted. He'd been a Marine, sure, but we'd done a lot of intelligence missions in the old days, and the essence of intelligence is deception.

The record ended and O'Rourke got up to change it. "You figure she stole some of their coke?" he asked.

"Seems logical," I said. "She got mad at them for something they did, or something she imagined they did, and double-crossed them."

"And so they sent Rivas after her."

"Right." I got up and went to the mantel. He still had his Christmas cards tacked up from last year. "But there's a couple of things that bother me."

He carefully replaced the record in its cover and selected another, giving me a chance to marshal my thoughts.

"First," I said, "there was no cocaine found at the crash site. Oh, I know it could have been thrown clear, or destroyed, or be at the bottom of the swamp now. But it would be nice if some bags of the stuff turned up."

"And second?" he asked, placing the new record on the turntable.

"Rivas was pretty busy. He took care of a whole plane

125

load of people and then hopped over to St. Croix and threw a grenade at Stokley. I don't like coincidences."

The room was filled with a fatuous voice: *"When I was a lad I served a term as office boy to an Attorney's firm."*

I smiled in spite of myself.

"You think Stokley was part of the dope deal?" O'Rourke asked.

"I don't know. It wouldn't be the first time a politician talked against something and did something else under the table."

"No, it wouldn't. But I've never heard anything about his being involved in dope deals. Not that I necessarily would, of course. It's not something he'd talk about."

"Doesn't fit his image, though, does it?" I agreed.

"Not unless they're holding something over him."

"I thought of that, too," I said. "But if you're blackmailing a man and he refuses to go along, you expose him first, right? You don't kill him."

"That's logic," O'Rourke said. "But it's ours, not theirs. Besides, they didn't kill him. They just came close. Maybe he wasn't meant to die. Ever think about that?"

He had me there and he knew it.

". . . You can be the Ruler of the Queen's Navee!" the record promised.

I went back to my office to wait. On most Saturday afternoons Katherine and I would take a long ride, or head for Gulfport and the beach, or laze around. In fact, one of the little delights of the past year had been wondering what whim would seize us the following weekend. But today was different. The only hook I had on the case now was Sandy and the hope that she could find out something from Julia's sister. A name, a date, a casual reference that might be remembered, and repeated in a rare moment of sanity. Anxiety gnawed at me. Partly it was fear for Sandy, and the not knowing. But it was also the fear that she would find out something I didn't want to hear: that whatever demons ate at Jenny's soul might also have inhabited Julia's and that her

126

wild flight from Jamaica had been part of a deadly fantasy. She had spent most of her adult life courting society's disfavor. Was it any different to now take on the drug cartel?

But this was only the second full day. I had given Sandy until Sunday. On Sunday her "parents" would come for a visit and she would pass me a message: *No go; Get me out;* or *Need more time.*

The problem was I didn't want to wait until Sunday.

I popped a beer, went into my bedroom and switched on the TV. The Astros were playing the Cubs. I watched without interest and then switched to the weather channel. It looked like the hurricane was going to turn toward Florida. I wished them no ill there, but with winds at a hundred miles an hour we didn't need it here. The phone rang then and I picked it up.

"I could come over." It was Katherine's voice, matter-of-fact, promising. "I'm tired of the house already. I haven't been to your place for ages. Maybe you don't even live there any more."

She waited patiently as I fought the urge to say yes. But Rivas was still out there somewhere. Odds were he was in hiding, but there was no guarantee. Best to keep her away from my place.

"Let me call you later," I equivocated. "It would be better that way."

"I was afraid you'd say that. Actually, I was just calling on the off-chance." She sighed. "Scott and his friends have asked me to go with them on a canoe trip into Barataria. Can you imagine? Asking an old person like me? I was so surprised I said *yes.* But I'm willing to cancel for a better offer."

Scott could handle himself and there would probably be another boy or two along, from the sound of it. In all, the swamp wilderness of Jean LaFitte might be the safest place for her to be.

"I'll catch you later," I said. "Maybe we can do something tonight."

"If I'm not worn out and mosquito bitten," she said.

127

"Let's hope not."

"Let's. Oh, and Micah . . ."

"Yeah?"

"I love you." The phone went dead and I replaced the receiver.

I was still looking down at the telephone, wishing she'd given me a chance to respond, when it rang again.

"Mr. Dunn, please," said a voice I'd heard but couldn't place.

"Speaking."

"Mr. Dunn, this is Theo Schwartz, at Charity. We talked earlier?"

Of course. The pathologist.

"Yes, Dr. Schwartz?"

"Well, this may be nothing." He gave his nervous chuckle. "But you wanted to know if we came across anything strange."

All my senses were on alert now.

"You've found her."

"Well, no, that's not it. This is something else. It's something somebody brought in, something I just got to. A plastic bag. And you won't believe what's in it."

17

I thought about what other ears might be listening and decided on caution.

"I'll be right over," I said.

It took me twenty minutes. I was sweating as I accepted the ticket stub from the parking-lot attendant. The day had turned sultry, with banks of cumulus clouds drifting in from the south, but it wasn't the heat that was making me perspire. It was the thought of the plastic bag.

Its contents weren't hard to guess.

She'd taken some of their coke, of course. The bag was probably small enough to be hidden on her, and there had probably been more of them. Pregnant women had been found to be carrying five or six kilos of the stuff instead of a baby. Handicapped men had filled up their prosthetic legs. There were all kinds of places to hide it, even inside the body.

But the fact remained that with experienced customs agents, used to all the ploys, and dope-sniffing dogs, it was still a sucker play. Lots got through, but lots didn't. So why take the chance with some half-assed stunt like that?

Because she was Julia Morvant, courtesan, not Juliette Folsom, farm girl, and she was living a fantasy that couldn't be spoiled by something so prosaic as a customs agent.

I'd have felt a lot better if she hadn't been a whiz at the market. What bothered me was that it was the kind of thing

129

poor, dim Linda would pull, not Julia, who could juggle
market figures, and who saved her money in bank boxes,
and who kept her client list under the same security.

There was a security guard at the front door and I showed
my license. He asked who I wanted to see and when I told
him he picked up the phone.

I knew something was wrong when he couldn't get
Schwartz. He said a Dr. Aucoin would be out. I told him
Dr. Aucoin wasn't who I'd come to see. He told me Dr.
Aucoin would explain everything.

All I could do was wait.

Dr. Aucoin took his time. When he arrived, it was in a
flurry of white, his lab coat flapping behind him like wings.
He was a big man, with a belly that lapped over his buckle,
and I was reminded of some great swamp bird settling onto a
log to peer into the murky waters for fish.

He didn't offer his hand, just his name.

"I'm Dr. Schwartz's supervisor," he said officiously. "I've
been talking with Dr. Schwartz. He really should not have
called you. This is an official matter. We're subject to rules.
We cannot divulge aspects of our investigation to members
of the public."

So Schwartz had gotten a chewing-out.

"Suppose I have Detective Mancuso call you," I said.

He shook his head. "A city detective? No. This is federal
jurisdiction. Dr. Schwartz really exceeded his authority."

Cox, I thought. *Cox had gotten to him.*

"Can I at least talk to Schwartz?"

"I'm sorry, it's out of the question. Now, if you'll excuse
me, we're working overtime on this and there's a lot left to
do . . ."

"All right. Then just answer one question: What's in the
bag?"

"I said I could not and would not answer questions. Now,
if there's nothing else . . ." He nodded meaningfully at the
security guard who took the cue and started up from his
chair.

"Thanks for the help," I told them and left.

*   *   *

I drove over to the Clarion Hotel. Too angry to call first, I went straight to the fifth floor and banged on the door. I was still hammering when a maid stuck her head around a corner.

"No hay nadie," she said.

"They've gone out?"

"Esta libre, el cuarto."

I didn't have to know much Spanish to understand that she was saying they were gone.

Next I drove to the safe house where they'd taped up Solly, but now there was a For Sale sign on the lawn, the doors and windows were closed, and there was no car in the drive. Just to be thorough I got out and went to the door and knocked, but there was no answer, and the window air conditioners were off.

I didn't want to have to wait two hours in the muggy New Orleans heat, so I found a phone booth near Charity and looked up the number of the security desk. When the guard answered I gave him my best imitation.

"Man, listen, this the attendant at the doctors' lot. You got Dr. Schwartz working there today? Tell him I don't want to make no trouble, but somebody just busted into his car, made a real mess."

I hung up and walked over to where I could watch the doctors' lot.

There wasn't long to wait.

He flew through the door and down the steps, half running, half skipping, his face screwed into a mask of anxiety.

I caught him just as he came to the garage, stepping out from behind a pillar and into his path.

"Hold on, Dr. Schwartz. There's nothing wrong with your car."

His jaw gaped and he raised a hand, as if to ward me off. "What?"

"I just wanted to get you alone. You called me. You said you found something, a plastic bag. I want to know what was in it."

"I . . . mistake. Shouldn't have talked. Excuse me." Before I could grab him he turned and dashed back for the building. I watched him go, a sense of failure settling over me.

When I got back it was after three. I parked in the patio and went through the back door into Lavelle's shop.

"Any visitors?" I asked.

He turned slowly from his vantage point behind the counter, from where he had been moodily eyeing the scatter of tourists passing outside on the sidewalk.

"None for you, damn near none for me," he said glumly. "I don't know how I can keep open at this rate. It was a mistake taking this place. I knew I should've taken a place closer to Canal. Down on Royal or Bourbon or Burgundy: That's where the business is. Christ, nobody comes here." He moved from behind the counter and gestured theatrically at his full shelves.

"Some of this crap's been here for two years. And I just spent five hundred on black candles. They *promised* there'd be an upsurge of satanism."

"I can see you're having the devil of a time."

"It isn't funny, Micah." He followed me up the steps and watched as I opened my door. "Those cattle in Tangipahoa, the ones that they found all gutted? I thought there might be a cult, maybe we could stir up some interest. Then that damn vet at LSU said it was coyotes. *Coyotes,* for Christ's sake! I can't make a living off coyotes. And if that damned hurricane comes, I can write off a whole week . . ."

"I thought it was headed for Florida," I said.

"Just shows you what the Weather Bureau knows. Last bulletin has it headed straight for the mouth of the river. If nothing changes, the son-of-a-bitch could be here by this time tomorrow."

I went for the refrigerator and took out a beer. He was still standing there, his eyes lingering on the can in my hand, so I moved aside.

"Help yourself," I said.

"Thanks." He slumped in my chair, one eye cocked at the

132

stairs in case anyone entered below. "I may go to L.A.," he declared.

"Well, there's no shortage of oddball cults there," I said.

"Oh, the hell with this scam." He gave a disparaging wave. "I was thinking of setting up a university."

"A university?"

"Yeah, you know, the kind that gives nonresidential degrees. I've been looking into it. You can charge ten thousand for a doctorate, five for a masters, and two-five to three for a bachelors, depending in what field. I mean, like, English degrees are cheap, but in engineering, well, you could ask four, probably. The overhead's next to nothing, just a box, and you throw together some crap for the state licensing board, but that's a formality. I got it all planned out, see." He leaned forward now, eyes dark coals above the spade beard. "You get some Ph.Ds that didn't get tenure, and you put them on as faculty for a percentage. Hell, I can put out a catalog that's as slick as Harvard or Stanford or even Tulane. We may even invent some new degrees. I was thinking of a doctorate in public analysis. We'll come up with the subject matter later. I figure I could clear sixty, seventy grand a year at the start."

"Good luck," I said.

"Well, it beats selling love potions."

There was a sound downstairs and the bell on his door tinkled. He rose and peered down the stairwell.

"One minute," he whispered and held up a finger. "Business."

He bounded down the steps and I heard voices at the bottom. He returned a minute later with a large brown paper bag.

"It's a shipment I ordered," he proclaimed. "From a lab in Arizona. Guaranteed to be a best-seller."

"What is it?" I asked.

"Ah!" He reached into the paper bag and produced a withered, brownish object wrapped in polyethylene. "A freeze-dried monkey paw." He sniffed and swore under his breath. "Damn. I'll be back in a minute." He bounded down the steps again and I heard his voice yelling in the street.

I looked down at the paper bag. A nauseating stench was already filling my office. A minute later I heard his feet on the steps again.

"Bastards are gone already," he muttered. "They promised the process was foolproof. Lab animals, parts that were going to be thrown away anyhow. They were selling 'em cheap." He came over and put a hand on my arm. "Micah, listen, I need a favor. I'll make it worth your while."

I shook my head from side to side. "Whatever it is, if it has to do with *those*"—I jerked my head at the bag—"you can forget it."

"Aw, Micah. Look, I don't have any way to keep them from going bad. In this heat an hour could make the difference. Nobody wants to buy something that, well, isn't *fresh*."

"No way," I said.

"Just a few hours, till I can work something out. They won't take up much room. Your icebox is almost empty."

"And it'll stay that way."

"Micah . . ." He gave me his hurt look and gathered his paper bag. I noticed he was having trouble not making a face at the smell.

"No," I said, guiding him toward the door.

"I'll give you a potion, guaranteed to keep it up for two days straight, even with the Pet of the Year . . ."

"Good-bye, David."

He huffed indignantly down the stairs and I shut the door. I found a can of air spray and used most of it on the place where the bag had been sitting.

Even so, the room still smelled uncomfortably like the morgue.

18

The call came at seven-thirty while I was sitting on the porch watching the last light play tricks with the spray from the patio fountain. I was thinking about Katherine, envying her the visit to the swamp, where the only dangers were elemental ones, like gators and snakes. But the news about the storm bothered me. I wanted her out of there, because Barataria was no place to be if a hurricane sent tides of ten feet crashing against the coast, and even New Orleans might not be safe. When the phone rang I thought it would be her voice telling me she was back.

I was wrong. It was Sandy.

"Micah-man, listen up: Be at the place at midnight. Can't talk more."

"I'll be there," I promised and heard the line go dead.

She'd obviously been calling from one of the administrative offices, which meant she'd sneaked away from where she was supposed to be. I tried to recall if there had been any anxiety in her voice, but she had seemed in control.

But if she was asking for my help it meant she planned to get out on her own. Which meant she needed surprise.

Either they were onto her and she couldn't alert them by having her make-believe parents come to the rescue or she planned something really spectacular.

All of which was why I was waiting across the street at a

quarter to twelve. I'd notified Vic Mancuso and he'd agreed to stand by his phone. Officially, of course, he could do nothing. It was out of his jurisdiction, and something he couldn't afford to involve himself in. But I told him if he didn't hear from me by two to call out the National Guard.

I'd agonized waiting for her call and now I'd gotten it, so why didn't I feel reassured? Maybe it had something to do with the fact that Katherine hadn't called, either. The authorities were recommending a general evacuation of the coastal areas, remembering Audrey, in fifty-seven, which had killed four hundred in Cameron parish, and Camille, a few years later, which had devastated the Gulf Coast.

One thing at a time, though, I told myself. That's what they'd drummed into us in Nam. Put away the problems at home and the Dear John letters and think only about the mission, or there won't be any going home at all.

A single thought kept circling through my mind like a hawk after prey: She must have found Jenny.

It was five after twelve when an ambulance coasted up to the guard post and was waved through. I reached under the seat and placed my revolver on the seat beside me. I didn't know what to expect, but I wanted to be ready. I watched the vehicle go to the side entrance, where I glimpsed figures unloading someone from the back.

Another poor soul, I thought. More figures moved in the distant lights and a driver went around to the cab and a door slammed.

Something was wrong.

Even as I tried to comprehend what was out of place, a bell started ringing inside the compound. The guard came out of the shack and looked back at the clinic building. The ambulance started to move and at the same time the guard began to pull forward the chain-link gate, closing the entrance.

And suddenly I realized what it was I had seen: It was Sandy driving the ambulance and the bells were signaling an escape.

The ambulance was going faster now, but the drive wasn't

long enough for it to get up much speed. Instinctively, I knew what I had to do.

I leapt from my car and, gun in hand, ran across the street toward the guard post. The ambulance was almost there now, but its momentum would never carry it through the gate. There were voices all over the compound and floodlights springing on from the perimeters and from recessed places in the lawn.

The gate was closed and the ambulance was slowing. . . .

I reached the sidewalk, bulled into the gate and started to shove it back. I had it halfway across the drive before the guard turned.

"What the hell?"

He saw the gun and froze. I got the gate back all the way and stood aside as the ambulance peeled rubber. The guard glowered at me, but made no attempt to approach. There were white bodies charging toward us now, outlined in the powerful lamps.

I wheeled quickly and ran back to my car. I heard other motors starting and jumped into my own vehicle, savagely twisting the ignition key. The engine roared into life and I nudged my way out into the street as the first car reached the gate. I cut in front of him, glad now for the special knob on the wheel that allowed me to steer like a man with two good hands. I shot in front of the pursuit car and heard his horn blast angrily.

The ambulance was two blocks away now, headed for Jefferson Highway, which led back to New Orleans, and I took the center of the street, preventing the car behind me from passing.

The horn became a furious staccato and I'd only gone a block when I felt a tap on the bumper. My own car jumped ahead and I swore under my breath. I jammed the accelerator and opened out the distance between us. The ambulance had its lights and siren on now, and a three block lead.

The pursuer tapped my bumper again and I slued into an S, barely missing the cars parked on either side.

137

They had a hand-held spotlight now, and they were hitting my mirror. The beam arrowed down, blinding me and I wrenched my mirror downward.

My car jumped forward again as they slammed me with special violence. Once more I jammed the gas, leaving them a few yards behind.

The ambulance had turned onto Jefferson now, headed east.

"All I had to do was hold my own and they would lose.

It was something they must have realized because even as I came to the intersection with the highway I saw another car speeding east toward me, a small red flasher on the dash.

I shot through the stop sign and cut it off, dimly aware of a squeal of brakes behind me.

If they were real police I was in a hell of a lot of trouble. If they weren't, I'd have to settle for the present trouble.

The ambulance was a blinking light in the distance, and most motorists would probably assume it was headed for Oschner Clinic. It was a good start, but I had two fast cars behind me now, one in each lane, and there was only one way to stop them.

I started to slue snakewise across both lanes. A few cars were still out and I looked for a situation that would give me some freedom. I found it in a lumbering Galaxie, sputtering along in a cloud of fumes in the right lane. Just ahead of it, in the left, was a milk truck. If I could slide between them, I might just cut off my pursuers. Not much of a choice, but it was the best I had.

Unfortunately, I never got a chance to maneuver. A popping sounded behind me and all at once my car was sluing again, except that I wasn't pulling the wheel. Instead, I was trying to hold it steady, but the tire had blown and it was all I could do to keep control.

Maybe a man with two hands could have held it. But the wheel whipped out of my grip and I felt the car spinning clockwise. The world turned and somewhere a silly voice was chiding me for not having fastened my safety belt. The steering wheel slammed my chest and my breath flew out. I dimly heard doors slamming and fumbled for the gun on the seat. It wasn't there.

I was alive, but just barely, the way I felt. There were faces outside the window, grim-faced men with guns. My hand touched something cold on the floorboards just as my door jerked open. I came up with the gun in my hand and jabbed it in the face of the man closest.

We stared each other in the face and my blood went cold. It was Solly.

His gun was inches from my chest, his finger on the trigger. He wasn't looking at my gun, though; he was looking at *me*.

Voices and shouts came from behind him and now somebody was yanking at my other door, but it was locked.

Solly's gun moved up slowly to train on my head and my finger tightened on the trigger of my own weapon.

Then, slowly, his gun lowered and he backed away.

"Let him go," he said, still staring at me.

I heard an oath, and a startled protest. Solly wheeled like a savage dog.

"I said let him go, fucker, or I'll blow your brains all over the pavement."

I pulled my door slowly shut, aware that my motor was still running. I was sideways across both lanes and traffic had backed up behind us. I jabbed the gas and the car lumbered forward, the blown tire flapping along underneath.

A block later I took a right-hand turn, off the highway, into concealing darkness, painfully aware that if they changed their minds I'd be easy to pick up. I was on the rim now and the noise could probably be heard for two blocks in either direction. I made a few more turns and ended up on River Road.

It wasn't the best part of town to be in with a disabled car on a Saturday night.

The rim wasn't going to hold up forever. I left River Road for a sidestreet that looked dark, passed a few houses, then stopped in front of one. I got out and opened the trunk. Pulling with all my strength, I heaved out the spare and dropped it in the street. My chest was hurting anew from the crash and I sagged against the car for a moment. Then I found the jack, got it out, and managed to wedge it under the bumper. I got the jack handle and started to work on the lug nuts, but it was slow going in the dark. Worse, I needed a hand to hold the tire tool onto the nut as I levered the nut loose. I swore as the tool fell into the street and heard a chuckle behind me.

"Work a lot better in the light man," said a voice. "And with both hands."

I stood up slowly, my hand in my shirt pocket, where the gun now rested.

"I'll get by," I said.

"Yo' choice," the voice said. I could just make him out now, a black man a head taller than myself, standing in the middle of the street with a beer can in his hand. There were other forms behind him.

I picked up the tire tool and started again and heard a grunt of surprise behind me.

"Dude ain't got but one hand," another voice said.

"I'll be damned," said the first one and stepped forward where I could see him better. "Better gimmie that tire tool 'fore you kill yourself," he commanded.

Wary, I took a step backward.

"You wanna be here all night?" he asked.

"Not especially." I handed him the tool. He squatted and in a blur of motion had the nuts loose.

"What happened to this tire?" he asked, running his hand over it.

"Somebody shot it," I said.

He nodded as if it made perfect sense. "I dig." He got up and went to the jack, his friends forming a circle behind us.

"You lucky," he said, muscles bulging as he pumped the jack handle. "I seen people killed with blowouts." He chuckled. "I seen 'em killed without 'em."

"Right," I agreed. "Look, I'd like to pay you."

"Sho'. Tell you what, you do this for me sometime I'm stranded in honkey town."

There was a ripple of laughter behind him.

"You got it," I said. "But it may take twice as long."

This time the laughter was raucous.

"I hear that!" my helper declared good-naturedly. He pulled the ruined tire off, threw it into the trunk, and fitted the spare on. Then he put on the nuts and started to lower the jack.

"Two minutes," he declared, "you be on yo' way." He tightened the lug nuts, then, satisfied, dismantled the jack, put it into the trunk, and closed the trunk lid.

"I reckon that'll do it."

"I'd still like to pay you," I said, reaching for my wallet.

"Man drive a car like this, go around getting hisself shot at, ain't in no position to pay nobody."

I held out my hand and he shook it.

"Thanks," I said.

And meant it.

Half an hour later I stopped at a K&B on Carrollton and used the outside pay phone. I tried my office—no message on my machine—so next I tried Sandy's number, but there was no message for me on her recorder, either.

Cox didn't have that many people, I told myself. She'd had a clear shot. Knowing Sandy, she'd have abandoned the ambulance as soon as possible and called somebody to pick her up. Maybe she was still waiting.

There was nothing I could do until she called. I used my last quarter to call Katherine. To my relief, she answered on the second ring.

"Hello?" Her voice was alert, even expectant, as if she hadn't been awakened from sleep.

"Thank God, you're okay," I said. "Look, I need to lay over."

"Where are you?" she demanded. "We've been worried to death?"

"*We?*"

"Can you come here? I'll explain."

Five minutes later I parked on Pitt, the next street up

141

from her house, and walked the rest of the way. Maybe Cox and his people knew about Katherine, but I'd seen enough to convince me they were far from infallible. No need to leave a flag, like my car, in front of her place.

I knocked once when the door opened and Katherine pulled me inside.

"What's going on?" I asked, and then I saw Sandy on her couch.

"We were sure they were drawing straws to see who got the ears and who got the tail," Sandy said, getting up, a glass in her hand. I recognized a sweatsuit of Katherine's.

"They almost succeeded," I said, watching Katherine pour from a decanter. She handed me a glass and I took a swallow, grateful for the slow burn as the whiskey made its way down into my belly. "Where's the ambulance?"

"Over on Sycamore," Sandy answered. "I called Katherine from a pay phone and she met me there, took us back here for safekeeping."

I turned to Katherine. "And where were you?" I asked. "I was worried when I couldn't get you."

"Scott's boat trailer," she said with a wry face. "Burned up a bearing on the way back. All I needed for the end of a lovely outing." She lifted her pant leg to show a welter of ugly red insect bites. "Give me a call from Sandy any day."

"Micah," Sandy drawled, looping an arm around Katherine's waist, "I never realized before how lucky you were. This is some lady you got."

"More like some pair of ladies I've got," I said, sitting down.

"What's wrong?" Katherine demanded as I winced.

"I'm okay," I said. "Just a bruised sternum." I described my escape, then turned to my assistant. "Now tell me about the clinic and why it was so important to get out when you did."

"Well," she began, but a movement behind her caught our attention.

I turned to see Julia Morvant standing halfway down the stairs.

19

After the initial shock wore off I could see, of course, that it wasn't Julia. This woman was younger, her face thinner, but there was still a remarkable resemblance.

"Jenny," Sandy cried, turning toward the girl on the stairs. "You should go back to bed."

I couldn't tell if she'd heard, because she didn't move. She was still clad in the shapeless white gown of the clinic and her hair was mussed. But instead of a wild look in her eyes all I saw was blankness.

"I'll take you back to your bed," Sandy said and took Jenny's hand. "That's a good girl."

I watched Jenny follow her back up. Katherine shook her head.

"Poor child."

Now I understood better about the precise timing of the escape. Sandy had planned to take Jenny with her from the first.

"Has she said anything at all?" I asked.

Katherine shook her head sadly. "Not since I picked them up. She was in the back of the ambulance. I didn't know what Sandy was up to"—she chuckled—"until she explained."

"I'm sorry to drag you into this," I apologized.

"Who else was there to drag?" she asked wryly.

Sandy came back down the stairs.

"I think she'll be quiet for a while. At least, I hope."

"Want to tell me what happened?" I asked.

The black girl smiled demurely. "Just a con-cat-e-nation of circumstances." She picked up her drink and swirled the liquor around. "As soon as they put me in, they fed me some pills, which I, of course, managed to spit out."

"Of course," I agreed.

"But I played groggy all the first day and kept my eyes and ears open." She kicked off her shoe and drew her leg up beneath her on the sofa. "It's not a very big place, you know. Just twenty or thirty victims. Er, I mean, patients. Mainly attendants and nurses. The hit squad, the patients call them. And then there's this Dr. Laurent who comes once a day to check."

"Dear old Dr. Laurent," I said.

"Right. The rooms are semiprivate, no ward like in *Cuckoo's Nest.* This is a high-class dungeon. The torturers all wear white."

"You found Jenny," I said.

"The very first day. She was two rooms down, across from me. I managed to sit next to her in the dayroom. I found out from the other patients they'd had her on drugs. It's amazing how much you can find out from so-called crazy people. Some of 'em are saner than the folks that run this city. But nobody pays any attention to them because they're supposed to be nuts. Anyway, the girl Jenny had been there just over a month. Sometimes she was hyper, and when that happened they shot her full of something to quiet her down. They seemed to be specially careful about her, watching her a lot, which is no wonder, because the others were telling me she managed to escape just a few weeks ago."

"What?" Katherine and I reacted together.

"That's right. Snuck out one night. They said the hit squad about went crazy, Laurent came down looking all red in the face, they thought he was going to have heart failure. Everybody got locked up for a few hours and then, just before sunrise, they brought her back. They took her right to

144

the shock room and after that they gave her some injections to make her a zombie. After that, they weren't so uptight about her, but the head nurse always checked personally to make sure she'd gotten her downers every morning and night."

"What was she like before she escaped?" I asked.

"Well, that's the interesting thing. She could carry on a conversation, but she was paranoid (the patients love to throw psychiatric labels around). She thought somebody was after her. She kept talking about somebody trying to kill her, got real uptight whenever the head nurse came around, once tried to brain her with a chair."

"Odd," I said.

"Had to be the authority thing, way I figure. She didn't like Laurent, either, but she wasn't violent with him. Just tried to avoid him."

"Psychiatrists have that effect on some people," Katherine said drolly.

"Did you ever get her to talk?" I asked.

Sandy smiled. "Not until yesterday. Course, you have to understand I only had a couple of days. Miracles take time. This was just *difficult.*"

"You'll get a raise," I promised. "As soon as the client pays us."

"'Bout what I figured," she said. "Anyway, I kept trying to talk to her, like morning, noon, and night, at meals. It was kinda hard, of course, because they had *me* scheduled for some activities, too. I kept being scared they were going to use the shock machine on me, and then there *would've* been some bashed heads. But all they did was give me an intake interview with Laurent, which wasn't anything. I've been through worse applying for jobs at hash houses. He wasn't really interested. You could see it in his eyes: one more screwed-up little nigger gal. As long as the money's green, color of the skin don't count, but no special favors. I mumbled a few things to him about how there was gonna be a day of reckoning for all those chickens they killed for Popeye's, and how God appeared to me and he had feathers, and he just wrote it all down and had them take me back to the dayroom."

Katherine and I were laughing now and Sandy was enjoying our reaction.

"After that, my time was pretty much mine, except for a couple of times the nurse would come around and ask how I was coming, and I'd say fine." She shifted on the sofa. "Anyhow, yesterday at lunch I was sitting next to Jenny and I was trying to get something out of her, why she was here, what had happened to her, and I kept using her sister's name, and all of a sudden she turns and when I look into her eyes she's as sane as you or me, and she says it, just the name, that's all."

"The name?" I asked.

Sandy nodded. "That's right. She looked right at me and said, 'Did Mary Juliette send you?'"

"My God," I muttered.

"I know. Unfortunately, right then I realized one of the nurses was standing there looking over her shoulder. I hadn't seen her come up, but I was sure she heard, so I did the best thing I could think of. By luck we were having chicken so I upset my plate and started screaming about cannibals. I hated to do that, I can't tell you how much."

"I'll get you some more," I said.

"No hurry. They took me away, stuck a pill in my mouth. I pretended to swallow it and calmed down, but I had the feeling they had their eye on me after that. I caught some of them whispering. I figured I might have to do something drastic. It was pure luck something happened so I figured I could maybe have a fighting chance."

She leaned toward us, knowing she had our complete attention.

"Just before I called you, Micah, the head nurse got called out of the dayroom. It seemed real urgent, so I waited a second and then followed her. She was in a big hurry and didn't lock the door into the hallway. Now, there's a staff snack bar off to the side and there wasn't anybody in it, but there *is* a telephone. I saw one of the buttons lit so I picked

146

up and sure enough a second later the head nurse picked up. It was Laurent, calling from somewhere else. He told her there was a new patient coming at midnight, in an ambulance, and that it was important for everything to go right. Well, she sounded griped, said she got off at five, and they were predicting a hurricane, and she had to store up on supplies and they almost had an argument, because then he said she was being well paid. He told her the ambulance would be at the side door at midnight and he wanted everything taken care of."

"And that's when you called me," I said.

"As soon as she hung up. I called quick, said my piece, and hung up, because anybody could've come into that room at any second. As it was, I didn't quite make it back to the dayroom in time, because the head nurse caught me in the hall and wanted to know what I was doing. I played dumb, but I could tell she was suspicious. For the rest of the day I laid low, stared into space a lot, but I could feel their eyes on me."

"You're lucky you made it," Katherine said.

"No lie," Sandy agreed. "But they were all caught up in this new victim that was coming. They had a big meeting and had to move somebody out of a room, and everybody was complaining about having to do all this at the last minute, but the head nurse didn't want to hear any of it. So I just laid low. I'd noticed something earlier: The main fuse box is in the snack bar, so when it was midnight and I saw them getting ready, I waited. When I saw lights outside and saw them come down the hallway with the stretcher I made my move. I'd jammed the lock on my door with some chewing gum, earlier, and I got out into the hall right after they passed. Then I went over to Jenny's door and opened it. They don't have anything complicated in the way of locks; I've seen better in parish jails. Anybody outside can open the door, see. So I got her up and dragged her down the hall with me. There was somebody at the desk but he was asleep." Her lips twisted in a smile. "Well, he was asleep after I hit him, anyway. I got Jenny into the back of the ambulance without any trouble, but that was when they saw me." She heaved a sigh. "Micah-man, I sure am glad you knew what to do."

"Anything to please," I said. "It's interesting the people that chased me belonged to Cox. It proves a tie-in, of course, with Dr. Laurent. But what the hell can Jenny have to do with it? I thought she was peripheral. But maybe Laurent's the key."

Sandy shrugged. "He's got a sweet setup. And he can handle all kinds of ticklish things. Where's it safer to be than in a nuthouse?"

Permutations of everything I'd learned in the last few days went tumbling through my head and I knew it was no use to try to make further sense of it tonight.

"Let's get some sleep," I suggested. "Maybe it'll be clear tomorrow."

"I don't know about the second part," Sandy said, "especially with a storm coming, but the first sounds like a fine idea. Who wants the first watch?"

It was just after four when Sandy nudged me awake. I stared up into the blackness for a moment and then swung over to sit on the edge of the bed. Beside me, Katherine moved onto her side and I got up carefully, so as not to awaken her. I hadn't undressed, except to take off my shirt, and for an instant I nursed the illusion that I'd just lain down a few minutes before.

I got my .38 from the night table and stuck it into my belt and followed Sandy to the hall. She eased the bedroom door closed and started for the stairs.

"I'll sack out on the couch," she said. "Coffee's in the kitchen. So far, everything's quiet."

"Good." I went to the downstairs window and lifted an edge of curtain. Still dark, but everything seemed quiet enough. I went back to the kitchen, poured myself some coffee and took a seat in one of the chairs.

So far nothing made sense. But there had to be sense

someplace, because two people were dead. It was the manner of their deaths that kept bothering me.

One, Julia Morvant, had died in a spectacular bombing that had killed over sixty other people and had left her body unidentifiable. Her roommate, the dull-witted Linda Marconi, had been kidnapped and then thrown from a car. Her almost casual death in the canal was as far removed from Julia's *gotterdammerung* finale as anyone could imagine.

A cadre of government agents who might or might not be completely legitimate had done everything they could to obliterate the evidence left by both girls at their apartment, and suddenly seemed to have an interest in keeping Julia's younger sister in an isolation ward.

Julia Morvant had presumably been killed over the drugs that had just been found in a bag in the swamp, and a madman named Rivas was stalking a congressman who had zeroed in on the drug cartel. The congressman was deafened and his wife disfigured by a bomb.

But most of all it was a casual boast that Julia had made before her death. A reference to the play *Julius Caesar*. A speech that everyone learned in the eleventh grade. A speech that I somehow felt would show me something I hadn't seen.

Unfortunately, only she knew what she had meant, and the only link left was her sister.

Was her sister insane or just smart enough to be faking it? Or had she been sane enough before someone put her away in a clinic run by an unscrupulous doctor?

She'd escaped, and it was then that she'd contacted Julia, asking for help. Julia had called their father and gotten no assistance. Her next action had been to make an appointment with the man who ran the clinic, give him some fake symptoms, and have him write out a prescription for depression—all to help assess him and try to decide how easy it would be to free her sister. So far, so good.

But then she had dropped the whole matter and gone to Jamaica, of all places, to steal money from a dope ring. Had she needed the dope to hire a person who could get Jenny out of the hospital? Not likely; she already had over a hundred thousand in her bank box.

I got up and tiptoed back across the room, past Sandy's sleeping form, up the stairs, and into the hallway. Jenny was asleep in Scott's old room, and I hesitated a second outside the door, before pushing it slowly open.

She lay motionless on the bed, so still that for a moment alarm trembled through me. Then the sheet rose slowly and fell and I knew she was all right.

An examination by a physician would tell whether she was or had been a junkie, but my guess was no. At least, Sandy hadn't seen any needle marks in the usual places when they'd put her to bed. She hadn't seemed to be suffering withdrawal symptoms in the clinic, either, though they might have gotten her through it before Sandy entered.

Her father had implied that she'd gone the same route as Julia. Did that mean Jenny had been a pro, as well? She looked peaceful, with her dark hair splayed out on the pillow, and I wondered if her father had ever stolen into her room to look down at her when she had been little.

I turned to go, sad with the memory of the old man across the lake, and it was only when I reached the door that her voice spoke out of the darkness, freezing me in my tracks.

"Don't leave yet," she said.

20

I turned back around slowly, closing the door. Her head had moved now and her dark eyes were on me. "Please," she said. "I need help to get out of this place. I can't take another beating."

I tried to absorb her words. Was she truly mad, or had she awakened from a dream that still clung to her consciousness, making it impossible to tell the dream from what was real?

"Nobody's going to beat you," I said.

"I don't want to be beaten." It was a little girl's voice now, childish in its pleading and I thought once more of Will Folsom.

"I'm not your father," I said.

"Of course not," she said reprovingly. "You don't even look like my father. Will you help me get out of here?"

"I'll help you," I said. "That's why I'm here. Where do you want to go?"

Her voice hesitated and her head turned back to stare at the ceiling. "I don't know. Just away. Where they can't find me."

"They? Who is *they*?"

"You know," she declared tightly, then sat up slowly in the bed. "If you help me, I'll treat you good. I'm good to men I like."

A pale slice of light from the street lamp splashed down

151

across her torso and she slowly pulled the hospital gown up over her head until she was sitting naked in the bed.

"Do you want to touch me?" she asked.

Her breasts were firm globes, inviting in the milky light from the window, but it was something else that made me move to where she sat.

At first I'd thought it was a shadow but as I got close to it I saw that it was what I'd suspected: An ugly scar, running from her right shoulder down her arm.

"You can touch me now," she said, "but we have to get out of here before you can do more. Unless . . ." Her hand reached for the buckle of my pants but I moved to the side, so I could see her back. It was a hatch-work of scars.

"Who did this to you?" I asked.

"I'll never tell." She giggled, then her voice fell serious. "You ask too many questions."

"Put your gown back on," I said. "Tomorrow we'll get you to a doctor."

"No doctor . . ." she said, alarmed. "Please, no doctor . . ."

The door opened then and Katherine stood looking over at us, still tying her bathrobe around her.

"Is everything all right?"

That was when the girl began to scream.

It took us both by surprise and Katherine backed away.

"It has to be me," she said. "The white robe. I probably remind her of one of the nurses."

She retreated to the doorway and the screaming subsided, but only slightly. A second later Sandy was up the steps and into the room.

"Let me handle it," she said quickly. "I think I can quiet her. She knows me."

Katherine and I left gratefully.

"My God," Katherine said. "I had no idea." She tried to laugh it off. "Usually I don't have that effect on people."

"Like you say, it was probably the bathrobe and the fact that you're a white woman." I told her about my conversa-

152

tion with the girl. "She's been beaten, but not in the last few weeks. The scars are pretty well healed."

"So it was right around the time she was put in the clinic."

"That's how it looks."

"Poor thing."

"Yeah," I said and wondered if any of the neighbors had heard the yelling. I checked the clock downstairs. Four-thirty. There were already occasional cars in the street outside and the sky was beginning to lighten. I knew there wouldn't be any more sleep for the rest of the night.

At seven I called John O'Rourke. His voice was sleep fogged and I knew he'd planned on at least another hour in bed.

"I need your help," I said simply.

"Couldn't you need it on Monday?" he groaned. "Haven't you heard? We're about to get blown away.

"Sorry. Wouldn't wait."

"Well, it doesn't matter, I guess. She didn't stay over, anyhow. I had *Casablanca* and *The Maltese Falcon* both all ready to roll, and champagne in the icebox. What's wrong with the women today?"

"Keep trying," I said drily. "Look, I want to know my legal status."

When I'd finished explaining he groaned again. "Christ. Kidnapping, ADW on federal officers." He thought for a second. "But, on the other hand, they seem to have been holding this woman against her will. As you know, in this state, an involuntary committal to a mental institution can only be done through the action of the coroner, and I have to wonder if the coroner knows what's going on."

"It's Jefferson Parish," I said.

"Yeah." Everybody knew that money talked in Jefferson, even louder, some said, than in neighboring Orleans. "Well, what do you want me to do?"

I told him.

153

It was ten before he called back.

"You're right," he said. "I called Mr. Folsom and he agreed—grudgingly, I have to admit—to let me act on his behalf. So I called the coroner in Jefferson Parish and he hasn't got any record of an involuntary committal for Jennifer Ann Folsom, or any other Jennifer or Jenny that he can remember. He was pissed, too. I made him late to his niece's wedding. He wanted to know what was going on."

"Good work," I said, breathing relief. "I guess that takes the weight off of us."

"I guess so. It isn't any crime *I* know of to free somebody that's being illegally held."

"Welcome news," I said, and thanked him again.

The next person on my list was Mancuso. His wife sighed when she recognized my voice and I guessed I'd just spoiled another family day. But when he came on he told me not to worry.

"Haven't you looked at the weather channel? The winds in that storm are up to a hundred and fifty. So I think we'll just stay in and tape windows."

I lifted an edge of the curtain and looked out. A thick fog hid cars and trees.

"I've been through a little bit of a storm, myself," I told him and explained what had happened.

"Thank God Sandy's okay," he said. "I never was comfortable with the arrangement. But look, you must've decided to ruin my Sunday for *something*."

I told him about the pathologist's call. "I think I know what was in the bag they found," I said. "But I'd like confirmation."

"I'll do what I can."

"And I also need somebody to take Jenny someplace safe. Couldn't we store her in the hospital at Mandeville for the time being?"

He whistled. "You don't want much. If the storm comes in this direction it'll close the causeway."

"If you can come right now, you'll make it there and back before the storm can move more than a few miles."

"Got it all figured out," he muttered, but I knew he was thinking the same thing I was: That if Cox was onto us, he'd have to think long about trying to take her from a policeman, even outside the policeman's jurisdiction.

When I was done with Mancuso I called a man who owed me a favor and told him where I'd left my car.

"Check the tire size and get a rim somewhere and then go out to K-Mart or Sears or whatever's open and get a new one and put it on. But save the old one."

"Save it?" he asked, surprised. "You selling old rubber or what?"

"Just do it, send me the bill, and we'll be square."

"Naw," he said. "You kept my ass out of Angola. Tire's a cheap price to pay. Look, the hurricane's fifty miles off the coast. You want some water wings, too, while I'm at it?"

It was just before noon and a feathery rain had already started when Mancuso pulled up outside. I gave a quick look through the curtains and then nodded to Sandy. She went upstairs while Katherine discreetly melted away into the kitchen. Seconds later Sandy reappeared with Jenny. The blank expression had returned and I couldn't help but think it was real. I watched them descend the steps and opened the door as they made their way slowly across the room.

The girl stopped suddenly and turned to Sandy. "Are you coming?" she asked suddenly.

"Sweetheart, I'll be right there every second," Sandy replied. That seemed to reassure her and they moved out onto the sidewalk.

The fog had lifted but a grayness still clung to the sky, and the temperature had dropped ten degrees from what it had been at the same time yesterday. I scanned the other houses and the cars along both sides of the street, but everything seemed in order. Mancuso had the back door open and the girl entered willingly. It was his own car, no markings, no

155

flasher on the dash, but he had a radio, which made me feel better. Sandy slipped into the backseat beside Jenny and I closed the door.

"Thanks, Sal."

He waved and I watched them go.

At one-thirty I got a call that my car was ready. I thanked my contact and turned to Katherine.

"I have a feeling things are about ready to break open. I know Solly. He let me go last night. That may mean he's on the outs with his people. I have to put myself in a place where he can find me if he needs to come in. Because until Jenny talks, nobody else can finish putting things together."

"Then I'll go with you," she said quietly.

"You'll stay here," I said firmly. "You've seen how rough these people play. It's bad enough just to have a hurricane to deal with."

The phone rang then and she froze, startled. Finally, on the third ring, she picked it up and I saw her face relax.

"Well, it's all right with me if I won't be a drag. . . ."

She turned to me. "It's Scott. They're having a hurricane party and they want to know if they can come over."

"Problem solved," I said. "They'll need a chaperon, anyway."

"Micah . . ."

"You couldn't be in better hands." I kissed her good-bye and closed the door behind me. Half an hour later I was getting out of my car in the courtyard of my apartment. Old Mr. Mamet, the caretaker, had cut off the fountain. Now he looked down at me from the balcony opposite, as I hurried across the yard for my stairs.

"Gonna blow," he called. "It's got that feeling. Better get your flashlight batteries before they're sold out."

I nodded acknowledgment and saw through the back door of the voodoo shop that Lavelle was fastening his storm shutters. I hurried up the outside steps and went in the back way, stopping to sniff the air. But there was no tobacco odor and everything seemed as I'd left it. I checked my answering machine but there were no messages. Then I got some flashlight batteries out of the bottom drawer of my desk. Fortunately, as a PI, they were something I always had enough of.

I put the radio on the public station, to get some decent music as well as the latest weather news. The Saints were supposed to be playing in the Superdome, but they'd postponed it, because the last thing they needed with a hurricane was fifty thousand tourists to worry about.

In the last day I'd had about three hours' sleep and it was catching up with me. I propped a chair against the front door and another against the door onto the balcony, then sat down in my easy chair, eyes closed. The gun jabbed my flesh through the pants, but after a few minutes I stopped noticing, as dreams slipped in to wrest away my attention.

I must have slept half an hour when I heard the noise. At first I thought it was from outside, but then realized it was coming from the door that led down to Lavelle's level. As I watched, the handle turned and the entire door jerked back against the chair that was tilted against it. Then it stopped, pulled back, and slammed forward again.

My hand snaked down, grabbed the pistol, and I jumped up, gun leveled at the doorway. I silently lifted the chair away and stood back as the door came forward again.

"Holy Christ, don't shoot!" It was Lavelle's voice, raised at least three octaves, and for an instant I thought he was going to topple backward down the steps.

I lowered the revolver and thrust it back into my belt.

"Close, David," I said. "Very close. Next time try knocking."

"I didn't know you were here," he protested. "You told me to use the key you gave me if there was ever an emergency, so I figured you wouldn't mind."

"What's the emergency?" I asked.

"Well, I thought maybe I ought to check your windows, make sure everything was shut up. If the hurricane comes through here there's no telling what'll go. This building is over a hundred years old."

"I appreciate the thought, but I think I'll be okay."

"Right." He half turned. "Oh, and there was just something I wanted to pick up."

"What was that?"

"Oh, nothing," he mumbled and headed through the office toward the kitchen, and I got a sinking feeling as I saw him head to the refrigerator and open it.

"David, by God, if you . . ."

"It was just for a couple of hours, that's all." He held up a plastic pouch with a disgusting brown object that caricatured a hand. "I found a man in St. Bernard Parish who's into occultism. I told him this was a mummified human hand, a hand of glory, from a condemned killer, that had been electrocuted at Angola, and that was why it would be so shriveled. He's on his way in, he said never mind the weather, he's been trying to get something like this for years. . . ."

"Get out, David!" I shouted, advancing on him. "And take that damned thing with you."

"You were right, Micah, the rest of the shipment wasn't any good," he babbled, making a beeline for the stairs. "But with what I'll make on this one it won't matter. I'll even buy you a new—"

"*Out!*" I commanded and slammed the door so hard after him that for a few seconds I didn't realize my phone was ringing.

I lifted the receiver and heard static, then a voice that was vaguely familiar.

"Mr. Dunn? This is Nelson Benedict, Congressman Stokley's aide. I wonder if you could come down to Godsend. It's urgent."

"Right now?" I asked, taken by surprise. "There's a hurricane on the way and—"

"Yes. As soon as possible." His voice was trembling and then, finally, he blurted out, "Please. It's a matter of life and death."

21

The sky was leaden as I backed out into Barracks, and bits of paper were already dancing down the narrow street. A few tourists hurried along, looking confused, but a gaggle of college kids stood at the corner of Barracks and Chartres with beer cans in their hands, laughing and enjoying the thought of a real hurricane. Only the bums who inhabited the steps of Our Lady of Victory seemed unimpressed, but then, another disaster would only be a footnote in their lives.

I took Esplanade to Claiborne, trying to skirt the downtown traffic. The old homes looked desolate and I wondered what another hurricane would do to many of them.

I didn't like the idea of driving twenty miles across the river in the teeth of a storm. If there was danger at Godsend, it was the job of the police. But then I realized they would never call the police because that would open them to public view. And I had the feeling that by going there I would finally make the pieces of the puzzle fit.

O'Rourke said I was a fool. He offered to go with me, but I told him to stay home, by the phone. He said two of us could do more than one, and I knew he meant it. In the days of protest he'd shown unusual courage in the face of police brutality, but nonviolence was too much a part of his character for him to be useful in a situation that could become explosive.

Finally, he agreed to keep calling Mancuso until the policeman returned.

The powdery rain turned hard while I was going up the east ramp of the bridge. Traffic was light in my direction but there was a heavy stream heading west, into the city and away from the mouth of the river. By the time I hit the down ramp, the rain had become a blowing succession of sheets, so that the Fischer Project, off to the right, was shrouded in a gray curtain.

The last few hurricane seasons had been lucky ones for New Orleans, but the radio said this one was headed straight into Plaquemines Parish, immediately to the south. Once over land the storm would start to break up, but that would take a while, and in the first few hours after landfall there was time for a major disaster.

I couldn't do much about it now. I had a small travel bag with some necessities, my slicker and a spare flashlight. I also brought an extra box of .38 ammunition, which I'd leave in the car, and a tiny Navy Arms replica of a Sharps pepperbox, the kind of four-barrel hideout gun that used to be favored by gamblers—.22 caliber, without enough punch to stop anyone who was determined, unless you hit him in the head, but, as my old DI used to say when teaching unarmed combat, better than a sharp stick in the eye. I'd keep the pepperbox taped to my ankle and hope things wouldn't come to that, but it was a measure of my uneasiness.

The congressman and his wife were away, so what made it necessary for me to visit Godsend on the worst day of the year?

Maybe it was a setup, another trap, and if so I was the world's biggest fool for allowing myself to be drawn in.

But, of course, it was Julia who drew me there. Julia who had died and yet somehow seemed still alive.

The wind was bending trees as I ploughed my way down General de Gaulle, headed for the Intracoastal Bridge. Already water was backing up in the street, and in an hour or two there would be flooding. I realized that I would have to stay the night at the plantation.

160

It was Rivas, had to be. There was no other reason to call me.

As I crawled to the top of the bridge, the wind shoved the car sideways and I fought to keep to my lane. The view from the top was unrelieved grayness, in all directions, and as the storm's fury increased even that scene was blotted away by a hail of raindrops. Approaching the bottom of the bridge I saw the flashing lights of a traffic-control point, where the four lane met River Road.

A state cop in a yellow slicker stuck his head at the window and I rolled it down.

"Road's closed," he informed me. "We're evacuating people. Do you live down here?"

"I'm working for Congressman Stokley," I said. "You can call his aide to confirm."

The cop took my driver's license and went back to his car. I rolled up my window and waited. Three minutes later he returned with my license and handed it through the window, shaking his head.

"Okay. But I'd tell them to come up to higher ground. And be careful: Parts of the road are starting to flood."

"Thanks." I took my license back and went right, onto River Road.

Now I was on my own. I turned up my radio.

The latest weather report had the eye of the hurricane near the river's mouth.

A blue pickup emerged from the storm, ploughing water out from the sides, and I slowed. As it passed waves rocked the sides of my car and I heard splashing against the floorboards. The water was already to the hubcaps, and if it got much deeper the engine would stall. If I stopped, though, it would flood into my exhaust and that would be just as bad.

I tried to remember—the Stokley place had to be just after the next bend. But there were so many bends it was hard to know if my memory was playing tricks on me.

All at once the car hit a dip and I heard water gush out as the vehicle started to sink. But miraculously the wheels bit into something solid and I felt myself skidding up onto a hard surface.

The victory was short-lived. Suddenly we were floating, and then the wheels touched again and the engine sputtered at the same moment. I pressed the accelerator, trying to squeeze out enough speed to keep up forward motion, but the water was too high. The engine quit and the car came to rest at the side of the road.

I swore aloud and got out my extra flashlight. Then I emptied a handful of the extra cartridges into my top pockets. I untaped the pepperbox from my leg and this time retaped it to my useless left arm, just above the elbow, on the inside. I took a piece of oilcloth from my traveling bag, wrapped up the .38, and stuck it back inside, with the spare flashlight. Then I struggled into my slicker, took a deep breath, and stepped out into the flood.

The wind, loud enough inside the car, was deafening. Bits and pieces of debris shot past my body but I hardly noticed. All I could do was keep my balance as the water swirled around me.

It rose midway to my knees, and already had a good current as it cascaded down off the levee and onto the road. I held the car with my good hand, trying to keep my balance and avoid dropping the flashlight. My watch said only four-thirty but it was dark enough to make me wonder if I could find my way. There were fence posts on my right, and what appeared to be a copse of trees. With luck Godsend would be just the other side. . . .

I let go of the car.

For the first fifty yards I did reasonably well. The water stayed at about the same level and I managed to keep my balance. The next fifty were my undoing.

I stepped in the first hole but managed to maintain my balance. The second hole sent me swaying and I reached out for something to hold me up. By luck there was a tree limb, a branch thrusting up from the water and I clung to it for a second, trying to keep from falling.

The third hole was just the other side, and this time there

was no hope. I felt myself going down and instinctively released the traveling bag. Water splashed up into my face and I threw out my good arm to break my fall. On hands and knees I caught a last glimpse of the bag bobbing away before it vanished in the gloom.

I struggled up, shaken and angry. Just ahead, the road rose slightly and I found the water receding to my ankles. Through the trees I thought I saw lights, flickering in the tempest.

Water sloshed in my shoes and rain pounded my body and face. The woods were a dim screen and where they stopped the grayness was only slightly lighter. I bowed my head and forced myself into the wind. A sudden burst of air blew me sideways, but I plunged forward. When I reached the edge of the woods I saw the guard shack beside the driveway. It seemed to be deserted, and a heavy branch had fallen onto the gate bar, splintering it.

I made my way through the branches and took my bearings.

The mansion was a pale outline through the leaning trees, the drive a gray river paved with water.

I started forward again, my feet crunching into the shells that were now covered by the flood. The wind rose to a howl and for a second I thought I heard a human scream, but then I realized it was a trick of the storm. A branch splintered with the sound of a gunshot and fell twenty feet to my left. I came even with the gazebo and saw that the trellis on the near side had been blown away, and a combination of light and shadow gave the strange impression of a figure seated motionlessly inside.

I stared an instant too long. Something hit me on the head and the watery ground came up at me. Somewhere, vaguely, I was aware of voices and lights, and then I realized hands were dragging me forward. There was light all around me now and I was seated in a chair, in what appeared to be a kitchen. A television was broadcasting weather reports from one corner and I watched the radar needle trace a line of solid white across our area. The atmosphere of the room was stale and if I needed a further sense of claustrophobia, it was provided by the closed shutters, that had the effect of converting the house into a sealed box.

The black manservant who had greeted me on my previous visit poured whiskey into a tumbler, and a man I recognized as Nelson Benedict stood across from me, his face twisted with anxiety.

"Thank God you're all right," he said. "I was so afraid."

I took the glass of whiskey and downed a swallow.

"Piece of wood hit you," the manservant said. "Bad out there, bad as I ever seen it."

"Why haven't you evacuated?" I asked.

The manservant looked away, leaving Benedict to answer.

"Congressman's orders," he said. "The storm was supposed to miss us and there're a lot of valuables in Godsend."

It was a feeble explanation, but I didn't see any sense in making an issue.

"Come on," Benedict urged. "I'll get you some dry clothes. I think you and the congressman are about the same size."

I stood shakily and followed him to a downstairs bathroom. A few minutes later he reappeared with some fresh clothes, a towel, and some shower shoes. "I'm sorry," he said, nodding at the latter. "They're the best we can do."

"They're fine," I said. "By the way, do you have any adhesive tape? I hurt myself a while back and I'm trying to keep my ribs taped up."

"Of course." He went away and came back with some tape. When he'd gone I removed the pepperbox and discarded the old tape. Then I dried the little pistol as best I could and, after making sure my own skin was dry, retaped it to my left arm. When I emerged from the bathroom my head still ached from the blow and I had some bruises where I'd fallen, but I was dry, and that alone made me feel like new.

Benedict was standing in the hallway, dithering. "This way," he said, gesturing toward the living room. I followed, conscious of the branches battering the eaves and the banshee howl of the wind. To the left was a closed door that apparently led into a study.

He stood aside and nodded at the door.

I went to the door, opened it, and went in. The room was filled with acrid cigarette smoke and at first it seemed empty, but I knew better.

"You can come out now, Cox," I said.

There was movement to my left and a form disengaged itself from the shadows.

"Very good, Dunn. How did you know?"

"I'm used to being bait," I said. "But tell me one thing, Cox: Who do you really work for?"

"Justice," he said. "But we're not FBI. We're a special task force, just as I told you before."

"Naturally, there's no way for me to verify that, because the secretary will deny all knowledge."

He gave me a thin smile. "The attorney general. Same principle, though."

"But why in a hurricane?" I asked. "That doesn't make much sense. You don't really expect Rivas to pull up in a boat."

He shrugged. "What the hell? We can't control the weather."

It wasn't convincing, but I needed some time to sort out the possibilities before I called him on it.

"Where's Solly?" I asked.

He sighed theatrically. "Flown. You were sharp. Dunn: You told me there was a leak but I didn't want to believe you. I thought my people were the best. They'd all been vetted, and vetted again. But sometimes you pick a rotten one."

"Solly?" I asked, shocked.

"Afraid so. If it helps, I was as surprised as you were."

"I don't believe it," I protested. "We were together in Nam. We were . . ."

"Yeah, tell me. He's done some sensitive jobs for us, too. I had him all wrong." Cox came out into the center of the room and drew on his cigarillo. He was in his shirt sleeves,

165

and the nickel plated PPK gleamed in the lamplight. "But you know, Dunn, sometimes there's something inside, a flaw." He removed his pistol from his shoulder rig and jacked back the slide, chambering a round. "I had this revolver once, a .357, one of the prettiest jobs of workmanship you've ever seen. I could take the pip out of an ace at a hundred feet, during rapid fire. I loved that weapon. Saved my life more than once in-country. Then, one day, I had it out on the range, at Quantico, of all places. Load five and fire at will, you know the drill." He brought the automatic up and sighted along the barrel, aiming for an imaginary point on the curtains that shrouded the windows. "First shot, bull's-eye. Second shot, overlapped the first. Third and fourth, all touching." His finger touched the trigger and I tensed. "Fifth shot . . ." He made as if to fire, jerked the pistol up, and then laughed, lowering it. "Fifth shot the son of a bitch blew to pieces." He lowered the hammer and then removed the magazine. "I checked the ammo. It was regulation, range loaded, nothing wrong with any of it. All I could figure was a flaw in the metal. I never forgot that experience." He jacked the slide back, ejecting the chambered round, and caught it neatly in the air.

"You have proof about Solly," I said.

He shrugged, reloading the magazine and shoving it back into the handle of the gun. "Proof? He broke. That's proof enough."

"Broke? How so?"

"Last night, at the clinic. He had a chance to take you and he didn't. At that point, we were unsure about you. You caught us by surprise. His orders were to stop you and he failed. And threatened the other members of the team. That was the tip-off he was under too much pressure to handle. So I spent the next few hours checking out times and places, and what it came down to was he was always gone at strange times. You know the kind of guy he was. He wasn't good at deception. It was like bending a piece of metal backward and forward. After a while it was too much. So I pretended I was being called back to Washington and had him listen in on the tap when Miss Benedict out there"—he made a derisive limp-wristed gesture—"called you to come. I figured that would flush him. It did. He vanished. AWOL. Gone."

"If that's true, why did he save me from Rivas the other night?"

"I'm telling you," Cox explained patiently, "he's a man trying to be two things. It was fine to feed Rivas intelligence about the congressman and about our investigation, but he didn't want you killed. You're his friend. Or were. But when you busted those folks out of the place, that tore it for him. You hadn't kept him informed. It was a sign you didn't trust him. And since he'd recommended you for this gig, he was the one knew he'd get a new asshole torn out." Cox jammed the pistol back into the shoulder holster. "His letting you get away was his good-bye present. His statement, according to his own muddled code of honor. But a code all the same."

I looked down at the rug. I hated to admit it, but it all made a kind of crazy sense, everything except how he could have been betraying his employers in the first place.

"You know," Cox said softly, taking a final puff and stubbing the butt out in an ashtray. "Solly Cranich wasn't the smartest guy ever lived. He wasn't made for spook shows. I figure he got set up sometime after he came aboard. Maybe a woman, hell, you know the routine: I've got an uncle in Malaga, will you take him a present? And the uncle has to send something back, of course, only it turns out to be some white powder, and a favor to a girl friend all of a sudden is smuggling."

I nodded. It was the sort of thing simple, good-hearted Solly could let himself get mousetrapped into.

There was a thumping behind the curtains and I walked over and parted them. The sound I'd heard was the heavy storm shutters, trembling in the wind.

"What about the girl? What was she doing in Laurent's clinic?"

"That's a long story," Cox sighed. "But she and her sister were mules for the drug cartel. This girl, Jenny, was a little unstable already. I don't know what she's said to you, if anything, but she's in outer space. And the drugs she was into made it worse. She knows a hell of a lot about the organization. We were protecting her. And trying to straighten out her head enough so we could get her testimony."

Outside, the usually tranquil grounds would be a lake by now and I thought of my traveling bag, with my gun inside, bobbing away on the current.

"How many men did you keep here?" I asked.

"One other," Cox said easily. "Why? Do you think Rivas has fins?"

I remembered the strange image I'd seen the moment the branch had hit me, of a form seated in the gazebo. It had been an illusion of the storm, I knew, but it still made me uneasy.

"I don't know," I answered. "But it might help if *we* did. This is lowland, with a bayou just behind the house. It can't take too much more flooding. And even the levee won't hold forever."

He laughed soundlessly. "Hurricanes don't bother me," he said. "And I didn't know they bothered you."

"I grew up in Charleston," I said. "Where did you grow up?"

"Touché, Dunn."

I started out.

"Oh, Dunn."

I stopped.

"What?"

"The offer's still open."

I shut the door behind me.

In the kitchen Benedict and the servant were assembling an array of hurricane lamps and batteries.

"How high has it ever flooded here?" I asked.

The old black man stopped, a candle in his hand. "In twenty-seven it was eight feet, they say. 'Course, that was before my time."

168

"But this house is on brick pilings," Benedict ventured. "That should help, shouldn't it?"

The servant and I exchanged looks.

"Pilings three-foot tall, Mr. Benedict. Water outside already almost a foot in some places."

"Is the phone still working?" I asked.

Benedict nodded. "Last time I checked."

"Then we should call and ask for help in evacuation. The Coast Guard station's just at the end of River Road. They ought to be able to send a boat."

"No!" It was Benedict's voice, shrill in its denial. "No, we can't do that. We'll be all right." He saw my surprise and licked his lips. "Don't you see? It's the congressman's house. He left it to me, as a trust, to guard. I just couldn't go away and leave it to be destroyed."

"Houses can be rebuilt," I said.

"Not Godsend. This is the family home. We couldn't leave, could we, Elias?"

Elias turned away to reach for another candle. "I reckon not, Mr. Benedict. But this gentleman got a right to leave."

Benedict picked up his glass and tossed down another swallow of whiskey. "That's for him to decide."

I took the glass out of Benedict's hand and set it down on the table. "How do you think the congressman's going to feel about your helping to lure me down here?"

Benedict's eyes bugged and he wiped a hand across his mouth. "I did what had to be done," he cried, shrinking back. "I was trying to save Godsend, to . . ."

Elias looked over at me. "Mr. Benedict gets upset sometimes," he said. I nodded and walked out into the foyer and picked up the phone.

The line was dead. I was just replacing the receiver when there was an explosion outside and the lights went out.

22

For a long moment I sat motionless in the darkness, listening to the wind's scream outside, while the sheets of rain pounded the walls and windows. Then a light flickered and Elias advanced into the foyer with a candle in his hand.

"Must be a tree across the power line," he said, handing me a candle stub in a brass holder. "We'll have the house lit again in a minute." He gave a little laugh. "We got plenty of hurricane lamps."

"We may have to go upstairs," I said.

He nodded. "In twenty-seven they took my folks off the roof of a house. They were lucky."

"Help will come here before that," I said. "When it's light a boat will get through."

"If you say so, sir."

I went over to the study door and tried it, but Cox had locked it behind me. I had a vision of him with the curtains drawn back, hands on his hips, daring the storm to do its worst. I'd seen a lot of men like him in Nam. They won medals for bravery, but they weren't brave. Mostly they got killed, and because they tended to work alone, they mercifully died alone, too. But a few survived.

Most of what he said made sense, but I still didn't believe him. Solly wasn't a traitor. And as for my being called here . . .

My thoughts were shattered by a crash from the back of the house and I whirled around. I was already halfway through the door when a shout sounded from the kitchen. In the lamplight I saw Elias holding a lamp up to the window over the sink. The storm shutters had torn loose and were swinging back and forth in the blasts of wind.

"I don't see nothing, Mr. Benedict."

"But my God, didn't you see?" gibbered the other man, his face convulsed. "He went right past the window."

"Mr. Benedict, it was the branches moving outside." Elias regarded me with deep-set eyes to see if I would accept the idea. "Big limb off the oak tree, should of been cut three months ago. Calm down now. I'll go up and put something over the window."

But Benedict was not convinced. Instead, he rose on shaky legs and grabbed my collar.

"I saw what I saw. He was out there!"

"Mr. Benedict, this window's nine foot off the ground, with the brick pilings. Man passed under the window you couldn't see."

"He didn't pass under the window," Benedict shrieked. "He was over near the tree line, near the swimming pool."

I wondered if Solly could be out there someplace.

"It's easy enough to prove," I said. "Who has some galoshes?"

Elias approached me. "Mr. Dunn, you don't have to go. It was just the limb."

"Then proving it'll make him feel better," I said.

I slipped into some gum boots and threw my poncho over my head. Maybe it was crazy and Benedict had seen nothing, but in Nam I'd learned to trust my guts, and right now my guts were telling me that things were wrong. I told myself it was only the storm, that the prospect of being flooded out would give anybody butterflies, but I'd been in danger from inanimate forces before, and this feeling was different.

Elias unbolted the rear door and handed me a flashlight.

"Be careful of the steps," he said.

He pulled the door open and I ducked my head and

171

rushed down the concrete steps. My boots sank into water almost to the knees and I steadied myself on the side of the house for support. In front of me were the surreal skeletons of the iron-filigree lawn chairs around the swimming pool, and behind them the outline of the pump house. I started forward, careful to walk around the watery pit that was the swimming pool. Leaves and twigs sailed past my head and I held up my hand to fend them off, the flashlight tracing crazy strips against the rain.

Could it be Solly? I halted, clutching the low fence around the swimming pool for support. A terrible thought grabbed me: What if Cox was right? Suppose Solly had been turned, had followed me out here and was waiting? Twenty years can change people, and how well do we ever really know anyone else?

I pulled myself along the fence, fighting the blast, and stopped in the lee of the pump house.

It had been a bar in Saigon, during R&R. A VC on a motor scooter had tossed in a bomb. I'd watched it bounce through the door and into the middle of the floor. But Solly hadn't watched—he'd jumped for it, picked it up, stiff-armed a couple of patrons between himself and the rear door, and thrown it into an alley.

Reflex. It didn't mean he'd done it for me. It had been as much for himself. That's what I told myself.

But, by God, he'd *done* it.

I came around the edge of the little structure and halted to look back over my shoulder at the big house. From where I stood I shot my beam at the kitchen window, where the storm shutter flapped back and forth like a broken wing, and I saw the limb of the live oak Elias had mentioned, hovering just a few feet away. Of course he had been right: It had been one of the branches.

And the man in the storm had been Nelson Benedict's imagination.

I felt my way along to the back gate and then along the other side of the fence to the door of the outhouse.

Below the house the land sloped downward, to the bayou.

The bayou had already risen over its banks and water slopped against my knees. Something brushed past my leg and I recoiled instinctively. I'd heard of the swamp creatures coming out in hurricanes, being driven to high ground. But it was only a clump of swamp grass, torn loose by the storm, and as I looked I saw others, uprooted by the rising waters.

I reached out for the door of the pump house and pulled. The wind battered against it, and for a while I thought it was hopeless. Then the wind fell for an instant; I yanked and the door came open.

I slipped inside and the wind slammed the door shut, closing me into the structure. I turned around and shined my light. It was, of course, the last place for anyone to hide in a storm and I knew already that it would be empty. The first probings of the light confirmed my suspicion. I saw a squeegee, a net, a bag of chlorine, and some old clothes floating in a corner.

My flashlight went over to the pump, and then back to the clothes, and I realized with a start that they were more than clothes.

I bent down to examine them, aware of the wind trying to lift off the corrugated roof. When I was finished I stood up again and sloshed to the doorway, leaned my body against it, budging it open just far enough so that I could squeeze out again.

Even in the teeth of a hurricane I felt relief after the claustrophobic little shack.

He'd been shot in the chest with a heavy caliber weapon and it had come out the back, leaving a hole big enough to put a fist through.

Judging from the freshness of the blood and the fact that the body was still warm, it had happened only minutes ago. I'd fished in the water for his weapon but had come up empty. Whoever killed him had been a pro, catching him at close range, putting a single round through the chest, and then collecting the victim's weapon before stowing him in the shack, knowing that the sound of the storm would drown out the gunshot.

173

The only question was whether the man Benedict saw had been the dead man or his killer. Not that it mattered: there was still somebody out here, now with two guns instead of one.

Reaching across my chest, I pulled the tape that held the little .22 to my left arm.

I started back along the fence, the wind at my back, trying to blow me forward. Three feet from the gate it knocked me to my knees and I almost lost the flashlight.

As I was rising to my feet the man appeared on the other side of the gate, pistol in hand.

For a moment we looked at each other and then I did all I could think of: I threw the flashlight in his direction.

It caught him by surprise and he ducked out of the way, firing off balance so that his bullets passed harmlessly overhead into the trees. I yanked the little pistol loose from under my arm, thumbed back the hammer, and when he rose from the water to take aim, I fired slowly, four times.

He looked surprised, staggering forward, then dropped his own pistol as his muscles quit working. He went onto his knees in the water and then toppled forward into the swimming pool, his slicker billowing out around him like wings.

Shaking now, gun emptied, I reached the back door and slammed on it with the flat of my hand. The door swung open and I staggered in.

Cox had joined the others in the kitchen and in the soft glow of the oil lamps I detected mild surprise on his features.

"Nice night out, is it, Dunn?"

I took off the slicker and slipped out of the gum boots. "Not my idea of fun," I said, walking past the table where Benedict sat. "By the way," I said. "You were right. There was a man out there."

The aide started, his fist clutching his whiskey glass.

"Nothing to worry about," I said. "He's dead."

The lack of sleep was catching up with me. I took a lamp and made my way to the front of the house, to the study, with Cox following.

"Water getting high, is it?" Elias called out from behind

us. "Got to watch for snakes. When the water gets high the snakes come out. During Camille people got bit by moccasins."

I slumped into the easy chair by the window and let my head sag back against the leather.

"You lucked out, Cox. Your plan worked in spite of everything. And all it cost you was one man." I exhaled. "They'll probably give you a medal. It'll be on Stokley's recommendation, of course. What do they put on spook medals? *For national security services rendered*? And nobody but you and Stokley will ever have to know."

"You're burnt out, Dunn. You aren't making sense."

"Probably not. But I'm making a lot more sense than that man of yours you sent outside after me. He's in the swimming pool now. And he's not practicing for the Olympics."

I thought I heard his breath rush out but it may just have been the wind.

"You killed one of my men?" His voice was icy.

"Well, it was only luck," I said. "He had a bigger gun. But for the record, I guess I have to say yes, I did."

"You son of a bitch."

"I was wondering what would get to you. But what's one man more or less? There's still you, and you've got the situation in hand, right?"

"What are you saying?"

"Figure it out." The lamplight danced on the walls, seeming to stir the curtains. I got up and went over to a framed picture of Stokley with the president of the United States. The president was signing a bill, and over his shoulder Stokley was smiling like the Cheshire cat. He was a handsome man, the kind cut out for television, with the good looks that attracted the female vote and yet the ruggedness that made men think of a good hunting buddy. His wife was beautiful, too, and in the picture beside it I saw her caught by the flash as she danced with the secretary of state. I moved over to the picture of a groundbreaking for a river diversion project. Stokley was wearing the obligatory hard hat, and the governor and a colonel from the Corps of Engi-

175

neers were at his elbow, all grins, as he bore down on his gold shovel. Behind him was another face I recognized, that of Benedict. He wasn't smiling. Probably the strain of orchestrating the event, the fear that someone would be late, that the ceremony would flop. Being the ever-present staff man was a job I would never have wanted. It suddenly came to me that digging up dirt was a bad habit for a politician to get into. The fatigue must have been getting to me, because for some reason I thought of Lavelle's monkey paws and how they would be best off buried in the hole Stokley was excavating.

"I like that one," Cox said from behind me, his voice suddenly silky. I looked up and saw a framed citation from the White House, commending the congressman for his efforts against drugs.

"Yeah, drugs are always good press," I said.

The next photo showed him in a schoolroom, handing a plaque to a student.

"I wonder if they still make them read *Julius Caesar,*" I said.

"What?"

I looked around the room, vaguely realizing there were bookshelves and I ran my eyes over the volumes.

"Do you think there's a Shakespeare here?" I asked. "I see a Dickens, and a Tolstoy."

"Dunn, you really have lost it."

The books were part of a set, the kind people buy to impress others, but I knew if I pulled down a volume at random I would find some of the pages uncut.

"No Shakespeare," I said. "Well, I guess it doesn't matter."

I looked back at the picture of the classroom.

"You know, when I was in the eleventh grade I had to stand up in front of the whole class and recite Antony's speech. I thought I'd never forget it, but somewhere over the years I lost the last lines. Whenever I get to 'Caesar was ambitious,' I start to bog down."

176

"'If so it was a grievous fault,'" said Benedict's voice from behind us. "'And grievously hath Caesar answered it.'"

"Right," I said. I looked back up at the man with the golden shovel and all of a sudden it came to me and I started laughing. I tried to stop, but I couldn't.

"What's wrong? What are you laughing at?" Benedict demanded. "Those are the words. I didn't misquote. . . ."

"Mr. Dunn's had a hard day," Cox said. "I think you ought to show him upstairs. Maybe he'll feel better in the morning."

"That's right," I said. "I will. But why do I have the feeling that if I close my eyes before then, morning won't come?"

"Delusions," Cox said.

"Sure." I was still laughing, because it all made sense, the Caesar clue, what the coroner had told me, and what I'd seen inside this house. There were other loose ends to tie up, but now I knew where to go. I turned to Benedict. "You've got him in a hell of a spot, Nelson, old friend. He can't kill me in front of you without killing *you,* and then Elias, too. You see, it would've been so much simpler if the storm hadn't interrupted. Then maybe I could've killed Rivas or vice versa, and one of Cox's people could have killed the one that was left in the crossfire. But your call threw him off and now he's left with his own dirty work."

"He's insane," Cox protested. "I'm not running Murder Incorporated."

"Of course not," I said. "Linda Marconi died accidently, jumping out of your car. The bruises and fragments of concrete and tar from the pavement prove that. And the water in her lungs shows she was alive when she fell into the bayou. You people are guilty of kidnapping her, not killing her. Except that her death was the outcome of a felony. So maybe murder *is* the right name."

"It was Rivas!" he cried, advancing on me as Benedict cowered to the side. "Rivas kidnapped her and killed her, not us. And when they catch him, he'll admit it."

"That's a pretty safe threat," I said. "But it's never been in the cards for Rivas to be taken alive. He knows too much. Rivas is history."

"Rivas is in the city," Cox said from gritted teeth. "He's a dangerous man and . . ."

I shook my head. "Rivas is harmless," I told him.

"What are you talking about?" he demanded. "How can you say that?"

"Because," I said, "I just left him. He was in the pump house next to the swimming pool, face down in the water. Somebody put a slug through his chest. So you see, Cox, you luck out again: Rivas is dead. There's just me."

23

For a long time he just stared at me and then he shrugged. "Did you kill him?"

"Does it matter?"

"No. He's dead. That's all that matters." He took out another cigarillo. He was trying to be nonchalant, but I could tell it bothered him to think that somebody else might be out there.

"You know, I've put most of it together," I told him. "There're one or two things left, though. Julia Morvant wasn't smuggling dope, for instance."

"You're in left field, Dunn."

"Am I? Then try this on for size: Dope wasn't involved at all. That whole story was cooked up by you as a way out."

I heard a squeal from Benedict. "Christ, he knows."

"Shut up!" Cox commanded. "He's imagining things."

I turned to the aide. "I'm not imagining murder," I said. "Sixty-seven people died in that crash just to get to one person. Then her roommate was killed. And there're a couple of bodies outside. Do you think you'll go to Angola, or to some federal joint like Marion? I haven't heard good things about either. Too bad." I shook my head. "Somehow I don't think you'll have a very easy time wherever you go."

Benedict swayed slightly and put a hand out to touch the wall, as if to reassure himself that it was there.

"I . . ."

"Benedict, don't be an idiot," Cox warned. "He's talking bullshit."

"Then the scandal," I said. "Every newspaper in the country, every wire service, all the networks. You'll be glad to get to prison before all the hearings are over."

"No!"

The rug had become spongy and I realized belatedly that as we'd talked, water had been creeping across the floor. The door burst open and Elias held up a lamp.

"Water coming in from the back," he said. "We got to go up."

"What?" Cox gave me a twisted smile. "Do you mean the great mystery is rained out?"

"Not for long," I said.

Cox smiled at the other two men. "Go on up. Mr. Dunn and I have some more things to discuss down here. Don't we Mr. Dunn?"

"You call it, Cox."

The others retreated and I heard their steps on the stairs. Cox dragged the door closed against the bloated rug and stood with his back to it.

"Now maybe you want to tell me all your theories," he said.

"Let's start with Rivas," I said. "He's not the most wanted terrorist since Carlos the Jackal."

A muscle flickered in his jaw and he turned, as if to leave, but then he spun back around, gun in hand.

"What else do you know, Dunn? Start from the beginning."

"Well, I guess I thought a lot about how a woman could fake her own death, and why she would. That stumped me for a long time. I knew Julia was melodramatic and pretty damned clever, but to kill nearly seventy people just for a stunt?"

"But you finally figured it all out," he said.

"Just about." I lifted my hand a few inches and his eyes went down to the little pepperbox.

"I keep underestimating you," he said with a nervous

chuckle. "But do you really want to go up against a .380 with that toy?"

"It's the best I have," I said, knowing how desperate the bluff was, that I couldn't even coax a .22 bullet out of the empty barrels.

Cox leaned back against the door and tried to laugh. "Dunn, you've got balls." He started toward me. "You know, this is crazy—"

"Don't take another step," I warned.

"Listen, for Christ's sake, man. There's no reason for us to kill each other. I was telling the truth when I said the offer still stands. Why not work together?"

"Because I'd always have to be watching my back," I said.

He walked away from the door like a dog circling another, looking for a vulnerable spot. I was playing for time, but I didn't know how long it could go on. I was no match for him physically.

"You know," he said, back to the curtain, "I'm beginning to wonder if that popgun of yours is really loaded."

"Find out," I said.

"What the hell is it with Julia Morvant?" he demanded, irritated. "Christ, you never even met the cunt."

"I don't know," I said truthfully. "Maybe it's just because she wanted my help."

"Well, you're crazy," he said. He was getting ready to say something else when the shutters outside slammed against the window, sending one of the framed photos to the floor, where the glass shattered. Cox spun, taken by surprise, and I kicked out at his gun hand.

It was a desperation move and it didn't work.

His arm went upward, the gun discharged at the ceiling, but he held it, and he started to lower it again toward my body. I hit him then with my shoulder, driving him backward, off balance. He crashed into the curtain, bringing it down on us as he fell and I heard him curse as the folds fell over us. I punched wildly but we were at equal disadvantage, neither able to see or effectively grab the other. The barrel of the pistol caught me in the head but, cushioned by the cloth, it did little damage. Suddenly I sensed him sliding away and realized he had freed himself. I flung my arm up, throwing the curtain off my head. As Cox rose to his feet I kicked hard at his kneecap, and he dropped the gun.

His mistake was reaching to retrieve it. My leg came back and then snapped forward, toward his head.

A quarter of a second and I would have finished him. But he managed to raise his left arm and deflect my kick, and I realized with a sick feeling that he wouldn't make the same mistake again.

He didn't. He rolled away from me, forgetting the gun, and then came back from a crouch, springing like an animal. He landed on my good arm, smothering my block, and I tried futilely to roll away from him. Water soaked into my clothes from the rug and I coughed as some of it splashed into my mouth. A fist crashed against my face and I thrashed out, but he brushed away my hand and brought down his fist again. My head slammed back, into the wet rug. Something flashed in the lamplight and I saw a stiletto, which must have been under his shirt. My hand reached out for a hold on something, anything, to pull me away, and touched something cold and hard. Instinctively, my fingers closed around it and I brought it up as his own hand came down. He gave a yelp as the jagged piece of glass from the broken photograph dug into his arm. My own fingers had been cut, but I shut out the pain, slashing upward at his face. He fended with his hand and I opened a gash across the backs of his fingers.

"Bastard," he spit, as I kicked sideways with a leg and knocked him off my body.

He fell onto the wet matting and I rolled forward, the glass shard poised to finish the job.

But this time he had found the pistol and I froze as the black hole of the barrel stared at me with the emptiness of death.

He pulled the trigger and the gun jerked in his hand as an explosion shattered the room. Cox stared at me, unbelieving, and then the room exploded again. He went limp and the pistol fell onto the rug.

Stunned, moving on instinct, I scooped up the PPK and rolled onto my belly, eyes searching the shadows.

"When are you gonna learn to take care of yourself, young 'un."

I relaxed. It was Solly's voice.

He was standing just inside the door, a big automatic in his hand and a grim smile on his face.

"Better get away from him," Solly said. "You'll get bloody."

There was something in his voice beyond tiredness. I scrambled to my feet and went over to where he stood.

"Are you all right?"

"Sure, kid. I seen a lot rougher people than these."

The gun in his hand was a Colt, government issue, and I thought about Rivas, with the big hole in his chest, and the even bigger one in his back.

"You killed Rivas," I said.

He nodded wearily. "I shot him. But it was close. He got off one of his own. Christ, I'm slowing down. It's the second time the bastard nailed me."

I saw a streak of red on his shirt and knew.

"You're hit," I told him.

"I'm scratched, for Christ's sake. There's a big difference."

"Let me see. . . ."

But he shook me off.

"Stand aside. Let me put another bullet into him to make sure."

I looked over at the man by the window, whose body now turned in the dark water like a grotesque piece of flotsam.

"No need," I told him.

He stared for a second, then nodded. "No. I guess not." He slid slowly down to a sitting position in the water. "God, I'm getting old."

"Damn it, Solly, you'll never be old. Look, we've got to get out of here. This whole place is flooding."

"I'll be okay. Just let me rest. Stay here and talk to me."

"Sure, Solly. I won't leave."

He nodded. "Good. We go a long ways."

"Saigon, Solly. We got back to Saigon. Remember the bomb in the bar?"

He nodded slowly. "Got a lot of mileage outa that one. Everybody in the whole fucking place thought I did it to save their ass." He coughed. "But I did it to save my own ass. Ain't that a laugh?"

"It's real funny, Solly, just like the man you brought back from patrol, shot to pieces, but you wouldn't leave him. You sent the patrol back but you stayed and dragged him back yourself. . . ."

"Hell, you fell for that? It was for me, kid, it always was. You save a man one day, he saves you the next. Nothing simpler. I wasn't being no damn hero. Heroes get killed. I wanted to stay alive."

I looked down at the red spot on his shirt and saw it was bigger now.

"What happened, Solly? What happened between you and Cox?"

"That son of a bitch," he snorted. "He used me. He used both of us. You got in by accident, because she called you, but when I saw your name, I thought if I built you up there might be something in it for you, but he never meant for you to be anything but a target."

The wind was stronger now, beating the shutters, and another picture tore off the wall and hit the water with a splash.

"I didn't know about the killings, Micah. You've got to believe me. I bought their story about Rivas."

"I know," I said gently.

"It was just the old days, that's all, Saigon and Pleiku and all the rest. The good guys had another chance and I didn't want to muff it this time."

"You never muffed it, Solly."

"They were holding the girl," he went on. "They told me it was for her own good, she was a druggie, Rivas was after her. When she broke out I thought it was Rivas. Then I saw

184

it was you. I couldn't let him do anything to you, Micah. I knew if you did it there was a reason."

"The girl knows the whole thing, doesn't she?"

"Far as I can tell. She was the last one. The last . . ." The lamp toppled from the shelf and crashed into the water, where it died in a hiss of steam.

"The last?"

"The pump house," he mumbled and I moved my ear down to hear him better against the storm. "Out by the pool."

"The pool? What about it?"

He stretched his hand toward the floating lump that had once been Cox and then his hand dropped to his side.

The memory of the dead man in the little tin shack flashed into my mind and I tried to make sense of what he was saying.

"She'd be the last one they killed?" I asked.

He nodded. "Wasn't, though." He started to point to Cox again but gave up.

"Afterwards, Cox jumped my case," he gasped. "Said I didn't know what side I was on. Told him he was full of shit, whatever side you were on was good enough for me. Asked did I want to be relieved then and there. Told him he couldn't relieve shit. I left." His breathing was labored now. "Spent a lot of the day looking after a bottle of Ezra Brooks. Then I figured they'd probably try to use you again, so I went to wait for you. When you came out, I followed." I sensed his smile. "Dumb bastard, Driving right into a flood. I found your car." He tried to chuckle. "Guess mine's under water now, too."

"Two dumb bastards," I said.

"I couldn't see you but I followed the way I knew you'd come. I didn't know just how to handle it. I couldn't exactly knock on the door. I went to the back and that's when I saw him, by the pool."

It wasn't hard to imagine the scene, because I'd been out

there myself. Rivas had materialized from nowhere and Solly had fired instinctively. . . .

"I thought I had it dicked," he whispered. "When I quit Cox, I took out my old Colt. Never could hit anything with that damned nine millimeter, and even when you do, you don't know if it'll do anything to 'em. But the old Colt nineteen-eleven . . ."

"You got him," I said. "He didn't live a second after you fired."

"Yeah. But what I can't figure, Micah, is how he hit me."

"He didn't," I said. "It was Cox's man. He was the one who nailed you." I knew it would please him. "But I got him."

"Son of a bitch," Solly muttered. "I didn't *think* it was Rivas." He shifted slightly and I realized he was looking up at me in the darkness. "You know if I'd seen him, I'd of gotten him, too."

"He wouldn't have had a prayer," I agreed.

For a minute I thought he had stopped breathing but then his hand moved out to grasp mine.

"Cox and his people, they were looking for her," he said. "They went crazy."

"After Jenny?" I asked.

"No." His voice came out in a painful rasp. "The other one. They were looking for *her*."

My head swam and I tried to keep my voice steady.

"You mean she really is alive?"

"Alive," he confirmed. "Oh my God, all of them. Everywhere."

"Who, Solly? Who's everywhere?"

"Outside. The storm. Oh, Jesus, the swamp."

"What are you trying to say, Solly? Tell me, please? Is Julia Morvant alive? She can't be in the swamp. Did you see her? Is she here? For God's sake, tell me. . . ."

But this time he was beyond talk. I felt his carotid and got no pulse.

The water was to his waist now and I stood painfully and dragged him through the half-open doorway as best I could.

186

The stairs: I had to get him onto the stairs. Maybe with mouth to mouth and chest compressions I could start him breathing again. He was tough. He'd been through other tough spots in Nam. A little piece of lead no bigger than a pencil eraser wasn't going to kill him.

The bottom floor of the house was dark, a watery cavern of sloshing waves.

"Benedict! Elias!" I called out. "I need help."

The wind answered with a howl and something crashed down in the darkness beyond the stairway.

"Benedict! Is there anybody there?"

I was trying to keep his head above water, but the effort was getting to me. My instincts told me he was dead, but I couldn't let him go. He had saved me and I wasn't going to forget.

A light flickered above me, to the right, and I made out the outline of the stairs.

"Mr. Dunn, is that you?" It was the voice of Elias and a moment later I saw him coming toward me, flashlight in hand. Benedict followed a second later and soon they were lifting him together.

"He's stopped breathing," I said. "We've got to get him started again."

Elias lifted him with surprising agility and deposited him at the top of the steps.

"I have CPR," Benedict said to my surprise and started giving mouth to mouth. I staggered to the top and collapsed.

Elias looked from the prone Solly to me. "Old house won't last forever," he said. "Won't do your friend no good if the house goes."

I lay back, exhausted, my head against the wooden balustrade.

She was alive. That's what Solly had said. All along she had been alive. . . .

The floor gave way and I reached out to keep from falling.

It was Elias's hand shaking me awake.

"Mr. Dunn, wake up. It's your friend. He's breathing again."

187

24

It wasn't much, just shallow respirations, but it was something. Benedict sat to one side, his face disbelieving.

"I took the course," he said unnecessarily. "I didn't know I'd ever have to use it. And I think he started breathing again in time so there wasn't any brain damage."

Elias held up a small transistor radio. "Thing ought to be passed out inside a couple of hours."

"Let's get him into one of the bedrooms," I said and watched as the two other men carried Solly across the hall to what I judged to be a guest room.

I watched as they placed him onto the bed.

"So far so good," Benedict said, still shocked at his own success. He straightened up from the bed. "What about Cox?"

"Dead," I said. "You won't have to worry about him anymore."

A slight ripple of relief passed over his features.

"He was . . ."

"Crazy," I finished. "Yeah, I know. That's why you called me, wasn't it? You couldn't feel comfortable with him." I hesitated. "But there had to be something more. Did you know Rivas was here?"

"Here?" His face went white. "No. How could I?"

I started to pursue the matter, but I was tired, and my

hand was cut, and with the wind threatening to tear the roof off the house, it seemed a waste of energy. Instead, I half nodded and lay back again, pastiches from the last days moving through my dreams. I was talking to the medical examiner and he was holding something up in a plastic bag, and when I looked closely I started laughing, because it was a monkey's paw, not a human organ at all. I was sitting beside the lake listening to a stockbroker telling me to buy Transcaribbean Securities and he was showing me a portfolio with an airplane on the cover. I was in a white room and gowned surgeons were standing over me. The main doctor was speaking, telling me that he could help me, that the odds were ninety percent I'd have full use of my arm, and then I realized it was Laurent's voice and I jerked awake.

A milky light was filtering into the room through the cracks in the storm shutters at the end of the hallway. The house still stood. I heaved myself up and checked Solly. He continued to breathe. Elias stood at the head of the stairs, regarding the muddy waters that swirled ten feet below, but Benedict was nowhere to be seen.

"A couple of hours," I said, "and they ought to be out here to get us. Sounds like the wind's died down."

Elias nodded grimly. "Couple hours," he echoed. "I been with this family for thirty-five years, longer if you count I was brought up here. I seen the congressman when he was a little boy, and I remember when he married the missus. A beautiful couple they was."

"The house can be rebuilt," I said.

He looked up and our eyes met for a long time, and then he turned away.

He went to the end of the hall, where a window looked out onto the grounds, and with a sudden effort of rage as much as strength, drove his fist through the glass of the window and into the closed shutters. The shutters sagged and he struck again, this time knocking one of the shutters off its hinges and letting in the daylight.

"Might as well give them a chance to see us," he said, turning back around to face me.

A door opened behind me then and I turned to see Benedict carefully relocking Stokley's room.

"I was checking," he said. "To see what of the congressman's things could be salvaged."

"I think," I said, "that a good place to start would be with the congressman."

His face blanched. "What do you mean?"

Elias had turned back around to look out the window, unable to face what was coming.

"Don't you know?" I asked, taking a step forward.

He backed up against the door, his eyes frightened.

"What are you talking about? What. . . ?"

"You called me down here because you needed somebody to protect your boss and you didn't trust Cox. You knew Rivas was here and you were scared."

"*No!*"

"Get out the way," I ordered.

He didn't move and I swept him aside.

"You can't—" he began but I pulled back my leg and kicked the door open.

It flew inward and I followed, without giving him a chance to block me.

Emerson Stokley was sitting on the bed, his face ashen.

His eyes went from alarm to resignation. He tried to stand and then caught one of the bedposts for support. His head was wrapped in gauze and he wore a coffee-colored dressing gown and slippers.

"Mr. Dunn . . ." he said. "I thought we might meet again."

"My God, Stokley," I said and then wondered if he'd heard me. But the expression on his face told me he had.

"Congressman, I tried to keep him out," Benedict jabbered, flying to Stokley's side. "I tried to tell him. . . ."

The congressman nodded and Benedict fell silent.

"What now, Mr. Dunn?" Stokley asked. "You wouldn't be here if certain things hadn't happened."

"Certain things," I said, shaking my head. "Like Rivas

being killed and me surviving. People are dead because of this."

"Mr. Dunn, I can't hear everything you're saying but I'm sure there's a way we can handle this."

"Is there? Are you ready to tell the world about Julia Morvant? Do you know what I'm saying, Congressman? Or do I have to write it down?"

"You can't understand," Stokley said hoarsely. "No matter how hard you try, you can't."

"No? I can understand how you got involved with Julia and why she got close to you. I can understand about her sister and about how she managed to get the story to Julia before your lap dogs recaptured her. You're the one who made the marks on Jenny's body, didn't you? What was it, a belt? Are those the kinds of games you like to play? Bondage and discipline? You're a pretty face, Stokley, and everybody says you've even got a good brain. You could've gone all the way to the top. But you had a problem that would've stopped you sooner or later, didn't you? You're a real sicky."

Benedict stared at Stokley, searching for an order, a direction, but the other's face was frozen.

"It's ironic. You could've had any woman you wanted but you had to choose one named Jenny. The mistake was that she had a sister and her sister was a pretty smart person, herself, not a street whore, but a high-class call girl with a flair for the dramatic. You did your thing with Jenny and when you were finished, you and Cox got her into a very exclusive clinic. Now Cox was an interesting case. He said he was working for the Justice Department. I think that was a lie. I think he worked for Defense. And he probably did have some legitimate commission, if these outfits are ever legitimate. But I think he saw himself as having another, more important function. You sit on a couple of committees that are important to the military. House Armed Services, for one. You can schedule bills for a hearing, have riders attached that favor certain projects. You're a great favorite

191

among certain admirals and generals. It would be a hell of a thing for them if you lost your seat in Congress. It would upset a lot of plans. So it's in their interests to protect you. I'm not saying the Joint Chiefs sent Cox's raiders down here to protect you. I just think Cox saw a niche for himself, a way to ingratiate himself with his bosses and with you by taking on a difficult problem, one he probably didn't share with anyone above him. It's been done before, hasn't it? A loose cannon, that's what he was, but with the quiet backing of the official establishment."

Stokley was trembling now and Benedict had shrunk back a couple of steps, as if he didn't know whether to run or stay.

"So Cox saw it as a case of damage control. Grab the girl and hide her away until somebody figured what to do with her. Maybe wipe out her memory and then let her go. Cox's idea of an enlightened solution. But then Jenny escaped and got in touch with her sister."

I didn't want to go on but there was no stopping now.

"Julia called her father and tried to get his help, but he's a stubborn old man. His daughters failed him and he wasn't about to be moved. So next Julia tried to figure a way to get to Jenny. She tried the man who ran the clinic, Dr. Laurent. She went to him with some bogus mental problem and he prescribed a tranquilizer. She was feeling him out, trying to get an idea of where he might be vulnerable. Maybe she thought she could use her wiles on him. But it didn't do her any good. Her sister was stuck in his clinic and there was no way out. After all, what could she do? Go to the law? Who'd believe a whore, trying to save another whore?"

My mouth was dry. I was seeing her now in my mind, desperate, trying to maintain a facade. . . .

"So she decided on the next best thing: She made herself available to the man who'd been responsible. I don't know how she managed to get to you. But with your weakness it probably wasn't hard. All she had to do was inveigle an invitation to some social function. She has a little book, you know. They all do. There are people in her book that she

192

knew would help her. So she found some event where you'd be dedicating a school or giving a speech and made your acquaintance, and it didn't take long for you to realize she had some of the same hang ups you did. Or that's what she let you think."

"I can't understand what you're saying," Stokley said, shaking his head. "Anyway, you'd better wait until you have legal counsel. He'll tell you to be very careful about what you say."

"I know. And then he'll tell me nothing can be done as long as I can prove it's the truth. And I can prove it, can't I?"

Stokley raised a hand, as if to push me away, but it was useless.

I turned to the frightened aide. "You know it's true, don't you, Benedict?"

His mouth moved but his eyes were on those of the older man.

"So Julia became your new playmate," I went on. "You thought she was a political groupie with odd tastes. She let you believe that. But once she realized there wasn't any way to get to her sister, she hit on another plan. And it was very simple. And effective. She decided on revenge."

I didn't know if he could hear or not but by now it didn't matter.

"You two played your games. My guess is she kept you pretty well at arm's length—or should I say belt's length?—with promises and then, when you invited her to meet you in the Caribbean, she figured it was a good chance to do what had to be done, where you wouldn't have all the cards stacked in your favor. So she flew to you and I hope, for your sake, you had an idyllic little interlude. Because it was the most expensive of your life."

"Please, Mr. Dunn—" Stokley sat back down on the bed—"I'm tired. This has been a trial for me. Nelson, can you get on the roof, through the attic? Make some kind of signal, a flag? They'll be coming. Any time now they'll be coming—"

193

"What's wrong, Congressman? Your bomb wounds hurting now? Your deafness *is* better, isn't it? I mean, it's not like you really lost your hearing. You just have a lot of gauze to hear through. You can really hear my voice if you try, can't you? It's not like you're really deaf—"

"Stop!"

Benedict turned away from me and Stokley's eyes seemed to go dead.

"All those pictures downstairs," I said. "There must've been ten or twelve of them. Hell, you must be one of the most photographed men in America. I remember the campaign, last year. Shots of your wife and you on picnics. Probably taken right here, but they didn't show the house. Just faces. Especially yours. And the one on the offshore platform, where you were talking to the workers about keeping their jobs by passing a foreign-oil tariff. I liked that one. You were in a khaki shirt, remember, with the sleeves rolled up? And your hair was blowing in the wind and you had a tan that looked like it could have come from being out there for thirty days at a stretch, even if it was really just from the beach at Cancun. I wondered why you made all those ads. You didn't have a serious opponent. So why go to the trouble? And I finally figured it was just because you were used to the cameras, used to being in the center of things, used to seeing your face on all the channels and in the papers."

His head was going slowly from side to side but he knew it was no good, he wasn't going to convince me.

"If I saw all the ads, and the pictures, so did Julia. And being a smart girl, with this turn for drama, she decided on an appropriate revenge." I paused and took a deep breath, trying to keep my voice steady. "And what's a good vengeance for somebody whose life is the way he looks on TV? Whose stock-in-trade is being photogenic?"

I was dimly aware of Elias, standing in the doorway and I wondered how much he knew. But even as I glanced in his direction he turned and walked back out into the hall.

"It wasn't your wife that needed the plastic surgery, was it? It's you."

There was a little gurgling sound in Benedict's throat.

"The congressman and his wife aren't that close anymore, are they?" I asked. Benedict started to answer and then caught himself. "Where was she, sightseeing while the little fling was taking place? Stokley, you and Julia got cozy, is how I make it, and maybe she slipped something into your drink. And while you were asleep she did what she'd come to do."

Stokley had his hands up to the sides of his head now, as if to keep out the words.

"When you woke up and found out what had happened, you sent Rivas after her. But he had to do something that would distract suspicion from you. What better way than to blow up a whole plane? Who'd have looked at Julia Morvant in particular?"

I went over to the wall, where a picture of a Civil War general stared down and I thought idly that all the Stokleys had been photogenic.

"I haven't quite got the timetable down pat, I have to admit. How did you get Rivas there in such a hurry? And what did you and your people do? I'll bet we could dig up some local doctor that treated you. Your wounds, after all, weren't life threatening, just disfiguring. With painkillers, you could afford a few days before you got to a plastic surgeon. So you used the time to charter a special flight to U.S. territory, St. Croix, in the Virgins, and then you cooked up the bomb story. I don't know where you got a hand grenade, but then you don't need one to blow something up, do you? Just turn on the gas, let the house fill up and add a match. If an elite group from the Pentagon, headed by your Mr. Cox, suddenly showed up to investigate, the locals would be glad for the expert help. Or maybe you even called Cox and had his people arrange for the bombing. What really isn't clear to me though is how you told Cox and his people about Rivas and what they thought of your allowing a plane to be blown up."

Stokley sighed. "Mr. Dunn, you've got it wrong. If you think I had anything at all to do with that terrible crash, you're wrong. My God, man, I don't kill people. Look at my record, my whole life." He took a step toward me now and I realized his eyes were mere coals, sunk deep into his skull behind black hollows of fatigue.

"This Morvant woman was insane. I didn't realize it at first. She was beautiful and highly intelligent. I won't lie to you. I enjoy the company of beautiful women. And I *had* known her sister. But it was nothing serious. My wife and I, as you say, are not close. I wish it were different, but she's been ill a lot and . . ." He managed a shrug. "I can't make excuses, but my God, man, I'm only human. There was nothing sinister in my relationship with this girl, and I certainly didn't beat her. She was unstable. That's why I had her placed in one of the finest facilities in the state, a private clinic. I tried to help her, Mr. Dunn, whether you believe it or not. She had delusions, real paranoid delusions, this poor girl. She did violence to herself and claimed I was responsible. Well, what would *you* have done? Anyway, she got out and told Julia about our"—he bit out the words as if it had a bad taste—"relationship. And Julia decided that it was too good a chance to pass up. She wormed her way into a party I was giving, told me her name was Julia Morvant, but who knows what it really was? Anyway, she was a woman of apparent breeding, or so I thought. She said her father was a Houston oil millionaire. I invited her to go with us to the islands."

I waited, conscious of his eyes measuring me.

"She got me alone, and made the most incredible proposition: If I didn't give her money, she'd ruin me. It was the most outrageous blackmail I've ever heard of. Naturally, I refused, told her to leave, but by then it was too late. She'd put something in my drink and I lost consciousness. I awoke in terrible pain. I realized then what had happened."

I had an image of him waking up, blood streaming off his head, onto the white sheets. . . .

"Yes, I admit we devised a story about the bombing. And I suppose you can use that to discredit me and destroy my entire career, if you elect to. Before you do, though, I'd

196

appreciate it if you'd consider some of the things I've done and some of the things I'd still like to do, and decide if you think it's worth it. You're a man who's given up something for his country."

I tried to keep down the anger. "There's still the matter of an airliner," I said. "And sixty-seven dead people."

He frowned, then nodded. "Oh. The airplane. I'm sorry, I couldn't hear at first. Yes. Yes, there is that, Mr. Dunn. And I wish there were some way to undo that, but there isn't. I'm afraid she's gone now. Probably to Brazil or some country without an extradition treaty."

"What are you saying?" I asked, but I already knew. Solly had as much as told me: *She was still alive!*

"She was never on that plane," Stokley rasped. "She put the bomb aboard in a suitcase, I'd guess. Maybe she bribed some other poor woman to go in her place. The perfect way to disappear. So you see, Mr. Dunn, my sins are venial compared to hers."

It was my turn to shake my head, trying to deny what I'd heard, and I knew they were staring at me.

"I don't believe it," I started and then stopped.

"I'm sorry," Stokley said, coming forward. He knew better than to put an arm on my shoulder.

"It really is in your hands, Mr. Dunn. I know things were mismanaged by Cox. And I'm at fault for letting myself get into this kind of situation. You can destroy me. Just call the *Picayune* of the *Washington Post*. It's your decision to make."

I tried to make sense of what I was hearing. Julia. A murderess . . .

A moan echoed from the hallway, breaking into my consciousness like a cry from hell. Benedict turned and the congressman frowned, trying to understand what was happening. I walked out to see Elias standing before the window at the end of the hall, looking out.

I went toward him and he turned to face me, his cheeks stained with tears. His mouth moved to talk, but after a few tries he gave up and he turned back to the window, and I realized he was looking at something outside.

I gently moved the old man aside and looked down.

The scene before me was an unrelieved gray of trees in a gray sea. The storm had pushed the bayou behind the house over its banks and now a shallow lake surrounded us, with a few aluminum posts marking where the swimming pool lay. A metal frame cut the surface, all that was left of the pump house, for the wind had carried away the corrugated top. Behind the pool a few stumps jutted up from the swamp, and just below us some clumps of debris floated, five or six agglomerations of swamp grass torn loose by the fury of the tempest.

The flood had done damage, but it would recede. It was not the mere fact of the flood that had caused Elias's pain.

All at once a fragment of the fight with Cox came tumbling back from memory and I fixed on it. No, not the fight, afterward, kneeling by Solly, my eyes on the body across the room, turning slowly in the water like flotsam, turning . . .

In sudden horror I looked down at the clumps of floating debris and saw that they weren't debris at all. What I'd taken for grass was clothing, now sodden from exposure to the flood, and I made out arms and legs, as white as the underbellies of dead fish, and streamers of weeds framing their heads.

I counted five, six, and then looked away, my stomach churning and bile coming up into my mouth.

Even from the window I could see what they were: They were the bodies of women.

25

My knees tried to buckle but I forced myself to stay upright. Nausea threatened to flood over me and I knew the best antidote to it was anger.

Benedict was beside me now and when he looked down his eyes bulged out. He turned quickly away and stood bent over at the head of the stairs, retching.

"What is it? What's going on?" Stokley demanded.

I wheeled on him, grabbing his dressing gown and jerking him forward. "Do you really want to see? Then come here. I'll show you."

I dragged him to the window and shoved his head out.

"Down there," I said. "Do you want to tell me now that Julia Morvant killed them all? They're the hookers that have been missing from New Orleans, aren't they? Somebody buried them on your property and the flood brought them up."

He drew his head in and his eyes searched for an escape but there wasn't any. "I didn't do it. I swear to God, I don't know, I—"

I shoved him against the wall and then let go, disgusted. The truth was clear enough now and it was bittersweet.

"She was on the plane, all right," I said, as much to myself as to him. "She's dead. And sooner or later they'll identify her. You bastard—you had Rivas blow up a whole plane to hide the reason for killing one person."

"No." His voice was a croak.

"Yes. To hide the truth about what she'd done to you. Well, there won't be any more hiding. When they come to get us I want everybody to see!"

I reached out, catching him by surprise, and jerked the gauze loose. He gave a yelp, but I was against him pinning him to the wall, tearing with my one hand, until the gauze and bandages lay in a bloody heap. His hands flew to the sides of his head but not before the other two had seen what I had: The sides of his head showed two bloody holes, as if someone had driven an auger through the middle of his skull. It was an illusion, of course, because what I was seeing was his ears, or what was left of them. And a plastic surgeon would be able to do a creditable job. But they would never look the way they had before she'd cut them off.

He cowered in the corner, hands hiding his disfigurement, and I heard my pulse throbbing. Benedict and Elias looked at each other and I wondered if they could hear it, too, and then it came to me that we were hearing something else, something that I'd heard often in the past, on battlefields, and tried to shove out of my memory. It was the sound of beating rotors, hammering toward us in the mist.

Benedict stepped forward then.

"I can't let this happen," he said. "I can't let him take the blame. I confess. I did it. I killed them all."

Stokley watched, frowning, and I wasn't sure how much he'd understood.

"Nelson . . ." He reached out a hand, but his aide brushed it away.

"No. That's okay. The congressman didn't know anything about it. It was all me. I was the one who killed the girls. I picked them up, had my way, and then killed them."

"Really?" I said. "Why?"

He shrugged. "I . . . just something inside. I couldn't help myself. It was something I kept doing. I knew I had to be stopped but . . ."

"And you brought them all here and buried them behind the house," I said.

200

"Yes. I didn't think they'd ever be found. The rising waters must have . . ."

"And Rivas?" I asked.

"I hired him to help me. He brought me the girls. The congressman didn't know any of this. I'll sign a statement, swear in court." He turned to Stokley. "You can't be blamed for any of this because you didn't know. There may be some bad publicity, but it'll go away. The plans for ninety-two won't be affected. You weren't involved at all."

Stokley nodded and started to reach out a hand, then drew it back as if it might be a mistake.

"Nelson . . ." he said.

"Nice try," I told them. "But I don't believe it. I think the congressman had everything to do with it."

"No!" Benedict shouted. Stokley watched, hope fading from his face and his tongue flicked out over his lips.

"Benedict, I guess you get points for loyalty, but I've never understood that kind of devotion, myself. Do you really want this man to be running our country?"

Before he could answer I stepped around him and stood facing Stokley, himself.

"And you'd have let him do it, wouldn't you? You'd have gone on with this cockamamie story about a bomb, used your injuries to drum up support for the crusading politician out to protect the nation's youth."

The rotors were closer now and I went into the bedroom where Solly lay and reassured myself that he was still breathing. It was almost over now, but there was still something that was bothering me, something he'd said, that was stirring inside my mind. He'd been right all along, so why would he have been wrong about this?

The chopper was over the house now and I wondered if they'd noticed the bodies in the swamp below. I went out into the hallway and to the window. The congressman had returned to his room and Elias and Benedict were staring at each other, as if each were willing the other to make the decision.

I looked out the end window and saw another chopper,

standing off about a hundred yards away and I made out the call letters of one of the local TV stations. Of course: Someone must have told them Stokley was here. The rescue of a congressman was a good story.

Except, why did he need to be rescued at all? That was what bothered me. Why the hell had he come back in the face of a hurricane, when he should have been at a private hospital getting his beauty restored?

I flashed back to Sandy's escape and all at once I understood. I'd been two steps behind the truth all along and it hurt.

An olive-drab figure was in the window now, dangling from a safety line, and I recognized the State Police insignia.

"Is the congressman here?" he asked, dropping through the opening.

"The congressman's fine," I said. "But there's a man in the room here with a gunshot wound. He needs immediate attention. You'll want oxygen and blood plasma."

The trooper gave me a strange look, but nodded and spoke into his belt radio. Stokley's door opened then and the congressman emerged, his head rewrapped and his face pale.

"We'll have you out in a minute, Congressman," the policeman promised and I understood he hadn't seen the bodies. Stokley's eyes darted to me and then back to the policeman and I knew he was struggling to come up with a story.

"We'll need a litter," I said. The cop relayed my request and a few seconds later another officer appeared, and then another, and behind them an emergency medical team with a backboard.

"What happened?" one of the later policemen asked and I saw that he had lieutenant's bars.

"I'll tell you when we get onto dry land," I said. "And I think you ought to get a statement from the congressman."

The radios crackled then and the lieutenant frowned. He went over to the window and looked down and I saw Stokley begin to slump.

202

"Oh, holy Jesus," the trooper ejaculated. "What the. . . ?"

"I'm sure the congressman will have a statement," I said. "Won't you, Congressman?"

The trooper looked at the politician for an answer but Stokley only stared back.

The emergency team had Solly on the backboard now and were rigging a cable that had been lowered from the chopper.

I watched them steer him through the window and then he swung for a moment in the air as the winch started him upward.

"Congressman . . ." The lieutenant started, but Stokley's back was turned and I could see he was having trouble controlling himself.

Next Elias and Benedict went out, each attached in turn to a safety belt that was clipped to a lifeline.

"You next," the policeman told me.

I looked over at Stokley. "I think the congressman ought to go."

The lieutenant nodded. "Congressman . . ."

Stokley stared up at us through lifeless eyes and didn't move.

"Sir, you have to come," the officer told him. "We can't leave you here."

The politician started forward, as if to obey, and then halted and made a half turn toward the other end of the hallway.

"I . . ."

"We'll come back and get your things," the trooper promised.

"Come on, Congressman," I shouted above the helicopter's noise, wondering if he was even listening. "There's nothing here you can't leave, is there?"

The policeman urged him forward by the elbow and Stokley took a step, then halted. Suddenly he wheeled around and started back down the hall for his room.

"What the hell?" muttered the lieutenant.

"His better nature won out," I said. "He realized there was something he really couldn't leave after all."

We followed, inured by now to the deafening beat of blades above the house. The policeman went through the doorway first, into the bedroom, and I followed. The room was empty.

Then I caught movement to the right and pointed to the open door of the bathroom.

Stokley was seated on a stool, reaching out toward the tub. I went over to the door and looked through. Even through the beating of the rotors I heard a muttered curse behind me.

She was lying in the tub, her naked body alabaster white, her dead eyes staring at something beyond space and time.

The last time I had seen her in this room she had been on the bed, her eyes bandaged, her husband beside her. Now, at the end, he was beside her once more.

It was clean, as befit a lady, I thought, with the blood having neatly drained into the bottom of the tub and with very little along the sides. She'd kept her cut wrists inside the tub, of course, so as to not make a mess for someone else to take care of.

Stokley was holding her hand and rigor hadn't yet set in, but I guessed she'd been dead for a couple of hours.

"Aline," he said to nobody in particular. "She locked herself in. I didn't know until an hour ago, when she didn't come out. Oh, God . . ."

"Maybe," I said, "it was for the best."

The trooper started to say something but I shook my head.

"I'll explain when we get back," I told the policeman and turned and walked out of the room to the window.

Five minutes later I saw the city, its buildings floating in a sea of mist. A hand came up from nowhere and caught my wrist.

"Saigon or stateside?" Solly asked.

I looked down at him and smiled. "Stateside, Solly. This time we're going stateside."

EPILOGUE

W hen the minister finished we all shook hands
with him and then with Will Folsom. Besides
Folsom, his sister, and a few locals, there was only myself,
Sandy, Mancuso, O'Rourke, and Katherine. So I was glad
we'd come, because funerals are bad enough without there
being no one there.

They'd identified Julia the day I got back, through a can-
vass of the dentists in the city. One had matched the dental
work of a patient named Julia Griffith with the teeth in one
of the bodies. A few days before and I would have demanded more proof. But it was too late for that. I just listened and nodded, because I'd already accepted the fact that
she was gone.

We came down the grassy hill, still wet from the storm,
and stood looking back at the awning with the now-empty
folding chairs, and I knew everyone was thinking the same
thing, that there ought to be more.

Mancuso glanced at his watch. "Funny, the two funerals
being the same time," he said.

I thought of the other interment, across the lake in one of
the city's most exclusive cemeteries. Unlike this one, there
would be reporters and videocams and police to perform
traffic control.

"Think Stokley will be there?" Katherine asked.

"I understand," said Sandy with raised brows, "that he is

205

under sedation, as they say when they can't think of anything else."

O'Rourke started to say something but didn't. I knew it had been hard for him. Unlike the rest of us, he'd known the man.

"I still can't believe it was the missus," Mancuso declared. "I mean, she seemed like such a lady, so . . ."

"That's the worst kind," Sandy said. "He was two-timing her, when he made those weekend trips home to attend to his constituents, which was bad enough. There wasn't anything she could do but sit there and watch him pick up all these bimbos and play his games with 'em. She could live with that, as long as there was some kind of payoff. But when his games got rough and one or two of 'em started to complain, she realized he might just upset the whole game plan. You're looking at a pretty determined lady. She wanted big things from her little congressman. And I'm not talking about having to run for reelection every two years."

"So she decided to get rid of them?" Katherine asked. "I go along with Sal: It seems like a big change for a society woman. And a big chance to take."

"There've been society killers before," I said. "And women at that."

"But how did she ever get hold of this Rivas?" Katherine asked. "A congressman's wife doesn't exactly hobnob with his type.'"

"Well, I think we've figured that out," I said. "I had a long talk with the congressman. Stokley's on a subcommittee investigating drugs, and his investigators turned up Rivas as a hit man based in New Orleans. They were going to have the DEA stage an arrest, in front of the cameras, of course, to show what good work the committee was doing. Mrs. Stokley managed to get hold of some of her husband's papers, probably when he brought them home one weekend, and found this out. She also came across an intelligence report on Rivas and where he could be found. It was a hangout in Harvey. As best we can put it together, she called and asked for him. Naturally, nobody would say anything. So she

206

told the bartender to tell him not to be there in two hours, and then gave him the number of a public telephone to call at a certain time if he was interested in talking with her. Naturally, the message was passed to him and he kept clear of the bar, so the DEA turned up an empty nest. It impressed him. What did he have to lose by calling the number she'd given him?"

"And when he did she laid it all out," Sandy said.

"More or less," I agreed. The afternoon sun was hot, a last gasp of summer, and the air was heavy with water vapor. I was sweating and looking forward to Katherine's, and the barbecue grill waiting on the patio.

"She told him she had a source that could help him. Then she offered him money to work for her. He was to follow Stokley and scoop up the women when Stokley was finished with them. The idea was to kill them before they could spill the goods on her husband, by talking to a friend or a cop."

"But there had to be more to it," Katherine said. "She was taking a big chance, bringing them back to the estate. . . ."

"Honey, there's nothing like a mad woman," Sandy laughed. "She probably enjoyed the long ride with Rivas holding them down in the backseat, with a knife at their throats. Watching him kill 'em back by the bayou was icing on the cake."

"Actually," Mancuso said dourly, "some of them were found with ropes around their necks. I wouldn't be surprised if she'd strangled them herself."

"And Jenny was the only one who escaped," Katherine said. "Hey, that night at the house, when she saw me and went crazy . . . do you think she mistook me for Aline Stokley?"

"Seems likely," I agreed. "Do you remember what you were doing?"

"Doing?" Katherine's face went blank.

"You were twisting the belt of your bathrobe. A scared girl in Jenny's condition might have thought you were getting ready to strangle her. Especially if somebody about your build and general appearance had already tried it one night not long before. After all, I'd noted that you two share a general resemblance."

"God," Katherine shuddered.

"Yeah," Sandy said. "A high-class lady playing second spot to a bunch of bimbos. You don't think she hated them?"

"That's how I make it," Mancuso agreed. "But what a hate."

"But bringing them back was stupid," Mancuso grimaced. "Plain stupid."

"Well, there was a certain logic to bringing them all back: She could be sure their bodies wouldn't turn up somewhere else, and who was going to look for bodies on a congressman's plantation? She was a lady used to controlling things and she'd lost her control over her husband. But this was something she *could* control."

"Right," Sandy said, smirking at Mancuso. "And cops ain't going to work too hard when street girls turn up missing. If they get killed, that's different. But missing? Maybe they saw the light and went home to Momma."

"Next time *you* handle it," Mancuso declared. "I did what I could. Do you know how many damned crimes there are in New Orleans?"

"Calm down." Sandy jabbed him with an elbow. "I know you're special."

"When did Cox and his people find out?" O'Rourke asked. He'd been silent so far and I knew he had to work through it on his own.

"I don't know for sure," I said. "I think Rivas's escape from the DEA alerted them that something was wrong. Then, from their intelligence sources in the underworld, they probably picked up some rumblings about a rich woman running their man. The break was when Stokley picked up Jenny, Julia's sister. When Stokley dropped her they were watching and they saw Rivas and Aline Stokley swoop. She got away in the confusion and when they caught her she identified Rivas. They whisked Jenny away to Laurent's clinic, and tried to decide what to do with her. They also went to talk with Stokley."

"That's the son of a bitch I blame," Mancuso swore.

"Well, he couldn't reject the evidence any longer," I said. "He'd had an idea his wife was involved in something, but he didn't want to acknowledge it. Maybe he confronted her, maybe not. I don't know. What I do know is they were locked into it by now, all three of them—Stokley, his wife, and Rivas. Stokley couldn't turn in his wife even if he'd wanted to, without blowing his own little adventures with the ladies who'd disappeared. His wife knew him well enough to know he wouldn't stop his extracurricular activities, and she and Rivas each had enough on the other to keep things quiet. I doubt Stokley knew where the bodies were. But I think Elias knew a lot more than he's ever let on. Like Benedict, he just wanted to protect Stokley."

"Like Cox," Sandy said with disgust.

"Stokley was an important man," I said. "His influence and his vote meant a lot of power and a lot of military projects. Cox saw his mission as one of protecting the goose that laid the golden eggs."

Mancuso muttered something under his breath as we reached the cars.

"And that meant going after Rivas," he said. "Cut off the arm, not the head."

"It was the best he could do," I said. "Then, when it turned out I was involved through Julia's phone call, and Solly recommended me to help them, Cox got the idea of setting me up as bait."

"But they knew Mrs. Stokley was doing this and didn't do anything?" O'Rourke asked.

"They suspected, but they were in a tough spot. How do you tell a congressman you think his wife's a mass murderer?"

"Tough," Sandy agreed.

I went on. "Evidently, as soon as Julia got her revenge on Stokley and his wife found out, Mrs. Stokley knew she'd have to get rid of Julia quick, before she got back to the mainland and told everybody what she'd done. She called Rivas in a panic, I'm sure. Here was her husband in a clinic, in pain, maimed, and the culprit had disappeared. I don't know what she promised Rivas, but he was on the next plane. Maybe he even had one of his drug associates fly him out specially. Or maybe Rivas was even there all along, at Aline Stokley's orders, shadowing her husband."

"Meanwhile," Sandy said. "Back at the Flying A Ranch . . ."

"Okay," I smiled. "Cox and his people spirited Stokley over to St. Croix. Remember, the congressman's injuries were painful and disfiguring, but not lethal by any means. With antibiotics there was no need to rush him to surgery, which was only cosmetic. The main need was to explain how he'd been injured and that involved getting him away from the location where it had actually happened. Naturally, they didn't realize Rivas had been sicced on Julia. Things were pretty panicky and confused."

"Seems like," Sandy said.

"Rivas got word she was booked on a flight, ready to make her run. He concocted a bomb and bribed some local woman to make the flight, checking in the bag. She thought it was just a routine dope haul, I'm sure, not a death run."

"It wouldn't have been if the bomb had just held off another few minutes," O'Rourke said, shaking his head.

"It couldn't have been a strict time fuse," I said. "That would have been foolish. I think Rivas must've used a barometric detonator, the kind that responds to differences in air pressure, with a timer to close the initial circuit. That is, about halfway into the flight the timer would close the circuit to the barometer and when the plane began its descent, the main circuit would close. That way, the explosion would be far away from where he was. He didn't know the plane's approach route, but he figured there was enough water and swamp to make it difficult to fish up all the debris, like the detonator. He was right there."

"But there was residue on the frame of the airplane from

the explosive used," Mancuso said. "That was what gave it away originally."

We got into the car, Mancuso taking the wheel. It was a pretty cemetery, I thought, lots of trees and grass, and far away from the city. I couldn't help but think that she wasn't the first girl who would have been better to stay away from the bright lights.

"She must have been a strange person," Katherine offered as Mancuso started the engine and turned on the air conditioning. "My God, to bring back a trophy . . ."

"What do you mean?" O'Rourke asked from the backseat, and I forgot I hadn't told him about the medical examiner.

"When the pathologist called me," I explained, "he said he'd found something in a bag, something they'd gotten from the crash site, in the swamp. I thought he was talking about cocaine. Unfortunately, Cox got to his boss and scared them both into silence. Then the man downstairs, Lavelle, bought a bunch of monkey paws."

"Monkey paws?" the lawyer asked as we started forward slowly. "What does that have to do with anything?"

"Nothing. Nothing at all," I said. "Except that it started me thinking. I thought of Stokley and the way his head had been wrapped up, his claim that he had trouble hearing, which was probably true, considering the gauze pads over his ears, and all of a sudden it made sense: Dr. Schwartz hadn't found any dope, he'd found what Julia had taken from the congressman's body."

"Oh, Christ," O'Rourke said, his face greenish. "You mean his . . ."

"His ears, baby," crowed Sandy. "That was her revenge against somebody that lived for the cameras. He was the bull and she was the matador. And she brought 'em back with her to show around. Hell, I bet she was gonna mail 'em to the *Picayune*."

"I think I'm going to be sick," O'Rourke said and Mancuso slammed on the brakes.

"Not in my car," he growled.

"I'll be okay," O'Rourke mumbled, embarrassed. "Just don't hit any bumps."

"Well, I think Micah did good," Sandy said brightly. "Took a lot to figure this all out."

"Thanks," I said. "And I wish it was true. But I was way off a lot of the time, especially about Stokley's wife. I was so sure Julia was still alive I bit when he tried to blame her. Even though I had a lot of evidence to point to something strange going on with the missus."

"You mean the thing Solly said about a woman being behind it?" she said.

I nodded. "I thought he was talking about Julia. But I should've known there would have to be something pretty drastic to bring Stokley all the way back from a hospital up east, before he could even have plastic surgery, and in the face of a storm at that. If I'd just put things together, about the mystery patient they were bringing into Laurent's clinic in the middle of the night, I'd have realized it was Mrs. Stokley, that they'd drugged her and were going to put her on ice, like Jenny, until they could decide how to deal with the problem. It just never occurred to me that in the confusion over Jenny's escape *she'd* manage to walk out, too. That was enough to sound alarm bells everywhere and Stokley came back as quickly as he could."

"Must have been panicked," Sandy said.

"They all were," I said. "But Stokley had no sooner gotten back than they caught her on the grounds, at Godsend. In retrospect, it was natural for her to go back there: It was her home, the bodies were all there, and, most important, off and on she'd been hiding Rivas on the estate, in a shack on the other side of the bayou. She hoped he'd be there when she showed up and he was, though she didn't get a chance to talk with him before Cox grabbed her. Cox knew Rivas was around somewhere. I imagine they gave her Pentothal to get her to confess—at that point Stokley was willing to do anything to keep the lid on the scandal, even letting them drug his wife. With the storm, there wasn't a lot

Cox could do. Benedict, who knew what was going on and was as dedicated as Cox to keeping things quiet, didn't trust Cox one bit. Suppose Cox decided his boss was expendable after all? Cox was too much of a loose cannon, and Benedict needed somebody else there to protect Stokley. That's why he called me. After all, without me there, Cox might have used *him* for bait. I finally realized, after Cox was dead, that Benedict wouldn't have called me unless Stokley had been there all along, and that that was his real reason for calling me."

"One thing I don't understand," Katherine said, "is how they got messages to Rivas and made him believe they were Mrs. Stokley."

"Well, Rivas didn't use the plantation consistently. A lot of the time he was in the city: After all, he was a city boy. Once Cox and company were able to get Aline Stokley under control with drugs, after the so-called explosion, they used dead drops, trash cans and the like, where they'd leave notes. Since the notes were printed, it was hard to say they weren't from her. But for emergencies Rivas had a couple of buddies at a bar who took the calls and relayed them. They'd used the head nurse at the clinic to pretend to be Mrs. S. before, on the phone. It was risky, but it had worked."

"Did Benedict know about Stokley's women and the mass murders?" she asked.

"About the first, yes. Congressmen's aides learn to be blind to a lot of things. But the murders were something else. It wasn't until after the fake explosion when they were able to use drugs to get the truth out of Aline Stokley. Benedict was in Washington with his boss most of the time, so he didn't know what was happening when he and Stokley left New Orleans."

"And Elias?" Katherine persisted.

"He was loyal, too. He may have seen the car coming back and seen lights back in the swamp, even heard screams, but he made it his business not to be too curious."

213

"Emerson Stokley," Sandy sneered. "What a creep. And to think I voted for him."

"Lots of people made that mistake," O'Rourke said sadly.

"Makes you wonder about the rest of them," Katherine ventured.

"Nah," Mancuso said. "I don't wonder. They're all the same."

"I guess," said O'Rourke, "Linda was really killed by accident, then."

"Right. Cox and his people saw her meeting with me, were afraid of what she might know, and swooped down on her. They were in such a hurry she dropped her cigarette on the rug and almost burned the place down. Anyway, they were going to take her to the clinic and stash her until they could figure what she knew. But first they were taking her to a safe house to shoot her up with Pentothal. On the way she jumped out of the car and before they could get to her she'd gone over the side, into the bayou. They couldn't very well hang around and look for her, so they left and she washed up the next day, drowned. Of course, they went back to the apartment and tried to erase all the prints and everything else they could find to keep any of the locals from clouding their investigation with embarrassing questions."

"Gawd," Sandy breathed. "And I thought the projects were bad. Look, you think Stokley still thought he could weasel out of it after his wife killed herself?"

"Politicians never stop trying," Mancuso said. "He'd have claimed she couldn't stand her disfigurement. Everybody would've felt sorry for him."

I checked my watch. I was tired of Stokley, tired of the web of death he and his wife had spun around themselves.

"If we hurry, we can get back in time for me to see Solly at the hospital," I said.

"Yes, sir," Mancuso said dryly. "But only if you tell us one thing."

"I'll try."

He turned to face me. "That business about *Julius Caesar*

214

and Marc Antony's speech. What the hell was that all about?"

I smiled. "That," I said, "was the key to the whole business. It was vintage Julia, being melodramatic, and yet it was so simple I guess we all overlooked the obvious."

"Well, I wish you'd tell us what was so obvious," Katherine said. "I've reread the whole play three times and all I can figure is that Stokley, like Caesar, was ambitious."

"He was that," I agreed. "But that wasn't what she had in mind. It was something simpler, that fit in with the macabre aspect of what she was planning to do."

"Well, for God's sake," Mancuso said, "tell us."

"Remember what she said to Linda? That she was going to make Marc Antony look like a piker?"

"So?" Katherine said. "We all assumed that meant she was going to pull off an even bigger deception than he did in turning the crowd on Caesar's assassins."

"No," I said. "She was more direct than that. There was nothing complex or devious about what she was trying to say."

"Honey," said Sandy in her sugar-coated voice, "you don't tell us in five seconds I'm going to pull *your* ears off and these folks gonna help me."

"Okay, okay," I said. "So who can quote the speech?"

"'Friends, Romans, Countrymen . . .'" said Mancuso and Katherine together and then halted, looking at each other in disbelief.

"Oh, sweet Jesus," said Sandy. "Do you mean?"

I nodded and finished for them: "'Lend me your ears.'"

"I may be sick again," O'Rourke warned.

"I may join you," Mancuso said. "Holy name of God."

There was a car coming toward us now and as it passed I caught a quick glimpse of the occupants.

"Turn around," I said to Mancuso. "Go back to the grave site."

"What?"

"Please. Just for a minute."

He shrugged. "What the hell."

The car ahead of us wound up over the hill and finally halted near the place where we had parked. In the distance, I saw Will Folsom, standing alone under the little canopy over the fresh grave.

The car door opened and a woman got out. She stood shakily and a man came around from the other side and caught her arm. I relaxed finally, glad my phone call had done some good. I'd never met him, of course. All I knew was that he was a cousin and that when we'd spoken he'd shown concern.

Arm in arm they started up the hill toward the canopy.

"Hey," Sandy said. "That's Jenny."

I nodded, watching them approach the old man. He turned his head as they approached, as if unsure who they were, but when they got to where he stood he let her take his hand. They were still standing like that when I signed for Mancuso to take us home.